Jackson Speed:
The Hero of El Teneria

◊

by
Robert R. Peecher Jr.

Robert R. Peecher Jr. grew up in Watkinsville, Georgia, and graduated from Oconee County High School. He has spent his career working as a journalist at a number of different daily and weekly newspapers in Georgia. He is a graduate of Georgia College & State University. He is married and has three sons and lives with his family in Bishop, Georgia.

Jackson Speed: The Hero of El Teneria

Cover Painting by Sarah A. Gordon
Cover Design by Jean A. Peecher

For information the author may be contacted at
PO Box 967; Watkinsville GA; 30677

This is a work of historical fiction. While some characters represented in this book are actual people and some of the events represented took place, these are fictionalized accounts of those people and those events.

ACKNOWLEDGEMENTS

The pages of this book came rather quickly. Each day I was printing as many as a dozen pages of manuscript. As those pages came off the printer, I handed them to my wife, Jean Peecher. She served as equal parts reader, editor and cheerleader. As I dedicated my time to writing this book, so too did I dedicate her time. It is a great joy to me that when I shoved my nose in the computer to write late into the night and early morning or in a book to research for hours, she never complained and asked only when I would have the next chapter available for her to read. Jean also lent her talents to design and arrange the cover. My partner in everything, whatever is good in my endeavors I owe to her.

The painting on the cover is the work of Sarah A. Gordon, who took a couple of paragraphs worth of description from me and then brought my characters to life in a way that far surpassed my imagination. I am grateful to her for giving me the opportunity to see Jackson Speed, Eliza Brooks Speed and Marcilina de la Garza.

I am also grateful to my editor, India Powell, whose feedback and encouragement through the editing process were nearly as valuable to me as her friendship has been over the last two decades. I knew from the moment I decided to publish this novel that when it came time to find an editor I wanted India to do the job, not because of our friendship but because she would provide the professionalism and experience I needed. Through our work on this book, India and I learned more about the etymology of the various slang synonyms for "breasts" than I think either of us ever expected to know.

I delved into numerous sources in researching the Mexican-American War and life in the 1800s, and it would be impossible and unnecessary to attempt a list of all the sources: From biographies and memoirs to newspaper articles of the time to any number of military essays about the war. However, it is worth noting the primary source I relied upon for details about the Battle of Monterrey. "A Perfect Gibraltar: The Battle for Monterrey, Mexico 1846" by Chris D. Dishman was an invaluable resource for improving my understanding the battle and those who fought it.

Finally, I think it would be appropriate to note the influence of a couple of people who, while not specifically but certainly generally, aided tremendously in my ability and desire to write the following pages.

My father, Bob Peecher, instilled in me a love of history. From the youngest of ages I was always fascinated by his knowledge of our nation's history. When I was growing up, he read ceaselessly so that it seemed he always had a book about the Civil War on his bedside table. I have followed his example.

Also, Dr. Robert Wilson, one of my history professors at Georgia College & State University, proved to be a bigger influence on me than he probably could have realized. Our conversations, particularly those outside of the classroom, were invaluable to me as a young man learning that history was not just fascinating or interesting but also overwhelmingly fun.

Mr. Charles Rankin, one of my English professors at Georgia College & State University, convinced me that it was worthwhile to pursue a passion rather than a paycheck. I have avoided making a lot of money, but I do believe the course I have taken has made me incredibly wealthy.

The Jackson Speed Memoirs

Volume I

1830 – 1847

◇

Edited & Arranged by
Robert R. Peecher Jr.

Dedication

For my father,
who instilled in me
when I was young a fascination
with these things
that came before us.

And for Jean,
who is my first reader,
my constant encourager
and my best friend.

EDITOR'S INTRODUCTION

Anyone with more than a passing interest in the history of the United States, particularly 19th Century American history, will be familiar with the name Jackson Speed (1830 – 1922).

Hailed as the "Hero of El Teneria," Speed was credited by no less notable authorities than Abraham Lincoln, U.S. Grant and Allan Pinkerton with having saved the Union at least twice during the Civil War, and Robert E. Lee claimed that Speed's "exploits have been an invaluable service" to the Confederacy.

A Texas Ranger who also rode with the infamous Regulators, toasted for his bravery by Theodore Roosevelt and recipient of the Congressional Medal of Honor at Gettysburg, Speed's place in history at one time appeared to have been secured. Over the years, however, he has largely been relegated to the position of footnote. As time goes by and history books get longer, certain details and personalities have a way of being eclipsed.

While researching another project, I happened upon a letter written by Speed's granddaughter in 1906, which mentioned that her grandfather was "furiously laboring at his memoirs."

Intrigued, I determined that there was no record of Jackson Speed's memoirs having ever been published, and so I began contacting his known descendants – who fortunately still live in Georgia near where I live and work – in the hopes of finding the unpublished manuscript.

When it finally came to light, I was understandably astonished at what I read. The myth of the man was shattered by his own recollections.

As it turns out, the man who received a battlefield promotion for valor from Jefferson Davis was a confessed coward, a womanizer and adulterer, and perhaps the luckiest man ever to charge into battle.

After some negotiations with his descendants, it was agreed that I could edit and publish his memoirs.

While I make no judgment on the character of the man, I believe the memoirs are of extraordinary historical value. Speed knew some of the most important figures of the 19th Century and offers first-hand accounts of events that shaped this nation. In some cases, Speed's proximity to great men at great moments goes a long way toward clearing up historical mysteries and shedding light on the events and personalities that altered the course of the ship of nation.

As editor, I have endeavored to provide footnotes that help to give historical context to the very personal story that Speed tells through his memoirs. At times, Speed's recollections appear to be confused over the course of the years, and whenever necessary I have attempted to point out discrepancies between what Speed remembers and what history reports. I have also broken the memoirs into volumes and chapters, which I hope will smooth the flow of the story. Speed's spelling was at times incorrect or inconsistent, and so I have also corrected the spelling throughout.

At times, Speed appears to have been prompted by events or sudden recollections to begin writing about specific episodes in his life. As such, his memoirs do not follow a strict chronology of his life, but rather skip around — one volume may take place during the 1870s while the very next volume covers just a few months during the Civil War, a decade earlier.

I considered initially reorganizing the volumes into chronological order, but instead decided to release them in the order in which they were given to me. The exception to that policy is the following volume, which takes up his recollections from his early childhood and teen years into the Mexican-American War. It actually appears to be the third volume he wrote. However, it made more sense to release the following work as the first volume, as it deals with his childhood and young marriage and also establishes how he initially came to be in the army.

For better or worse, it has been a distinct pleasure to serve as the editor of his memoirs, and I am grateful for the opportunity.

Robert Peecher Jr.
Editor

CHAPTER I

When I look back over the wretched injustices I have suffered during the course of my lifetime, I can trace every misery that ever came my way to a single individual. It was, of course, a woman who set me on a path that led from one calamity to the next. Ashley Franks was her name, and a more beautiful, wanton trollop never rode bareback astride a more fresh-faced, impressionable youth in all the history of sexual congress. As she heaved and jerked and pounded and screamed and gnashed her teeth and clutched at the bed sheets while atop me, I had no idea that she was sending me forward to a life of peril and woe from which I have barely escaped more times than I care to remember.

And if I sound bitter, I am not.

Oh, aye, there were times, I'm sure, when I was quick to damn Mrs. Franks' rapturous blue eyes for setting me along a course that inevitably led me into so many hellish situations. That afternoon, for instance, when I huddled in that damned alleyway in Gettysburg wondering whether it would be Billy Yank's Minie ball or one fired by Johnny Reb that did me in ranks high in my memory as a time that I thought of that milky complexion – those great big round teats with their crimson points – and I cursed Mrs. Franks mightily and even wept with despair at the shape she'd put me in.

But here I sit now, in my sunset years, able to reflect on the memories of a long life, and I am a bit more generous toward the voluptuous Ashley Franks than I was, say, when the bullets started flying around Blazers Mill and I thought certain that fool Billy Williams (or Andy Roberts, as he'd have it) would lead me to an untimely end. Well, Buckshot got his, and here I sit in the comfort of my old age, sipping brandy and listening to my grandsons make wagers on the Giants and the A's in the World Series. [1]

My life had been easy enough at the start. My father was a man of wealth and influence in Madison, Georgia – the town you'll recognize as the one that Sherman did not burn. But my mother succumbed to a fever and died when I was just a toddler and my father – brokenhearted and lonely, they claimed – followed her to his grave not long after. My father had children from his first wife, but they were all grown or nearly so when he died. I was the only child to this unhappy couple. Orphaned, I was sent to live with my mother's sister and her husband in the nearby town of Scull Shoals.

Though my father was wealthy and influential, his children from the first marriage managed to secure for themselves nearly all of his worldly possessions, leaving me nothing to get through life but the old man's saber and his favorite horse.

My father's only connection to Scull Shoals was that he had served with Phinizey's Dragoons at Fort Clark, protecting the inhabitants of the village on the eastern side of the Oconee River from the Creek Indians on the western side. That was long before his first marriage and even longer before I came along. And though I am not the sentimental sort, I still have that sword hanging in a prominent location in my home – the leather gone from the hilt, and the blade more worn from my exploits than anything he ever did with it. But it's there, inscribed on one side: Phinizey's Dragoons, and on the other side my father's name: Andrew Speed.

I was named for United States President Andrew Jackson, who was in office at the time of my birth, and I will tell you that my name is one of the few things in which I take much pride. Jackson Speed – it's a good-sounding name, especially in a fight, and I daresay the name alone has backed down better men and therefore saved my neck a time or two. The sword, too, has come in handy when nothing else was to be found, and so I suppose when I count the number of times one or the other has seen me through the thick I can say with truthfulness that the little my father left me turned out to be useful enough.

The horse, too, served me well, for as a boy I spent more time on the back of that horse than I did anywhere else, and when I was in my prime you couldn't find a better horseman than me. I lived up to my last name on the back of a horse. That's a fact that I found more useful than anything else, for when the bullets begin to fly you could count on it that if there was a horse within reach Old Jackie Speed would be gone and away lickity split.

My days in Scull Shoals were not poorly spent. My aunt, whose husband was the blacksmith, had no children of her own, and so when I came to live with her she doted on me and showed me no end of affection. She took care to see that I was educated, teaching me reading and writing and arithmetic, and I took care to avoid her lessons at every opportunity I could find.

I rode my father's horse through the woods and fields around Scull Shoals, playing Dragoon with his sword and slashing at branches and corn stalks, and avoided scholastic endeavors as best I could. Not to be overly sentimental, but it was good business for a boy and time well spent.

My uncle, who was a hard man and believed in hard work, taught me a little of his trade, allowing me to apprentice in his smithy when I was aged twelve or thirteen. At an earlier age than that, he took me with him hunting, where he taught me to use a long-barreled rifle as well as a bow and arrow. We hunted deer, squirrel and turkey, and we frequently fished together. That I have always been a good shot with a rifle I owe to my uncle.

I grew fast, and by the time I was a teenager I was taller and stronger than any of the boys my age, and a fair bit taller than most of the men. And I suppose that's what caught Mrs. Franks' eye.

I was just fifteen-years-old – not nearly a man yet but too old really to still be considered a boy – when Mrs. Franks took me into her home that first time, using against me a fresh peach cobbler she had made. As I ate at her table with the spring breeze coming through the open window, she talked sweetly to me about nothing at all.

I had no idea at the time that I was being seduced, but I knew I liked the cobbler, and even as a young lad I knew Mrs. Franks was delightful to look at. At my age now, I can say that she was not much more than a girl herself. She was in her early twenties, I would guess, bright blue eyes and soft blonde hair and tanned skin. Her nose was pointed, and I remember when the mill's foreman came down from Athens with his new, young wife, Mrs. Ashley Franks was the target of all the town's gossip. She was twenty years his junior, maybe more than that.

She could not have been any more opposite from her husband. He was short and stocky, older, balding, tanned like leather from years of working in the sun. Uriah Franks was gruff and mean-spirited, and not a soul in Scull Shoals could determine why on earth this beautiful young creature had married such a man. He was no more wealthy than he was handsome. But he was a terrible bully, and there were those who spread the rumor that he had in some way blackmailed or threatened Mrs. Franks into marrying him.

"My, but I have taken a fancy to you," she fluttered at me on that first afternoon as I tucked into that peach cobbler. "You are so tall and such a strong looking young man, and the way you ride your horse, so erect, so dashing." And here she paused, eying me as I ate. "I do say, Jackson, you do enjoy your cobbler, don't you?"

I stopped the fork halfway between plate and still-full mouth and looked at her clearly for the first time, and whether I knew for sure what it was or not, I saw lust in that licentious face.

She was wearing a cotton dress with a square neckline, and I confess that, reading the passion in her face, as my eyes lit on those shoulder blades, my first instinct was to clutch her to me and get my lips on her neck and shoulders. But I restrained myself, still holding the cobbler on the fork.

She smiled, parting those lustful lips and fluttering those big blue eyes at me.

"Oh, it is ever so hot, don't you think Jackson?"

Knowing a bit about wooing women, I can tell you that the best way to get them naked and in bed is to get them laughing. And had I a little more maturity and knowledge, this is the point at which I'd have started in with some of my famous Speedy wit, got her pumped and primed and then lifted her off to the bed.

But not knowing anything at all, I just looked at her over that cobbler.

She giggled a bit, knowing I'm sure the state of confusion she had me in.

"Wouldn't you be more comfortable if I helped you out of that shirt?" she asked me. And she stood up, walked around the table to where I was sitting, took the fork out of my hand and set it on the plate – if you can believe such a thing – and then she grabbed my shirt at the waist and lifted it right up over my head. Without thought or comment, I put my arms in the air like a wee boy getting undressed by his mama.

As I said, I was tall and well built in my youth, and Mrs. Franks seemed to appreciate that. With my shirt on the floor, she began rubbing her hands along my chest and up and down my arms, feeling my muscles.

I sat there like an idiot, mute. I did not know what to say or do.

Had I been ten years older, or even five years older, and known just a little bit more, I'd have taught her a lesson for her forwardness. Oh, I've thought about it over the years, how I would have liked to have been able to go back and snatch that cotton dress off of her, twirled her around and smacked that round rump pink before throwing her on her back and giving her all I was worth.

But instead I let Mrs. Ashley Franks lead the way, and it

was slow as you please, gently seducing the fifteen-year-old until we were both naked and I was on my back on the bed she shared with her husband and she was on top of me riding like she desired to break me. And by God, I suppose she did, the tart.

She was all sweet and Southern and almost demur leading into the thing, but once engaged, she was randy as a cowboy just off the trail and loose in a cat house.

As I said, I'd have liked to have had a go at that again when I was older and knew better what I was getting myself into.

Now, I'm sure you cannot blame me when I tell you that I went around Mrs. Ashley Franks' house quite a bit during that spring. And more often than not, she had a cobbler waiting for me. And while I may not have gotten any more sure of myself, I suppose I did get better. At the least I got a taste for it.

Fifteen-years-old, and I'd gone in one afternoon from playing Dragoon with my dead father's sword to getting belly to belly with another man's wife.

Is it any wonder I turned out the way I did?

I suppose it occurred to me more than once that what I was doing was the sort of thing that would get me killed, but in my youth I had no discretion. I suppose, too, that I trusted Mrs. Franks' judgment, which was a damn fool error on my part.

Our afternoon romps often stretched into the evening, particularly after we'd had a few sessions and I'd learned more about my business. Mrs. Franks wanted to be in control from start to finish, but she was well pleased with me when I learned to pinch and bite, and she laughed with glee that first time that I wrapped my hands around her waist and lifted her straight off the ground and tossed her down on the bed.

But she was getting careless.

Uriah Franks was the sort of man who worked hard and that was all he did. He didn't become foreman by leaving the mill just because the sun was setting. But dusk was our cue for me to pack it up and get out before the neighbors got suspicious, leaving plenty of time for Ashley Franks to straighten the bed clothes and clean up the dish of cobbler.

One afternoon, though, after working on each other until we were all sweaty and spent, we collapsed onto the bed together and fell asleep in each other's arms.

I remember very clearly that I was dreaming that Ashley Franks and I were in the clouds, naked and with the breeze blowing against our bodies and she was floating beside me, her lovely face smiling at me and her wide blue eyes like sapphires. I suppose in my fifteen-year-old way I was besotted. But then there was something thumping and making a commotion so that I thought it was thunder clouds we were in. Then an angry shout: "Cuckolded, by God! I'll cut your throat!" and Ashley Franks was pushing me off our cloud.

I hit the hard floor of her bedroom and jumped with a start, sensing more than understanding what was happening.

The betrayed husband had caught his unfaithful wife, and his wrath could only be soothed by murder. It's a storyline I've been familiar with more than just this once, I assure you.

Like a fool I took the time to grab my britches and shirt from the spot on the floor where they'd been discarded and I started toward the open window. I looked back, thinking to get my boots, and saw Mrs. Franks standing beside the bed screaming at her husband. He'd already hit her across the face once – I could see the red hand print and her nose was bleeding – and he had her by the throat with one hand and was raising the other to strike her again. He was shouting, too, over and over again: "Cuckolded!"

Well, that's it for me, I thought. I abandoned my shoes and made for the window. Once through it I found myself on the roof of the front porch. I hesitated for just a moment to pull on my britches before launching myself into the bushes below where I received a number of scrapes and cuts.

From inside I could hear the sounds of struggle, glass breaking, Ashley Franks' screams of terror and hatred and that inflamed bastard shouting "Cuckolded!" all the while. It took just a second for my eyes to adjust to the dark, and I was off like a flash in search of safety.

The village of Scull Shoals sits low on the banks of the Oconee River. There, the warehouse and store, my uncle's smithy, the remains of the fort where my father served, the superintendent's big house (occupied at the time by Dr. Poullain) all surrounded the mill itself. The canal rerouting the waters of the Oconee River came in from the north and wrapped around to the power plant at the south of town. From the power plant, most of the mill houses and other homes rose up a hill above the town.

Uriah and Ashley Franks lived at the top of this hill in one of the few two-story homes in the village. My aunt and uncle lived in one of the others at the bottom of the hill, near the power plant.

It was to their home that I now rushed.

My uncle, being the smithy, was as respected as any man in the village other than the superintendent of the mill. He was also as powerfully built and as feared as any other man, and if there was a soul in that village who could protect me from Uriah Franks, it was no doubt my uncle.

So I rushed past the little mill homes, trampling their beds of daffodils, knocking over garden fences and stomping on every bit of vegetable in my path. And in my bare feet, I felt every bit of it.

By now the din that the enraged cuckold had caused had brought out all the neighbors, and I could hear the commotion of pursuit behind me as I fled. I lost my footing at one point and tumbled tit over head, but I regained my footing and never broke stride.

At length I reached the porch of my aunt and uncle's house and flung open the door crying bloody murder. To my astonishment and horror, no one was home. Chest pounding, legs weak with exhaustion and trembling from head to foot with terror, I called out for my aunt and uncle, but there was no response. Meanwhile, I could hear through the open windows the angry mob approaching in the street. It seemed the whole town of Scull Shoals was coming to get me. And above all the noise was that bastard Franks roaring for my neck.

I dashed to the trunk where I stored my belongings and slid a pair of moccasins onto my cut and sore feet and started to go for the backdoor when the glint of my father's sword caught my eye. For the first time in my life, I knew real fear. I'd seen that crazed man grab his wife by the throat, his knuckles white, and for all I knew he'd already done her in and sought to do me next. I intended to flee as far as I could go, but when I saw that sword the thought ran through my mind that if backed into a corner with nowhere left to run, an old cavalry saber might be the thing to have.

So I plucked the sword from my trunk and ran through the back of the house. Outside I made for the stone bridge that arced beside the power plant over the canal and ran straight for the grouping of mill buildings.

I doubt that those among the pursuing crowd had any idea what they were after me for, but Uriah Franks had worked that mob into a frenzy with his cries of vengeance. Having lost sight of me as I ran for the mill, they were fanning out through the village as they crossed the stone bridge – some headed toward the ruins of Fort Clark, others toward the mill and some following the canal toward the river.

I stopped against the wooden wall of a mill building and tried to catch my breath. For a moment I thought if I fell into someone's hands other than those that most wished to strangle me, I might talk my way out of it, or at least buy myself some time. But as the mob approached I could hear Franks' roars at the head of the pack and I realized that if the mob on my trail caught me it would be Uriah Franks himself that had me in a hold.

I thought about breaking past the superintendent's house and toward my uncle's smithy. Just beyond the smithy was the toll bridge that led to the western side of the Oconee River, and it seemed that only there would I find safety. But the mob headed along the bank of the river would catch me before I could get to the bridge, and with Uriah right behind me there would be no time to plead my case – whatever case that might be. Entrapped by the womanly wiles of a seductress? That would sound a pretty story as they nailed my ear to a board.

I wretched in fright, and that was enough to get me moving again.

I slid along the wall of the mill until I came to an open window, through which I tossed my sword and then followed.

When I got to the other side of the window I realized I was in the office of the superintendent. An oil lamp was lit and papers were on the desk. He'd been in here moments before, I realized, and he must have gone out the front door to see what all the ruckus outside was about.

My stomach dropped, though, when I heard some nosey fool cry out, "I saw him go through that window!"

I looked for my escape – the door across the room from me – but I was too late, for Uriah Franks' hulking mass was heaving itself through the window.

"Trapped! B'God!" he yelled, victorious.

"Let me explain," I whimpered, but he cut me short.

"You'll explain to your maker!"

And he lashed out at me – catching me across the side of the face with a riding whip that cut a deep gash in my cheek.

I fled behind the desk, and for a moment we were locked in a stalemate of a dance – as I went one way to escape, he'd move in that same direction, but he could not get at me and I could not get at the door or the window.

And that's when I felt the weight of my father's saber in my hand and knew for certain that the only way I would escape was if I not only bedded this man's wife but also bashed in his head or ran him through.

And so I mustered up what little courage I could find and struck out with the sword, swinging it as hard as I could at

Uriah Franks' head. I missed him by several feet, and the sword landed on the desk with an almighty crash of glass and oil lamp and splintered wood and flying papers and, my God! I'd set the entire room alight!

Franks' eyes grew wide at the suddenness and extremity of the fire that seemed to be surrounding us. All thought of me had rushed from his blasted head, and if you thought it was fear of burning alive – which was the very same fear now adding itself to my already troubled thoughts – I'll have you know it was fear of the mill burning to the ground that had this man rushing to the window.

Hanging his head out the window, he shouted, "Fire! Fire!" to the still-gathering mob outside. But it wasn't the same tone as when he shouted, "Cuckolded!" The latter had been a shout of rage, a shout of murder. But the former, his cries of "Fire!" were cries of fear. "Get the water buckets! Form a line!"

Well, old son, you had better believe Ol' Speedy wasn't forming a line.

Seeing my chance I dashed through the superintendent's office door and down the hall to the front door of the mill. It was standing open, and there in the moonlight I saw the thin, worried face of Dr. Thomas Poullain, still attempting to take in what was happening inside his mill.

He grabbed me by my shoulders, "What is going on, son?"

"Fire!" I yelled. "The mill is ablaze!"

Poullain's face showed horror. He released me, and while he ran inside to see what was to be done, I ran past the smithy and across the bridge over the Oconee River.

CHAPTER II

I fled along the wooded bank of the river, making my way south, though by now there was no pursuit, and so I gave up running but continued to walk at a good clip.

Whenever I turned to look over my shoulder and make certain I was alone walking along the bank, I could see the glow of the fire in the distance growing ever brighter. It appeared to me that I must have set the entire mill ablaze – maybe the whole village – for the light casting through the woods was of a brightness I'd not seen before and couldn't fathom.

I could only assume that the mob, engaged in fighting the fire, had all given up on finding me. Even Uriah Franks, enraged as he was, had abandoned vengeance in favor of trying to put out the blaze. But if I was worried what they would do to me for bollocking the foreman's wife, I could not imagine what they would do to me for causing such a tremendous fire in the mill. Nailing my ear to the boards would have been the absolute least of my worries. It would be the rope for sure.

At length I came upon what I'd been looking for: an old dugout canoe. I'd known it was there and had, in my youthful wanderings, used it to cross the river from time to time. So I knew it was sturdy enough. I turned it over and found a paddle under the canoe where I'd left it the last time I'd used it. I could walk for days along the banks of the river and never feel that I'd outdistanced my pursuers – for I had no doubt that once the fire was extinguished they would be on my trail – but by taking the canoe I could easily get well beyond the reach of that madman and whatever of the mob he could muster into a posse.

So I pushed the dugout into the river and began paddling to safety.

The panic that had swept through me since Ashley Franks had first pushed me off our cloud and onto her pine floor eventually subsided as I paddled down river, and through the night I dozed some, drifting along in the canoe. Once, exhausted, I even rowed into the bank and stretched out in the grounded canoe and slept. I do not know how much later it was when I finally woke, but I was left with a stiff neck and shoulders from the cramped, hard bed. I pushed the canoe off the bank and continued my flight to safety.

Day broke and I kept going without catching sight of a soul all morning and well into the afternoon. I was famished from the hard work of rowing through the night, exhausted and completely lost without any notion of what to do next, when at last I came upon a slave boy fishing on the bank of a river with a cane pole in his hand and a straw hat on his head.

"Hey boy!" I called out to him. "Where am I?"

"Yaz sah," he called back to me. "You ain't know whar you is?" And he sniggered at that.

"Damn you, boy!" I roared at him. I was in a foul temper and would take no insolence. "Answer me before I row this dugout up to the bank and beat you with this paddle!"

That shut him up, though he was still grinning. "You'se in Milledgevilles, sah."

In those days, Milledgeville was the capital city of Georgia, and I'd visited the city twice with my uncle when he was purchasing supplies for his smithy. Milledgeville was a bustling city with big houses, the Capitol like a castle on the east side of the town, Oglethorpe University out to the west, the penitentiary and asylum, hotels and taverns and stores of all sorts, and cotton bales lining every street. I was still north of the town, as evidenced by the fields of cotton stretching out from the banks of the river, so I continued to float along until a short while later when I came within sight of the city proper. Just upstream of the gristmill, I paddled toward shore and beached the canoe. I hid my father's sword on the bank with the intention of retrieving it later, abandoned my dugout canoe and walked the rest of the way into town.

It was two days, or maybe three, that I spent stealing what food I could find and sleeping in the woods on the outskirts of town, unsure of what I should do next. But I've always been fortunate that at my lowest points when I was out of ideas, some unsuspecting do-gooder came along to rescue me. And don't misunderstand me – I seldom set out to do wrong by people, particularly those who helped me along the way. But often in life circumstances dictate actions that can unintentionally bring pain and suffering to those we least want to hurt. Such was the case with William Brooks.

Old Man Brooks owned Brooks' Dry Goods and Hard Ware on the corner of West McIntosh Street and Jefferson Street, two blocks up from the Capitol and just down from the LaFayette Hotel.

The LaFayette Hotel was a grand place in those days. The lobby was richly furnished with dark wood tables, plush couches, a big chandelier and oriental rugs. A restaurant off the lobby was a kind of gathering place for some of the local men who breakfasted there in the mornings. For that reason, the lobby was always crowded with people in the mornings, and the previous day I had discovered that I could move around inside the lobby, reach into the cushions of the couches and fine loose and forgotten coinage.

I was now back snooping around in the lobby of the hotel in the hopes of finding some misplaced cash when I felt the sharp whack of a cane across my buttocks.

I jumped up with a start and turned to see what had struck me, and I was amazed when I saw that it was a bent old man with gray, mutton-chop whiskers and sagging skin. I was a pretty good-sized boy, as I've mentioned, and I towered over this ancient who had smacked me with his cane. But there was fire in this man's eyes.

I've seen it since, and I know it now to be a fire of

conviction, and it's the sort of thing that sets a fellow like me to squirming.

"I've seen you around here for the past two days," he began, "and I can see plainly that you are nothing but a rascal and a thief. But your victims will smell you coming because you stink, and your filthy appearance shouldn't be tolerated on the streets of a respectable town."

He looked me up and down, disgust written all over his face. "Your face is congealed with blood. Your clothes are ripped and stained. Potatoes could grow in the dirt on your hands."

It was true; I'd never tended to that gash on my face or made any effort to clean myself since my flight from Scull Shoals.

And as if I'd asked for a bath and clean clothes – which I had not – he reluctantly said, "Very well, then. Come along."

Sheepishly, I followed this queer old man who had just given me a loud and public dressing-down out of the hotel lobby and down the street to his store at the end of the block.

Brooks' mercantile was the typical sort of general store you would find in any town, though being in the state capital it was quite a bit bigger and with more merchandise than the mercantile in Scull Shoals or some other small town. The walls were lined with shelves containing anything from tobacco to powder horns to hammers to jams and jellies, coffee, tea and other edibles. In the center of the store there were more shelves with a variety of goods: glasswares, lamps, lamp oil, spectacles, cutlery and even chamber pots. Stacked at the front of the store were large bags of seed and feed and the back wall was filled with racks of farming tools. There was also a stock room in the back of the store where more merchandise was kept on hand.

The second story of the store held shelves and racks of clothing, hats, shoes and implements of sewing – thread, needles and bolts of cloth.

At the front of the store, Brooks had left plenty of room for folks to gather – even a couple of stools for people to sit on – because his store was a bustling place where the town's old-timers and farmers gathered for gossip.

When we walked into the store, Old Man Brooks agreed – without my asking – to hire me at forty cents a day to stock shelves and make deliveries for him. He would provide me, in his own home, room and board at a cost of 5 cents a day. All this on the condition that I get myself cleaned up immediately.

"There is no reason that, given an opportunity, you cannot make something more of yourself than thief and miscreant," Brooks told me. "If you promise that you will forego your thieving ways, I'll give you that opportunity."

Not seeing that I had any viable alternative, I gladly accepted his offer and swore that I was no thief.

Old Man Brooks turned out to be one of those truly generous Christians who will do anything for anyone so long as that person is half trying for themselves.

The job kept me busy from sun up to sun down six days a week, and on Sunday mornings I went to church with the old man and his wife (they were Presbyterians, which should come as no surprise) and had my afternoons free for "spiritual meditations," as Mrs. Brooks called them.

She was as ancient as her husband and not in particularly good health, so other than church on Sundays I saw little of the old woman. Mr. Brooks was ancient and bent and used a cane to get around, but he was still sprightly enough and his mind was sharp, and keeping active at the store seemed to be what gave him the energy to keep going at his age.

Their home was a fine two-story mansion – bigger than any home in Scull Shoals – with great columns on the front, big windows, a pleasant porch that wrapped around three-fourths of the house and a big garden in the back.

They had just a few slaves. A slave woman named Mamie who was not a bad cook and kept us well fed, Jimbo and Willie who did the hard labor at the store, and Bessie, a girl about my age who tended to the housekeeping. Jimbo and

Willie lived in a shack at the back of the garden. Mamie and Bessie shared a room inside the house.

Jimbo and Willie were solid workers who kept their mouths shut and got through their lives by doing as they're told with no comment other than a "Yaz sah," and as they principally helped me with deliveries and stocking, I appreciated their efficiency.

From the time I left Scull Shoals, maybe even before, most folks always treated me older than I was. They assumed because of my size that I was in my late teens rather than my early teens. Mamie, though, even from the first, treated me like a child to be worried over and cared for. And, the truth is, I can't say that I minded it much. When Old Man Brooks first brought me back to his house, she doted on me, heavens sakes-ing and oh my-ing over the gash on my face, taking care to clean the wound and blessing my heart over the scar it would leave. She wouldn't leave it to me to scrub my fingernails, and with a brush and soapy water undertook the job herself. She even sent Jimbo down to the Dry Goods and Hard Ware store to fetch me up some new clothes.

And it was all genuine. She made certain that I got extra helpings at supper, sent Bessie to the store with my lunch, and always asked after my health.

More so even than my aunt who raised me, I have always felt tenderly toward Mamie and the kindness and care she showed for me. She was fat as a cow and dumb as a sheep, no question, and clearly the worst judge of character there ever was to have taken so warmly to me, but I appreciated her kindness all the same.

Bessie was a different breed altogether. Plump in breast and thigh but thin at the waist, her hourglass figure was of the kind that had to be bred, and I was just the man to teach her what she'd been bred for.

I wasn't in the employ of Old Man Brooks long before my lingering doubts and fears over the situation with Uriah Franks began to dissipate and I suddenly found myself missing Mrs. Ashley Franks. Or at least I was missing those afternoons in her embrace.

Desperate for some relief, I took a notice to Miss Bessie whenever she brought me my lunch at the store. Her bosom pushing up out of the top of her dress, her big lips pursed in a coy smirk and her dark eyes fluttering mischievously at me. And when she turned to leave, the plump roundness of her rear end swished and swayed in a come-and-get-me way. At least, that's how I took it, and so I did.

I didn't waste time, either.

In the evenings it was habit for me and Old Man Brooks to retire to the front porch of his home where we would read the day's Southern Recorder and he would talk politics at me. I learned a lot from those evenings and came away with a much better understanding of the world than I'd ever had before. Owning one of the first businesses in the state capital, he knew his share of political leaders and had observed them all.

The Old Man was too honest and too hard working to cotton on much to politicians. Christian charity required that he treat he fellow man with respect and kindness and dignity, but Old Man Brooks found a way around that when it came to political figures: he simply deemed them a lower class of species and treated them with contempt.

Of course, he was all smiles when they came into the store and spent their money, so there's that and you can make of it what you will.

But he did understand the mind of a politician as well as any man can.

"They are all, always, with no exception, in the business of politics for their own personal gain: either in dollars or in power or in both," he raged at me one evening. "No matter how noble their cause may appear to be, no politician has ever acted out of nobility. It is always an issue of self-interest, and do not ever forget that."

Well, I've known a fair number of them: Abraham Lincoln and Jeff Davis, both; Boss Tweed and James Garfield and any number of mayors and representatives and aldermen and senators, and I can say that every one of them lived up to Old Man Brooks' estimation – except one. Sam Grant was a different kind of man, and whatever that was, he wasn't a politician. He was just unlucky enough to be elected president.

The Old Man also predicted for me the coming Mexican-American War which was to be another major turning point in my life. He could see it coming because of the money involved. The deepwater ports in California were critical for Northern manufacturing. Every Southern politician viewed Mexico as an opportunity to expand and further entrench the institution of slavery – thereby expanding and further entrenching his own political influence. Well, he called that, no doubt, and he was right about every bit of it.

So it was one of these evenings when the Old Man was waxing on about the troubles out West and how the politicians were getting us into a war solely for the purpose of helping themselves and their rich friends that I made some excuse and slipped off the porch and walked into the backyard.

It was full dark by now, but I saw a light glowing in the room Mamie and Bessie shared at the back of the house. The window was open, and I crept up to that.

Frequently in the evenings Mamie would be called to attend to old Mrs. Brooks whose various ailments kept her bedridden all days except Sunday but awake at all hours, and I was counting on it that tonight would be one of those nights. And, to my delight, when I looked through the open window it was just the young, supple Bessie who was to be found, rubbing her feet with oils.

"Psst! Bessie," I whispered at the window, and she jumped and yelped. "Hush, girl," I said. "You'll wake the house."

She stared wide-eyed at me. She was wearing nothing more than a white, cotton night dress, and in the heat of the early summer evening it clung to her sweaty body in a way that had me stirring something horrendous. I will confess that at that moment I was prepared to bully, threaten or force her if it came to it.

"Mr. Jackson," she cried. "You gave me such a start!"

"My intention is to give you more than that," I whispered at her. "Now hush girl and come out here and lend me some assistance."

"I only has on my night clothes," she protested, still more loudly than I cared for.

"I don't care what you're wearing," I told her. "Come around through the back door and help me in the garden."

It took her a minute to find some slippers, and she draped a shawl over her shoulders in a fairly unsuccessful effort to cover herself, but as I waited by the window she at last exited her room and a moment later was pushing through the screened door on the back.

I took her by the hand and led her from the back porch into the garden where it was well dark and we had only the moon to lend us sight. There was a small pond in a corner of the yard shielded from view by a variety of azalea bushes and rose bushes and hedges. It was a pleasant little place with a wooden bench and soft grass surrounding the pond, and it was to here that brought her.

"Mr. Jackson, what is you doing?" she asked.

"Keep your voice down," I said to her, and once we were in the garden I spun her quickly around, wrapped my hands around her waist and pulled her hard against me, pressing myself against her thigh so that she would have no misunderstanding about my intentions.

"Why, Mr. Jackson!" she squealed again, but I shoved my mouth against hers and kissed her hard so that she would shut up that fool talking.

As I said, I was prepared to take whatever action was necessary to have my way with her there and then in that garden, but I found that she was as willing as could be. Being strong and handsome has its advantages. My experience has been that even those women who were initially reluctant came around easily enough, and I've always credited this to my physical appearance. Sure enough, my natural instincts to charm women with good humor and easy talk helped along the way, but there were a fair number of them that I never had the opportunity to charm and they came around willing anyway.

A little kissing and it was only moments before I'd lifted off that night dress. That plump rear and those big melons were an absolute delight, and I went to work on her with a frenzy. She loved every bit of it, squealing and wriggling and giggling while I set to work on her. She wasn't of the same temperament as Ashley Franks. Uriah's wife was intent on being in control and would do what she liked with absolutely no interest in whether or not her dancing partner cared for the tune.

Bessie, on the other hand, showed no initiative at all. She was game enough, no doubt. As I soon discovered, she'd brought the shawl so that she'd have something to lie down on rather than the "itchy grass" as she called it, so I don't doubt Jimbo or Willie or perhaps both of them had at some time or another had her bare back on that itchy grass. Needless to say, she was well clear on my intentions and nothing about what I was doing confused her. But she wasn't what I would consider an overly active participant. She was pleased enough to wriggle and giggle and squirm a bit, but whatever use I was going to get out of her would solely come from the work I was willing to put into it.

And after a few weeks of missing Mrs. Franks' charms, I can tell you that I was willing to put good hard work into it.

When it was over, and I lay sweating beside her – on the itchy grass, you understand – she took the whole thing as a compliment to herself. "I knowed by the way you looked at me that you was gone ta want ta lay in the grass wit me," she said. "All the mens look at me. They likes my big breastses and they likes my big butt, and they likes my lips. And when I saw you lookin' at me I knowed you was gone be comin' to see me."

And she went on like this for an eternity, bragging about her plump assets. And then, to my astonishment, she started naming off the men in town who at one time or another had had their way with her, and there must have been a dozen of them that she ticked off.

"Now you listen here," I told her, pretty stern like. "This isn't the last of what I'm going to do with you, but don't you go blabbing it around town. D'ya hear?"

"Oh, I wouldn't never tell nobody," she assured me, but I wondered if the next man who put her down on top of her shawl wouldn't hear my name listed off with the others.

Not that it stopped me. Bessie turned out to be an easy way for me to exorcise my desires, and more nights than not she draped that shawl over her shoulders and met me out in the back garden.

I was living in a fine home in the capital city (though, to be sure, there were plenty much nicer) and making wages doing work no harder than carrying a fifty-pound sack of flour on my shoulder for a few blocks, and at almost no expense to myself, I was eating well and sleeping in a soft bed. And now I was almost daily enjoying the manna of Miss Bessie's honey pot.

And I can tell you that Ol' Jackie Speed spent that summer well contented with his lot in life.

Scull Shoals was a distant memory to me then – almost another life – and there was not a moment that I thought of my aunt or uncle or the time that I spent there. At times, I suppose, I reminisced about Ashley Franks and the afternoons spent with her, but not much. There were few women who I ever really loved – those who lingered in my thoughts well after my time with them was over – and I've found that one belly lass tends to make you forget the previous one pretty quick.

At night I'd sometimes awake in a sweat with Uriah

Franks' visage in my mind, but that was nothing more than my natural bent toward cowardice haunting my sleep.

The scar that bastard had given me across my cheek wasn't so bad a thing, either. Tall and strong as I was, with my wavy brown hair and dark eyes, that scar added to my face an air of distinction, I thought. Examining myself in the mirror, I thought it rather made me look a bit dangerous, maybe a bit mysterious. It was a white scar against my tan cheek, just a bit raised, and though it was impossible to miss, it was also the sort of thing that a person could quickly get accustomed to. And it also made me look a bit older, so that now no one looked at me and could believe that I was just fifteen years old. I easily passed for the same age as the boys who in late summer were arriving in town to begin studying at Oglethorpe University.

CHAPTER III

The students at Oglethorpe University were not the only ones arriving in Milledgeville that late summer.

"We're closing the store early today. Have Jimbo fetch up the carriage," Old Man Brooks said to me one August afternoon as we were working at the store.

"Closing early?" I asked. This was unheard of practice for the old Presbyterian.

"You and I are off to the train depot to greet my granddaughter who is arriving on the train this afternoon," he said. "She is coming to visit her grandparents for the next couple of months – maybe longer, if I can arrange it. She'll be bringing untold amounts of luggage, and so I'll need you and Jimbo to help me gather all her trunks and baggage."

I had heard the Old Man talking about his granddaughter's visit. The story was, she was coming from her father's farm in the little town of Bishop to visit the capital, but the truth was her father and grandfather had designs to find her a husband among the political class or prosperous trade men in the community. As much as Old Man Brooks might hate the politicians, he wanted to secure for his granddaughter the most profitable match he could find.

In those years the Georgia Legislature was meeting every two years. Biennial they called it, and 1845 was one of the years that the legislature met. Though they didn't convene until later in the fall, politicians were already arriving to town to, as Old Brooks put it, "begin the process of wrangling for themselves through their corruption and baser instincts more wealth and power than they rightfully should have or can comprehend what to do with."

I suspected that if Father and Grandfather were going to such pains to find a match for the girl she must be brutal on the eyes and certainly hadn't gotten my hopes up. Besides, there was no need for me to be hopeful as I had a steady ride in plump Bessie, and I didn't want to do anything that might upset what had become an ideal situation for me by bedding the Old Man's granddaughter.

So I was a bit taken aback as we stood there on the platform watching the passengers exiting the train and off walked what was then and remains today the finest example of womanly beauty I have ever had the pleasure to see.

She was tall and thin, with a long neck and big green eyes and milk-white skin. Her red hair – orange really – was pulled up under a white, wide-brimmed hat with fancy lace and flowers adorning the top. On each side of her face, drops of that red hair streamed from below the hat, framing her countenance. She wore a white gown with a high waist, accentuating her not overly large but ample enough breasts. The gown was detailed in lace and satin ribbons, and had the low-cut square neck that was popular in those days. She wore satin gloves up to her elbows, and as she stepped out onto the platform she raised up a white lace parasol to shield herself from the August sun.

My God! she was as fine a woman as I ever saw. I have always been inclined to affairs of the loins rather than affairs of the heart – as you may well have determined for yourself – but I will tell you that if my heart was ever to be won it was won on that day on the platform of the Milledgeville train depot.

And I nearly fell off the platform when she looked my way and smiled a smile of honest delight.

But it wasn't me she was smiling to. It was the Old Man.

"Granddaddy!" she squealed, and came forward to embrace the old man.

Jimbo and I fetched her trunks and baggage, and I can say I was more than a little indignant that the Old Man never even bothered to introduce us. I was no more than one of the slaves in his mind, though I lived in the house, ate at the family table and suffered his philosophical rants in the evenings. It's the little things that allow you to know your place in life.

Even as I loaded the trunk onto the carriage, helped Old Man Brooks and his granddaughter in, and took up the reins to take them home, the Old Man never bothered to introduce her. Jimbo and I took the baggage up to the room that would belong to Miss Brooks – conveniently located just down the hall from my own room – and it was only then, when Jimbo had gone, that Brooks finally made me known to his granddaughter.

The girl had just returned from visiting her grandmother's bedside. The Old Man and I were in the parlor off the foyer, and as we heard her coming down the steps the Old Man said, "Eliza, dear, come in here and let me introduce you to a young man who has been helping me at the store." She came into the sitting room and I stood to greet her. She eyed me up and down, and I was fairly certain she approved of what she saw. "This is young Jackson Speed. For several months now he has been in my employ and has proved to be a valuable asset at the store. He also has been paying board here at the house, and so I am sure you will get to see quite a bit of him."

I did not know yet what to make of Miss Eliza. Unimaginably pretty, but the idle chat in the carriage on the way back to the house left me wondering if she wasn't a bit vapid.

"Mr. Speed," she said, curtseying and then holding out one of those long, gloved arms so that I might take her hand, which I did. "It is a pleasure to meet you," she said, with all the emphasis on "pleasure" in a way that I might have taken as an invitation had it come from a different woman. Of course, with Southern women you never can tell if they are simply being polite or flirting.

I smiled my best crooked smile and gave her a wink. "Miss Eliza," I said to her, "your grandfather has told me so much about you (which was a lie, he'd hardly mentioned her directly to me) and I am so glad to finally be able to meet you face-to-face. I must say, you're even lovelier than your grandfather let on."

She smiled and cocked her head a bit at that. "I am so glad that you are of such a great assistance to my dear Granddaddy," she assured me. "Father and Mother worry all the time that he is doing too much at that store of his, and they will be ever so pleased when I write to them to let them know that Granddaddy has a helper."

There was something about her manner that left me convinced that she was probably a bit daft. But I moved ahead anyway: "It is a constant pleasure for me to be able to ease the burden on your grandfather. And at the same time, his tutelage has been of extraordinary value to me. I believe I have learned more about business and politics and the important things of this world than I ever could have at Oglethorpe University, or maybe even at Yale."

It's charm, you see. Give 'em a smile and a wink, butter 'em up a bit with fine talk on a subject they care about (in this instance, her grandfather) and then give them a laugh and they're halfway undressed.

"And with him paying me thirty-five cents a day," I said, working up to my punchline, "I can also say that his tuition is much more reasonable than what I might expect to find at some Yankee university."

Poor stuff, I admit, but that had her fluttering and laughing just enough that I gave her another wink.

At that moment I caught Old Man Brooks eying me with suspicion in a way he hadn't done since we'd first met that day in the hotel. Old Brooks and I had been getting along quite well, but in that instant when he thought I might be sizing up his granddaughter (right enough he was, too) I got a cold, hard stare from him.

I decided my best course of action at that moment was a hasty exit, so I made some excuse and left the house for a while.

When I returned for supper everything seemed right again,

and I enjoyed a pleasant meal with Old Brooks and his granddaughter. Through dinner, and afterwards when the three of us retired to the porch, she patiently sat listening to her grandfather and his talk of politics. He quizzed her quite a bit about the state of her father's farm – which I deduced was actually a cotton plantation of some size – and she was able to offer mostly unsatisfactory answers that gave him no more notion of the state of the farm than if he'd asked me about it.

But it is an undeniable fact that her presence dramatically improved the quality of the company.

If you think that Miss Eliza Brooks was enough to make me want to give Bessie a reprieve, I can tell you that wasn't the case at all. If anything, I was more adamant when I went to ride her that night. Shawl be damned, I dragged her all about that yard.

Still, I threw every bit of charm I had at Miss Eliza and, whenever her grandfather wasn't watching, made a real effort to woo her. But I liked her, and so I was willing to take my time.

Over the next few weeks Eliza joined her grandfather and me infrequently. Often she had formal parties to go to. Her grandfather never went, but put her under the chaperone of one of the local ladies who was only too glad to look after her and keep those political boys at a safe distance. But most nights in the week, she joined her grandfather and me on the porch, and together she and I patiently listened to what he had to say. Knowing she was looking for a suitor among the sons of congressmen and senators, Old Man Brooks tempered his opinions, some. He instructed her to listen carefully, though, so that she wouldn't "sound like a fool" at her parties.

A few evenings, as the weather started to cool, Old Man Brooks turned in earlier than usual, leaving me and Miss Eliza swinging on the front porch swing together, and here I started making real efforts.

She confessed that she found the parties dull and the boys duller, and so I made jokes at their expense. Most of them, of course, I knew a little from when they came into the store. I would tease about their big ears or large noses or weak chins; I would laugh about how fat their fathers were and how many of them looked to be following in their father's footsteps (planting seeds of doubt in her mind, you understand); or I would poke fun at their overall lack of self-sufficiency. Why, here I was just a teenager out on my own and making my way in life, and these boys in their twenties were still hanging onto Daddy's coattails.

And Miss Eliza loved it, mostly because she despised them.

In my jokes I always made myself out to be the better man, and it wasn't long before she was agreeing with me on those counts. Eventually, she was even comparing me to her father: "You're so like Daddy in the way you want to work hard for what you have."

Well, I've since met her father, and the fact is as a plantation owner he never worked a day in his life. He had a farm full of slaves to do the work for him. But truth didn't matter. All that mattered was what her mind conceived to be true. And if she wanted me and Daddy to be so much alike, all the better for me if she believed we were.

Sometimes we would read Shakespearean plays together – with me taking the roles of the men and her taking the speaking parts of the women. She adored the flowery language, and I knew once I opened one of the books in her grandfather's library that she would be mine for hours.

I discovered, too, that Miss Eliza enjoyed above all other things a Sunday ride into the country, and so every Sunday after church and supper I saddled up two of Old Brooks' horses and she and I would ride out away from town through the hilly countryside to look at the leaves changing color or watch the train on its way to Macon. We'd chat idly, she about her parties or her siblings back home (she had two older brothers and three younger siblings, two girls and a boy) whom she truly missed. Or we discussed whatever novel she happened to be reading or some article that had taken her fancy in the American Magazine of Useful and Entertaining Knowledge to which her grandfather subscribed and which she and I often read together. I always believed she liked it best because it was so full of engravings and very short on words.

I mostly listened, or rather pretended to listen, as she chatted away and I spent my time admiring her more attractive features.

Miss Eliza was eighteen years old by then. I suppose Ashley Franks had given me a taste for older women, because I've had them older and I've had them younger, and I can tell you that the ones I liked best were always older than me. Oh, aye, that didn't hold true for Pinkerton's Agent, but it was true in all other cases. And it was especially true with Miss Eliza, then and now. I've intimately known hundreds of women, I suppose – some for a night, others for a week and others for months or years – but I guess the truth of it is I've never liked any of them better than Miss Eliza. Except maybe Pinkerton's Agent, but that's neither here nor there. It was Eliza's prettiness that had me so overwhelmed, then, and even as she aged, she never really lost that.

Anyway, I'm getting all sentimental and going off of my story.

It was on one of these Sunday afternoon rides that I won Miss Eliza's heart, and would you believe for a minute that it was through my heroism that I did it? Well, it was cowardice, but when you're a big, strong lad like I was and your cowardice makes you think quick and act quicker, cowardice can often be misunderstood by witnesses, as I've seen countless times.

We'd ridden well out from town, past Midway, where Oglethorpe University was at the time, and we'd stopped and were picnicking on Fox Hill, looking down across a valley of brilliant red, orange and yellow hardwoods. It was cool and crisp, but not late enough in the season to be overly cold, the sky was cloudless and a pretty blue, and the afternoon could not have been more pleasant. Eliza was wearing a pale-blue riding habit that matched her orange hair superbly, and she was so fetching that I was having a bit of difficulty in restraining my carnal instincts. For this very reason, Sunday evenings after my rides with Miss Eliza proved particularly burdensome for young Bessie, who always took the brunt of the frustration that Miss Eliza stirred within me.

She was laughing gaily at some joke or another that I'd made, and I was at that very moment wondering the proper way to make the leap from our growing friendship to romance. I had nearly decided that the best way to do it would be to grab her left tit in my left hand, wrap my right arm around her waist and pull her lips to mine – right there on Fox Hill – when I heard the sound of an oncoming rider. I looked back toward town and saw approaching us two boys on horseback.

I recognized them right away as a couple of the dandies who frequented the parties Miss Eliza attended, and I thought one of them was actively after her. They rode up fairly fast and halted their horses just in front of where Eliza and I were perched on a blanket. It was pretty plain to me that this was no chance encounter – these boys knew Eliza and I were up here and they'd come to force an encounter with me.

"Hello, Miss Eliza," one of them said, still astride his horse. "And who is this?"

That was pretty forward of him, I thought, and damned rude.

"This is my friend Jackson Speed," she said. "Jackson, this is Alexander Franklin, a secretary of Governor George W. Crawford."

The way she spoke his name – or more accurately, his title – my stomach dropped, for I was certain there was some attraction there. Eliza was always drawn in by men of station and importance, and in her mind one could not get much more important than being a secretary to Governor George W. Crawford. Crawford, of course, was a Whig – the only one

Georgia ever had – but that was meaningless to her.

Franklin slid down off his horse, without taking his eyes off me, and I could tell he was sizing me up. His friend, who was not introduced to me, followed his lead. I was well aware that the peacock was about to fan his plumage. He had a hostile air about him, and I decided to meet it with grace.

I rose from the blanket where I'd been sitting with Eliza and stretched out my hand to Mr. Franklin.

"Pleased to meet you," I said.

I was well aware that he was all hot and full of hostility, and so I endeavored to be cool and gracious so that by comparison Eliza would view me as the more mature, level-headed and, (I hoped) desirable one.

"Sir, I demand to know what it is you think you're doing picnicking with my intended," Franklin said. Though the speech was clearly practiced, his voice quavered a bit. Franklin was shorter and thinner than me, though at least eight or ten years older. He didn't seem unhealthy at the moment, but he had the appearance of a man who has fought against ailments and might have won the battles but was losing the war. His cheeks, rosy enough in the cool weather and straight from a ride, had a tinge of gauntness to them, his eyes a bit dark and sunken.

His friend was something different. Big and buff – about my size, I seem to recall. He was what they call the strong, silent type and didn't utter a word during this brief interview.

"Intended?" I asked, startled. "I did not know Miss Eliza was betrothed."

"I am no such thing," Eliza exclaimed, now rising to her feet. "Why, you've merely mentioned to me that you would like to be a husband and I've only told you that I would like to be a wife. These were pleasant enough flirtations, but at no point have we ever been in agreement that I would be your wife and you would be my husband."

She sounded a bit perturbed, and this was all to my benefit. I believe that even then my charm had won her over, and being confronted with one of her young sparks in front of me and forced to deny his forwardness I believe also made her realize that if there was a man in the vicinity of Fox Hill that she truly admired, I was he.

"Well, not betrothed, exactly," Franklin stammered, having to back down.

My preference is to never have to win a woman's affections through confrontation, but if it must be done it cannot be done better than this. My adversary interrupted a pleasant picnic; he showed up with a strongman to help him with his weak and quavering voice; he came on too familiar with the girl in question by announcing her as his intended when she clearly had no such intentions.

I thought for a moment all the fight was out of him, having been reprimanded by Miss Eliza. And while I wasn't a bit concerned about Franklin, I can tell you the cold stare of his companion had me a little jumpy. I didn't care for the idea of having to fight one man, but the idea of having to fight two was beyond anything acceptable, particularly when one of them was clearly a brawler brought to the scene for no other reason than to put me down. But I breathed relief at the thought that maybe Franklin's warm attitude was cooling a bit.

But I was well off the mark.

Rather than lose his will, Eliza's rebuke just made Franklin that much hotter.

I was never particularly clear on the order of things (which is uncommon, for usually I'm very alert when there's danger going about and can recall with clarity what happened and how I managed to avoid it), but here is what I recall of the incident:

Franklin, still huffing and puffing, took a couple of steps toward me and poked me in the chest. He said something threatening, the sort of thing that usually makes me fall back a bit, but I don't remember exactly what it was he said. At that point, I believe, Eliza stepped forward, attempting to wedge herself between Franklin and me, and that's when the damned fool drew back his hand and backhanded Miss Eliza right across the cheek.

Though he was my rival, I will tell you plain: I do not believe he intended for a second to lay a finger on that beautiful face. I believe he was drawing his hand back with an intention to slap or punch me and, whether it was nerves at picking a fight with someone of my size or carelessness or a complete lack of bodily control, he inadvertently slapped Eliza across the face with the back of his hand.

She gasped, "I never!"

Franklin looked aghast.

Franklin's friend took a step back, clearly uncertain now whether he wanted to be the champion for someone who would manhandle a woman in such a way.

And here I saw my chance. In the flash of a second, I knew that if I wanted to avoid becoming a punching bag for Franklin's champion and if I wanted to also win outright any rivalry with Franklin and become a hero in Miss Eliza's eyes, there was nothing else for it. I had to act in a decisive way in her defense and do so before that fool Franklin had a chance to issue an apology for what was very obviously (to me, at any rate) an accidental slap. In an instant, I girded myself and took action.

"Scoundrel!" I shouted in outrage, and balling my fist, I landed a punch on his jaw that had behind it every bit of strength I could muster. As I've said, I was a big and well-built lad, and when I put every bit of my strength behind a punch it was quite a considerable punch. And my punch combined with Franklin's physical weakness was enough to win the day.

Franklin stumbled under the blow, taking two wobbly steps backward. His eyes glassed over and he reeled, and then he fell flat on his back, half conscious and sprawled in the grass. For a moment I thought I'd killed him.

Eliza gasped again at the sight of the violence, but she

threw her arms around my waist and pressed her cheek against my chest. I looked at Franklin's companion, who was rooted to his spot, unsure of what to do.

"The scoundrel slapped a lady," I said, baring my teeth and putting on a show of bravado. It was easy to do with her wrapped around me, for if he was to decide to come at me he'd have to get through Eliza first. "If you choose to fight for him, I'll give you more of the same. Otherwise, you should put him on his horse and ride away from here, and next time you should think better than to come along for a fight with a coward who slaps women."

It was all strong and manly stuff, and the brute saw the reason in it. Without a word, he helped the delirious Franklin onto his feet and then steadied him as he climbed, humiliated, onto his horse.

And that was how I won the lady's heart. Stand up strong and courageous for a woman's honor or defense, and she'll be with you as long as you'll have her. The fact is, she'll be with you even when you're done with her.

Of course, Eliza couldn't see it for what it really was. I was neither standing up for her honor nor defending her person. I'd seen an opportunity to put a quick end to this without having to find out if I could stand up to Franklin's friend's punches any better than Franklin could stand up to mine. Maybe I didn't flee headlong off Fox Hill and run for shelter, but that punch I landed on his chin was thrown in cowardice all the same.

A brave man would have instantly recognized the foolish mistake Franklin made in smacking Eliza on the cheek. A man of honor and chivalry would have stood by silently while the offender made his sincerest apologies. The decent sort of bloke they write about in the dime novels would have manfully allowed weak and sickly Franklin to step aside and would have engaged in fisticuffs with the big brute, shaking his hand and exclaiming, "May the best man win!" before the row.

Not me and no thank'ee!

It has been the rule that has saved my neck over and over again: If there is a way out, whatever the cost in fortune or fame, then b'God skedaddle.

That fool Franklin handed me the way out and in less than a second I was quick enough to see it and take it. Call me a coward if you like, but I was proud of my work on Fox Hill that afternoon.

And, of course, that wasn't all.

Eliza was still clutching me around the waist and her face pressed against my chest and her cheeks were moist with tears. I took a step back to break the embrace and looked down at her. "Come here, dear," I whispered to her, taking her chin in my hand and lifting her face to me so that I could see her cheek. The red mark from that idiot's knuckles was still plainly visible. Obviously he was drawing back to punch me, not to slap me.

"That infamous scoundrel really did give you a pop, didn't he?" I said, still holding her chin with one hand and wiping away the tears with the other. "Can't imagine what he might have been thinking, hitting a woman while standing within arm's reach of me. Why he's lucky I didn't give him more than I did."

"Oh!" she exclaimed, taking my hands in her own and working her face into a frown. "I don't want to talk about him anymore! He was too forward by far coming out here and making claims on me. And what did he have his friend along for?"

"Well, clearly Mr. Franklin was here to hit the women and his friend was here to hit the men," I scoffed. It was half joke, half making sure she was well aware of why Franklin's friend had come along. She smiled a bit at that. "I can't imagine what you saw in him."

"I saw nothing in him," Eliza confessed. "He has been a diversion at these socials and nothing more. And, the truth is, I was becoming increasingly annoyed with him."

"I can certainly see why," I said, wiping the last of her tears away.

And she smiled up at me with a light in her eye and I was simply overcome, and so I kissed her.

I cannot count all the women who have looked at me like that or had a Jack Speed kiss planted on them unsuspected like, but all except this one got it because I wanted to get my hands in their shirts and my hips between their thighs.

Not this one, though. I was just overcome. Eliza, with her flushed cheeks against her pale skin, and her pretty green eyes looking up into mine, and her long orange hair dazzling in the sun – well, there's no other word for it: I was overcome.

"Jackson Speed, I believe I am in love with you," she whispered into my face as our lips parted.

We settled back down to our picnic, both of us reclining on the blanket, but there wasn't much eating of what was left of our meal. I believe we had cold fried chicken and biscuits for our picnic that day, but at best we only nibbled at it.

"I think I've known since I first got off the train and saw you," she said. She was rambling idly away and I caught myself actually listening to her. "Granddaddy didn't even introduce you, but I could barely stop myself from gazing at you. You are the loveliest man that I've ever seen. You've never spoken of any of your girlfriends, but you must have dozens of them."

"Not a one," I told her wistfully, unless of course you count the slave girl that I rumble on nearly a nightly basis while thinking of you, I thought to myself.

Thinking back on it, I suppose it only made sense: All that Eliza knew of me was that I was lower class, a laborer, strong and handsome, maybe, but probably trouble all the same. And here she'd just had firsthand evidence that I was a ruffian. Girls her age are always drawn to men like that.

I brushed her hair with my fingers and kissed her each time she stopped talking long enough for me to pucker my lips, and soon the shadows started to get long and I suggested that we get back home before it was dark. I was worried, too, that her friend Franklin might have regained his courage and be waiting for me, maybe with a couple of thugs, and I didn't want to be caught out at night and not see them coming. But we arrived home without a problem and joined Old Man Brooks on the porch for our usual evening conversation.

I remember well that he railed against the politicians over the coming war. The Old Man was against the war, but he was just being contrary because most of the politicians were for it. Had the politicians and newspaper editors been editorializing on the dangers of hostilities with the Mexicans or waxing eloquent about the flower of youth and the futility of flinging our nation's future at a storm of Mexican bullets, the Old Man would surely have been leading the charge to slaughter the Catholic bastards.

By then all the newspapers were carrying dispatches of local militia companies that were forming to go west and kill the rancheros.

"I reckon we'll be at war soon enough. The Yankee politicians want the deep-water ports in California, and the Southern politicians want new slave-holding territories, and as long as they both agree that they want the Mexican territories, you can bet they'll figure some excuse to go to war," the Old Man was saying. "And every young rascal will gladly answer the call to glory. Listen to this, a company of volunteers has formed in Macon and they have offered their services to the secretary of war," and he picked up a newspaper and read from its pages: "'Our fellow citizens, and the public generally, we are sure, will join us in rendering a tribute of praise and noble zeal, and alacrity with which this gallant and spirited company have stepped forward at the first whisperings of danger.'

"Now you tell me, what young fool upon hearing those words – 'praise, noble zeal, gallant and spirited' – will decline the offer to rush into the fray and lose an arm or a leg to a Mexican bullet?"

It was all prophetic stuff, and every time since that I have read a newspaper editor wax eloquent about the nobility and gallantry of volunteering to be killed for some politician's war, I have thought of the Old Man and his tirades on that front porch.

But I had other priorities that evening, and was relieved when the chill calmed the old man's temper and he decided to turn in early.

Earlier, when we'd first arrived back from our picnic, I'd nicked a bottle of muscadine wine from the Old Man's liquor cabinet, and hid it under the straw cushion of the bench outside. Now, with the Old Man gone for bed, I slid the bottle out and popped off the cork.

Eliza gave me a coquettish smile as I handed her the bottle. "What are you about?" she asked me slyly.

"I thought I would toast the escalation of our friendship," I smiled.

"Oh-ho!" she exclaimed, taking a swig from the bottle, "Our friendship is escalated now, is it?"

She passed me the bottle, and I took the opportunity to slide from my bench to her porch swing.

"Earlier this afternoon you were professing your love," I whispered, putting my face near to hers. "That seems an escalation to me."

We kissed again and continued drinking from the bottle. I tested my limits by placing a hand on her thigh, then on her waist as we both continued kissing and murmuring.

The more we drank, the lighter our conversation became, so that I was soon making fun of her "beau" Franklin, and she was making fun of him, too. And then I was calling her "my intended" and she was making fun of that.

And I suppose at some point, as we neared the end of the bottle, one or the other of us said something about getting married – but I thought nothing of it at the time.

By the time the bottle was gone – which didn't take long – we were both feeling its effects, and when I stood up I felt myself get dizzier than I expected to be. I helped her to her feet and we both giggled our way into the house.

The front door of the Old Man's house opened to a large foyer. To the left and right were the parlor and dining room, and the hall extending toward the back of the house led to the living room and the slaves' room. I could just barely see Bessie peaking around the corner as Eliza and I came into the house. And, would you know, there was jealousy in her eyes?

Well, Bessie's jealousy was nothing to me, and I pinched Eliza on the rear as she began to ascend the stairs in front of me. She squealed and laughed and then shushed me. When we got to the top of the stairs the Old Man's bedroom was in front of us and his wife's room was beside it to the right. Eliza's room was at the far end of the hall to the right, and my room was to the left at the opposite end of the hall.

I was well pleased to see that without the slightest bit of prodding from me, Eliza stumbled off to the left.

It was the small stand in the hallway beside her grandfather's door that did it. Unaccustomed as she was to walking toward my room, and in the dark and a bit uneasy on her feet anyway, she bumped into the table. The small porcelain decorative pieces on the stand rattled and the table bumped into the wall with a bang.

Eliza laughed and turned and looked at me wide-eyed. She put a finger up to her pursed lips, "Shhhh!" and she spat out a fresh group of giggles.

I pushed closed the door to my bedroom and fumbled around on the night stand for the matches and struck one on the side of the box. I lit the oil lamp and replaced the glass chimney, and as I turned, Eliza was finishing pulling off the rest of her clothes. [2]

She stood there before me in the lamplight with nothing on, and I could have sworn I'd died and gone to Heaven and was now gazing upon an angel.

Pale as paper, Eliza's legs rose all the way to her shoulders. Her frame was lean – not a lot of curves to grab hold to – but the breasts were pert and peppy and topped off with big red points that I couldn't wait to get between finger and thumb. The look on her face as she displayed her body to me was one of pretty pride, and there was such gleeful expectation in her smile that I was fairly out of my boots, suspenders and shirt before you could whistle Dixie.

The truth is she's never really changed. Throughout her entire life, she was easily as ready to go as ever I was, and any time since that we've come to grips she was always like this: gleeful and energetic like a playful kitten, and long legs open.

She did a back dive onto the bed, everything exposed before me, as I shook first one leg and then the other out of my trousers, and I was prepared to pounce on that red-haired little puss, when from nowhere I heard a violent swish and felt what I instantly knew was the Old Man's cane.

Well, you'll remember I'd felt it once before, but that had been nothing. This time it was across my bare bottom and he'd swung that cane with the strength of a man 40 years younger.

I yelped and flew headlong to the floor where I balled up like an infant praying to God and damning his eyes.

I looked up and saw that he'd moved across the floor and had raised the cane over me and was prepared to swing it a second time.

"Granddaddy, no!" Eliza yelled, while pulling the blankets up to cover herself.

"I'll break your skull open, you rascal!" he said, and swung the cane at my head. I covered my skull with my forearms and felt the smartness of the cane crash down on me again.

"Granddaddy! I love him!" Eliza squealed. "Stop hitting him! We're going to be married!"

Well that sucked all the fight out of the Old Man, and it even stopped my whimpering.

"You're what?" he demanded.

"Married!" she said again. "We're going to be married!"

The Old Man studied her for a minute, and then he studied

me: naked and curled up and nearly weeping in pain on his floor.

"Married, eh?" and I could see that he was calculating.

He liked me, and that's all there was to it. He liked me, and he didn't mind the idea of his granddaughter marrying me – a hard-working laborer, like he was in his day – rather than one of those politician's dandy sons.

After a moment of considering, Old Man Brooks said, "Well, he couldn't continue on as a delivery boy at the store. That wouldn't do. But if he were a manager – perhaps even if we arranged for him to buy the store from me. Yes, that wouldn't be so bad."

And as he was caught up thinking about it, I chanced to slide my trousers across the floor and – without standing – slid them back on.

"There'll be no fornicating in my house!" he roared after a moment's consideration. Then he settled his tone, though, and said, "But I don't see why we couldn't get the wedding planned for three or four weeks from now. Surely you two can keep your clothes on that long."

It was Eliza banging into the table in the hallway that did it. She'd roused the old man, and sensing that his granddaughter's virtue was at stake, he'd come armed with his cane. And now – with me still sitting there on the floor wondering if my forearm wasn't broken – the two of them were actually making wedding plans.

CHAPTER IV

For the next two weeks the old man watched me like a hawk, seldom letting me out of his sight. The cool evenings no longer drove him to bed early, and he made certain Eliza and I were tucked into separate beds before turning in himself. And at that point, even though she was steaming fit to burst to get to business with me, Eliza was adamant that if we were to be wed we must wait as her grandfather insisted.

And all the Old Man's effortations to secure his beloved granddaughter's chastity until her wedding night meant, too, that Bessie was safe and I was left as frustrated as a man can be. It was made all the worse because we'd nearly done the deed – I'd laid eyes on the bare body of that wonderful Venus – and then been interrupted so cruelly. But it didn't matter much, I suppose, that even Bessie was unavailable to me as a release for my frustrations; she didn't seem to have much interest anymore anyway. Every look she gave me over the next two weeks was a scandalous look of loathing and jealousy.

The wedding was a fairly simple thing, held on November 10. I have decent enough memories of it, anyway. We were wed by the pastor at Eliza's grandfather's church (the one we all attended) up on Fox Hill.

It was one of those gorgeous November days that make you glad to live in the South. The sky was clear and blue, the air warm in the sunshine but with a hint of that autumn nip, and the birds, as if paid off for the occasion, were constantly singing their songs throughout the morning and afternoon. By God, I believe I even remember bells ringing throughout the day.

Eliza's mother and sisters all took the train to Milledgeville for the wedding, and they mopped their eyes and hugged Eliza both before and after the ceremony. Her grandmother even came out of her sickbed and rode the carriage up to Fox Hill to attend.

We returned too the Old Man's house and ate a big dinner after the ceremony, and a few of the Old Man's friends, neighbors and customers came by to say hello and congratulations. Eliza, too, had a steady stream of friends coming by to wish us well. I kept expecting young Alexander Franklin to come offer his congratulations as well, but he never showed up. I suspect he was holding a grudge.

The Old Man worked it with Eliza's father for me, too.

Eliza's father had bought a plantation and saw himself raising his status in society. He'd risen above the merchant class of his father to the plantation class, and he believed, therefore, that his daughters ought to be married to future senators and governors or the sons of other wealthy plantation owners – certainly not to delivery boys. So the Old Man had written to his son that long before there was any romance between me and Eliza there had been a decision made to sell the store to me. He put in there, too, that I was planning to enroll at Oglethorpe University and was considering a future career in law.

This all delighted Eliza's father who – while disappointed she hadn't found someone already building a political career – seemed grateful that I was a hardworking, enterprising young man with designs to continue improving my status. So much that he knew. He immediately gave his blessing to the whole thing, and the Old Man legitimately promised to use his influence to get me actually enrolled at Oglethorpe.

Eliza thought it was all a wonderful idea, and the truth is I was warming up to it myself.

You'll have to understand: I was still young with little ambition in life and absolutely no plan for my future. So far, I was simply coasting along the river of life and each bend in the river had led me from one thing to the next, and it seemed that the next thing was always better than the one before. I'd encountered very few rapids – the business with Uriah Franks trying to slaughter me was bad, and those first few days in Milledgeville before the Old Man took me in had been unpleasant, hungry days – and it seemed to me that if this family wanted to give me their daughter, set me up as a hammer and nail salesman and push me into higher education with a view of eventually becoming Governor of Georgia, all that was well enough.

And I even started daydreaming a bit:

"Governor Speed," my young secretary would ask, "how can I be of service to you today?"

"Why, son, how about you run into town and fetch me two whores and bottle of whiskey."

Yes, being the most powerful man in the state might not be so bad a thing.

So as all these people around me made my plans and decided my future, I just smiled and nodded and promised that it would all be delightful, and I could hardly stand my excitement at the idea of attending classes and arguing the law.

And it's no lie, either, that being married to Eliza – especially back in those days – sweetened the deal all the more.

We found a cottage in town over on McIntosh Street – a small place with a nice garden in back – and set up house there. Eliza cooked me meals that were passable enough – though not quite up to Mamie's standards – and I sold nails. And more evenings than not, we woke the neighbors as the headboard threatened to break through the wall.

She was an astounding rollick in bed. She'd giggle and laugh and tease, and we had such tremendous fun together that it was hard to see how anything could ever turn wrong for me.

Oh, the war drums were beating by then, for certain, but that was no business of mine. Here and there volunteer militia were forming up and offering their services to President Polk (should they be needed), but I don't recall anyone from Milledgeville ever talking about joining the militia. The big talk then, of course, was the renaming of Marthasville – and we see where that got Milledgeville. [3]

Those were good days spent with my new bride. The Christmas season was a gay time with balls every other night while the legislators were in town. When we were not at the balls, Eliza and I enjoyed evenings at home, reading Shakespeare and other popular Christmas stories of the time. And when the stories were put away, we enjoyed the benefits of marriage. Particularly during the Christmas season, too, the Old Man often came to visit in late afternoons. Though the colder temperatures ached his bones, as he said, both Eliza and I believed he was lonely and missed our evenings chatting on his porch.

The New Year held the promise of being prosperous and enjoyable. And do you know, even though we were attending these balls with all the loveliest of belles of the Georgia political class, in those first few months of marriage my eyes didn't wander from my blushing bride? Even through the spring when everything with two two ripe melons was as goatish as you could desire and readily had, I only had thoughts for Eliza.

In the winter I began attending lectures at Oglethorpe University, continuing to work at the store in the afternoons. To ease my burdens of attending lectures and working at the store, I had hired a new delivery boy, Dick Pruitt, and the Old Man still came into the store daily to see that I wasn't ruining the business he had built. But by the time I arrived in the afternoon, the Old Man typically ended his day early and went home.

All the plans concocted by the Old Man for my career and the situation of his granddaughter seemed to be falling perfectly into place.

Well, all of that was good enough, but we seldom have

control over the events of our lives. Everyone was making plans for my future, but often a person's past has more to do with his future, and presently my past had decided to change the course of my life.

As I was now the proprietor of the store rather than the delivery boy, I had adopted an appearance more fitting to my new station than the trousers, shirt and suspenders I ordinarily wore. Besides, I now had a wife who was taking a particular interest in my appearance as I left the house each morning.

I wasn't pleased, if the truth were known. The frock coats she dressed me in, which were all the style then, were uncomfortably tight in the shoulders for me. They were cut tight, and particularly when I was young I wore a tight coat very well and cut a pretty fair figure, but my shoulders and arms were too big to wear the frock coats comfortably. In the winter they weren't so bad, but by late spring these wool coats were insufferably hot. It was the expected uniform for students attending lectures, but when I arrived at the store each day, I always removed my coat and worked in just my shirt and vest.

On this particular day in June of 1846, I had just taken off my coat and hung it in the back storeroom and was still at the back of the store when I heard the front door open. The Old Man had already left, and only Dick and I were in the store.

To my horror, when I looked up I saw Uriah Franks standing there, the door still open behind me. He had seen me just as I'd seen him, and our eyes were locked. I cannot tell you what emotions my face revealed. But Uriah Franks' face contorted into an expression of recognition immediately followed by hatred. His eyes cut through me in a stare of fury. And then his lips curled into a smile full of revenge. He stood there for a moment – was it five seconds or five minutes, I do not know – holding his stare on me. Despite the heat and my back drenched with sweat, I felt a shiver run up my spine. Then Franks turned and walked out.

When I had seen him come in, I had expected, following the theme of our last encounter, Uriah Franks would launch himself at me in a rage, intent on murder and shouting and cussing. When our eyes locked – him coming through the front of the store and me at the back – I felt my insides dissolve and hot, prickly fear ran up my neck and into my hairline. For a moment I was ready to bolt for the back door and flee headlong down the streets of the state capital screaming bloody murder. But when he turned and walked out of the store, I was dumbfounded – caught completely off-guard by this unexpected move. I scrambled over to where we kept the hatchets, grabbed one up and walked up to the front window to see if I could see where he'd got to.

From the store window it appeared that no one was out on the street – including Uriah – which was uncommon. At first I attributed the absence of anyone about to the hot June weather. But then I remembered that there was hullabaloo down at the parade ground at the Capitol, and everyone in town would be there.

"We're closing early today," I said to Dick ushering him out the front door amid his protests.

"But what about the deliveries?" he asked me. "I've got three orders yet to deliver today."

"Tomorrow. We'll deliver the orders tomorrow," I said, too distracted to give him another thought.

I pulled down the shade in front of the window and locked the door on my way out.

I looked up one side of the street and down the other, but wherever Uriah Franks had gone I didn't know. The streets of Milledgeville were full of cotton bales, and it was easy to assume that he'd hid behind one of these and was watching for me.

Standing outside the door – still with that hatchet unconsciously clutched in my fist – I tried to think of what to do. The only option that seemed viable was to make my way home. I thought I might stay there for a day or two, maybe a week, to give Uriah Franks time to leave town. I could close the store or get the Old Man to go down there for the next few days. I considered, too, that maybe Eliza and I might get on the next train out of town and hide out somewhere else for a few days. Savannah, maybe. All I knew was that I wanted to keep distance between me and Franks.

He might not even have realized I owned the store. I was in the back when he came in. There was nothing to indicate that the store was mine or that I worked there.

Unconsciously, I found myself walking toward the Capitol and the crowd at the parade ground. A volunteer militia – the Jasper Greens out of Savannah – was making its way through the state, from Savannah to Columbus and then on to Mexico, and they were stopped today at the Capitol to be recognized for their gallantry and bravery by the Governor and some other dignitaries, and they would be taking the train that afternoon for Macon. It was all the gossip in the store the previous day, and the sons and daughters of Milledgeville were at the parade ground to wish them Godspeed and a mighty victory.

I kept looking over my shoulder, but there was no sign that Uriah Franks was following me. There were a handful of people about, but the street was so near to empty that I felt certain if he was there I would spot him.

Presently, I found myself staring down the long lawn of Capitol Square, leading to the front of the Capitol, with the parade ground off to the left. There was a crowd on the lawn, which rose at a slight incline so that even over the heads of the people gathered I could see the Irish Greens, formed up before the Capitol steps where, I believe, it was the mayor who was asking that while they were in Mexico would they please tell General Taylor that the Mayor of Milledgeville was praying for the rapid deliverance of California and all that new slave territory, or some such.

I crossed the lawn to the crowd and looked over my shoulder – surely here, if anywhere, I would see Franks following me. Of the three or four souls walking behind me across the lawn there were a couple of slaves and a woman with a parasol. Franks was not to be seen. Nevertheless, I had to assume he still had eyes on me.

Now I saw my way out. I pushed into the crowd and worked my way in through the semi-circle surrounding the lined-up volunteers. They looked an unlikely group, those volunteers, wearing nothing resembling uniforms, and they stood slouched on the parade ground – not so much soldiers at parade as a gang of layabouts loafing in the heat. Most of them wore brown trousers and green cotton shirts with big-brimmed straw hats. The officers, such as they were, could easily be recognized as they were wearing vests or even wool coats.

Obviously the War of '46 was going to be a come-as-you-are sort of affair.

I worked through the crowd, starting at the north side of the parade ground, making my way out to the east, and then to the south, sure not to get too close to the edges but always keeping to the middle of the assembly. Despite the heat of June, the crowd was packed in there tight enough – all hoping to hear something of what was being said to make certain they didn't miss an opportunity to cheer and applaud our daring young volunteers. And with the crowd so tight, I was making a terrible ruckus as I tried to move through it. This was all deliberate, though. Every once in a while I would pause and look back in my wake. If Uriah Franks was there, I'd see the commotion he caused as he moved through the crowd.

Each time I turned, there was nothing. Though, once, I did catch an older woman eying me coldly, and I suspect that was because I'd trodden upon her toes as I'd scooted past her.

Now that I was at the south end of the parade ground, I backed my way out of the crowd again. Our cottage was northwest of the Capitol, just a few blocks, but I could swing around the southern end of the legislative building and make my way down Washington Street and then turn back north.

From there, I was just three blocks from West McIntosh Street and two blocks to our cottage. I was relatively sure, too, that even if Uriah Franks had somehow managed to follow me, unobserved, through those deserted streets to the parade ground, he must surely have lost me among the crowd.

But two things I didn't know: Uriah Franks was a far better tracker than I would have credited him being and the man was so set on revenge he would have followed me to hell and back to see my insides torn out. And, it's an absolute fact that he followed me halfway along that journey.

I walked across the west side of Capitol Square – past the Presbyterian Church and the town market where the slaves were sold – and walked three blocks down Washington Street. Again, the streets were nearly deserted as everyone in town seemed to be crowded in at the parade ground. I was careful to keep a look over my shoulder, but there was barely anyone about, and certainly no one appeared to be following me. Here, too, were residences, not stores, and there were no bales of cotton lining the streets behind which a pursuer might follow unnoticed.

At Clark Street I turned north. I was just five blocks from home now – up a hill, a left on McIntosh, down the hill and there was our cottage – and I almost broke into a run.

As I turned up Clark Street, I realized I could hear a band playing. The Jasper Greens – along with the populace of Milledgeville – were marching toward me and heading to the depot. They were coming down Greene Street and, presumably, would turn south on Tattnall where they would then be just a block from the train depot.

I didn't want to meet the crowd at the junction of Greene and Clark streets because if Franks was in among them I would be easy to spot, but as I neared Greene Street I could see that I was still several blocks ahead of the band, the troops and the gawkers.

I felt an extreme sense of relief as I reached McIntosh Street and rounded the corner for home. Then I took one last look over my shoulder, and that's when I saw him: short and stout, lumbering toward me with a purpose. I couldn't see his face and so didn't know for certain that it was Franks, but there could be no question of whether or not the build of the man following me matched that of the man who sought to kill me, and there was something so purposeful in his stride that my guts melted for the second time today and, despite the heat, I felt the cold grip of fear in my chest.

In the distance, I could hear the triumphant band growing louder.

I knew that I could not now make it to my cottage, for it would be folly to allow Franks a glimpse of where I lived. He would sneak into the house and gut me in the middle of the night. I thought quickly of what my options might be, and decided that the only thing for it was to get back into the crowd. I could hope to lose him, possibly, but at the very least I could feel safe enough that there would be no attack there in front of an entire town of witnesses and a company of men headed to war.

So I made my turn down McIntosh and quickened my step without actually breaking into a run.

At Columbia Street, where I was within sight of my home, I made another left. I was two blocks from Greene Street now and would arrive there almost at the same time as the oncoming band. As I turned back south on Columbia, I saw that the man following me was closing the distance. Here, among the homes of Milledgeville, there was not a soul on the street other than me and Franks, and he must have seen that now was his opportunity. He wasn't running – not yet – but his pace had quickened and he clearly was no longer worried that I would discover his pursuit.

I sped up, too, and as I neared Greene Street I felt a rush of relief as I saw the sackbut players come into view, leading the rest of the band.

I reached the corner of Columbia and Greene just as the band was passing, and behind them were the Jasper Greens, followed by the enormous crowd that went on for blocks.

I took another look over my shoulder and saw clearly the burning hatred in Franks' eyes. He was less than a block away from me now. I stepped into the street just as the crowd caught up to me, and I took a couple of steps into the crowd and then started making my way along with them down Greene Street. The band was already turning on Tattnall.

The train was at the tracks, smoke billowing from its stack, and the Jasper Greens would soon be on their way to the coming slaughter in Mexico. I had blended in with the crowd, and felt a certain level of safety now.

The crowd formed up around the depot. There on the platform, Captain Jackson of the Jasper Greens stood before the crowd and made a speech – as he was known to do. He was a young man – twenty-six years old at the time, he looked like a hawk with his curved beak of a nose, his eyebrows perpetually turned down in an angry frown and stern, serious eyes. He had a deep and robust voice, and was talking now about the necessity of brave men answering the call when their nation needs them. It was all well and good, but I paid almost no attention to it. I was near the front of the crowd – sweating and shivering all at the same time. [4]

Then I heard the heavy breathing in my ear and could feel Uriah Franks pressing himself against me, standing on his toes so that he could whisper the threat into the back of my ear: "Momentarily, you perfidious recreant, you will feel the hot slice as I jab my knife into your lower back. I will twist my knife to cut through your entrails, and I will drag it back out slowly and painfully, and with it will come half of your insides so that I might see your true color. I will leave such a mess inside of you that you shall never recover, but it will take you days, maybe even weeks, to die. It will be an agonizing, painful death, but it will be no more than you deserve – so pray now for mercy from God that the infection kills you quickly.

"And as you lay here dying in front of all these people, I

shall disappear into the crowd and not a soul will know that I've killed you except you and me."

I then felt the tip of his knife push against my back, ever so slightly, and it is no exaggeration to say that I leaped forward – maybe six feet, flat-footed – and then took three big steps, and I was beyond the crowd and stood looking up at Henry Roote Jackson, his speech interrupted by my sudden appearance at the edge of the platform. The moment was surreal as all time seemed to stand still and the crowd looked at me and H. R. Jackson looked at me and I looked at him and wondered if Franks was about to jab that blasted knife into my back. And I did the only thing I could think to do:

"B'God, sir!" I croaked. "That was as rousing a speech as I've ever heard, and I would like to right here and now volunteer to join your fine company and serve beside these men of Savannah!"

The Jasper Greens, who were going about the business of loading their gear onto the train, stood and looked at me for a brief moment and then they hurrahed me and the crowd followed suit, cheering and applauding my gallantry.

I held Jackson's eyes and watched as he pondered. I swear I could feel the heat of hatred penetrating my back as Uriah Franks' eyes bore into me, but it wasn't his knife so I stood my ground. I did not turn around and face him for fear that that last bit of contumacy would be enough to send him over the edge and he would murder me there before everyone.

"Are ye Irish?" H.R. Jackson asked me.

The Speed family were Scotch, my great-grandfather having come from the lowlands of Scotland to Virginia where he was given land so long as he would serve as a buffer between the good English colonials settling along the coast and the savage Indians living to his west. But that was close enough for me, as long as it kept that bastard Franks from gutting me. "Of course I am!" I said. "My father was Andrew Speed, immigrated from Ireland and served with Phinizey's Dragoons!"

None of that meant anything to H. R. Jackson, who was looking around at the crowd and wondering what to do.

"Can anyone testify as to the worthiness of this man?" he asked in his loud voice.

A couple of hands raised from some of my customers and friends. Old Tom O'Connor, whose red face and white hair proved him as Irish as any man in County Cork, stepped forward and swore an oath that I was the finest fighter this side of the Mississippi River, that he'd known my father to be a fine Irishman and by God! but what I wouldn't do Milledgeville proud. Of course, Old Tom O'Connor, who barely knew me other than the times I'd delivered something to him or he'd come in the store and bought something from me, didn't know my father at all and couldn't have told anyone a thing about my ancestry, but he was so caught up in the moment that he'd have swore I was Chinese if it would have gotten me into the war.

Jackson – who was barely more than a boy himself – eyed me up and down and looked thoughtful for a moment.

You'll remember, I had that hatchet in my hand, I was flushed from the heat and my fear so that my face was as red as every Paddy in his company, and I must have looked like a madman intent on getting the Mexican hoard underneath the blade of my hatchet. From all of this and the size of me, H.R. Jackson knew that he wanted me with him if he found himself in a fight. And anyone who knew him knew that Cpt. Henry Roote Jackson loved to make a speech – he was a lawyer, don't ye know – and I believe he was sure that it had been his words that compelled me to step forward and volunteer. Convinced thusly, he could hardly turn me away for I was all the evidence he ever needed that he was the finest of orators.

"Yes then," he said. "Sgt. Devany – muster this man into our rolls!"

And the crowd exploded in cheers! Hats went flying into the air as the men hurrahed me. Women pumped handkerchiefs to their eyes as they wept with pride at my gallantry. Boys in the crowd idolized me. And the boys of the Jasper Greens hurrahed and Sgt. Devany smiled like a maniac and grabbed me by the shoulders and dragged me forward swearing to God Almighty that I was just the man he wanted beside him when the Mexicans came a-calling.

Just then I heard my name called from the crowd and turned to see my lovely wife with parasol in one hand and waving a handkerchief in the other. Miss Eliza was pushing her way forward through the crowd. "Jack! Jack Speed!" she called, unable to get through the crowd fast enough as Devany led me onto the platform. I could see Old Man Brooks just behind her, looking disgusted at me.

"I must do my duty!" I called back, trying to come up with some excuse for her. But the crowd thought I was yelling at them, and they hurrahed me once more and the band started to play and Old Tom O'Connor dabbed at his eyes with his handkerchief and commented to everyone around him that he wished I were his own son, and there I was, stepping onto the train, the 87th member of the Irish Jasper Greens, headed to war in Mexico.

Because I volunteered in Milledgeville under unusual circumstances, my name never appeared in the official rolls in Savannah, and when I tried to secure my pension for my service the damned Yankee bureaucrats refused me on those grounds. As you'll see – or may already know – my name was made in Mexico. Jack Speed, the Hero of El Teneria, they called me. How any damned fool bureaucrat can deny me my pension is beyond the pale. But that's the Yankee government for you.

CHAPTER V

You might imagine that volunteering to join a company of mad Irishmen headed off to war was one of the last things I might comfortably do, but you tell me what alternative I had to avoid a terrifying death at the hands of that lunatic Uriah Franks. He was prepared to gut me with his knife, right there in front of hundreds of witnesses, and if I hadn't stepped forward that would have been Jackie Speed's name on a tombstone. Stepping out of the crowd the way I did, I could think of nothing other than volunteering with the Jasper Greens to get me away from Franks.

I was quite the oddity to the boys of the Jasper Greens – a boy so hell-bent on joining up that I leapt upon the train bound for war. All those boys in the Jasper Greens took me in, and to this day I have nothing but fond memories and good thoughts about them. They were a carefree group of boys back then, full of pranks and jokes. Like any good Irishmen, they enjoyed their whiskey, and it wasn't long before I was enjoying their whiskey, too. If you know anything at all about the Jasper Greens or the War of '46, you'll recall the famous refrain that went 'round the troops: "Give the Jasper Greens some whiskey and they'll charge into hell." It was true, too, but it was no comment on their courage. It was entirely a comment on their desire to drink. With a little whiskey in them, those boys would go anywhere.

Like most of the volunteers headed to war, their chief aim was to see how many Mexicans they could kill. You'll hear talk that most of the volunteers in the war were a bloodthirsty, unruly bunch – and that's a reputation earned largely from behavior of the Texians. I know – before it was all over, I rode with them, too – that the Texians deserved every bit of their reputation. The Jasper Greens only deserved a part of it.

Despite the warm welcome I received from them, I decided that when the train stopped in Macon I would make an escape and go back to Milledgeville. It would be easy enough to explain to Eliza and anyone else in town that I'd been caught up in the moment when I volunteered but, as a newlywed, immediately regretted my rash decision to leave my still-new bride. And surely, if I didn't rush back to Milledgeville but took my time over the course of a couple of days, Uriah Franks would be well off my scent and once again out of my life.

When we arrived in Macon, it was more of the same as the company's welcome to Milledgeville – a band and all the citizenry cheering us as we unloaded from the train.

The Macon Volunteers, the Bibb Cavalry and the Floyd Rifles – who all looked a good deal more soldierly than we did, though we were the ones going off to war while those boys got to sleep in their beds at night – marched us from the depot to the Court House Square where the city's ancient Mayor addressed us in a speech full of flowery expressions of our noble and splendid and chivalrous sacrifice and how God would undoubtedly smile upon us and put thousands of Mexicans before the barrels of our rifles that we might smite the Catholic hoard and much more of the same, I'm sure, though I couldn't hear a word of what he had to say because he was so old and offered it all in the feeblest of voices.

It was a good thing, too, that all his talk of killing the Mexican Papists wasn't audible to those Irish Catholics he was addressing. Ancient as he was, those Jasper Greens who did hear him grumbled a little but mostly ignored and forgave what he was saying. [5]

Confident that I had confounded Uriah Franks, I kept my eyes open for an opportunity to abandon my new brothers in arms.

Captain Jackson made another speech in Macon, no doubt he fully expected some number of boys in the crowd to jump forward and offer themselves for service, but here Captain

Jackson was disappointed. He received plenty of cheers from the crowd, but no volunteers rushing forward claiming to be Irish.

After the speeches at the Court House, we marched up Second Street to where some of the local citizens had prepared a small meal for us, and from there we went to the Floyd House, where we stayed the night as guests of the city. By the time we arrived at the Floyd House, I was too exhausted for flight, and so I spent the night in a room I shared with the Gatehouse brothers. Willie and George Gatehouse were the company musicians (Willie played the tin whistle and George played a drum that he called a bodhran).

It was the last decent bed I would sleep in for months.

The next morning – it was a Saturday, because I recall thinking when I woke up that it was the store's busiest day of the week and here I was soldiering in Macon and not there to open for business – I considered how I was going to make my stint in the Georgia militia a short one. I thought of going straight to the man himself, H. R. Jackson, and just explaining to him that I'd made a rash decision, caught up in his impressive speech as I was, and that I'd like to go home now. But I knew that wouldn't do. I'd volunteered, and I couldn't see them letting go of me now.

And the next thing I knew, the sergeants were going about ordering us to get our gear together and fall in for the march to Columbus. I had no gear, even the hatchet had by now been discarded, but in the coming days the quartermaster would have me kitted out with a green shirt, canteen, Bowie knife, bedroll and haversack.

A march to Columbus is what it was, too. We bade goodbye to the pleasantness of riding the train across the state and hoofed it out of town. The local volunteer companies all showed up to march with us for a while, but when they started to break a sweat sometime before noon they about-faced and headed for home.

The Jasper Greens had no such luck: We trod on forward

toward Columbus, which was designated as the rallying point for all the Georgia volunteer companies. There, we were to form up the Georgia Volunteer Regiment and make our way by steamer from Columbus, down the Chattahoochee River to the Gulf of Mexico and then to New Orleans. From New Orleans, we would again go by steamer to the Rio Grande and there be in the theater of war.

We tried our hands at marching to the beat of George Gatehouse's bodhran, though we couldn't much get the hang of it. Some of the boys complained about the heat or complained about the walking or complained about the bedrolls they carried over their shoulders or complained about all of it. Some sang the tunes of their homeland, which I rather admired – all of them about women and whiskey, don't ye know. But they all kept up a constant chatter. Not me, though, I just groaned to myself and wondered how I would get out of this mess before we got to the Rio Grande.

One of the first things that I learned on my journey west is that once you are in the army – even a volunteer company of Irishmen – your life is no longer your own. You are forced hither and thither, someone is always around, and the opportunity for escape is almost nonexistent. And of course that's how it is – in the history of human conflict there are two absolutes: Death and Desertion. As long as men have been leading other men to kill or be killed, some men among them have been looking for a backdoor.

And though we'd been just a few days in Columbus, my desire to desert had nothing to do with fear of what was to come. It didn't seem real to me, I suppose, that in a few weeks I'd be ducking Mexican shells and trying to put El General Ampudia to the bayonet. But already I was bored of the company of the Jasper Greens, who gambled and drank to excess in their off time and drilled and marched to excess while on duty. Even there in Columbus, I was forever being ordered to guard duty – no matter how unlikely it was that Ampudia would be marching on Columbus, of all places.

I confess that I missed my lovely Eliza, too. We'd not been married long enough for me to fully grow accustomed to and exasperated by her inane chatter, and we were still in that honeymoon phase of our marriage where almost every night we enjoyed some new and wonderful encounter that had our bodies intermingling and her giggling and convulsing below me. Or atop me. Or beside me. Or over in the chair. Or on the rug. B'God I missed her!

Worse than missing Eliza, my new sleeping partner was Moses Gleason, with whom I shared an insufferably hot canvas tent, and every night I was subjected to Moses snoring in my ear and drooling on my shoulder and kneeing me in the thigh. Also packed into that tent were the Gatehouse brothers, along with Michael Downey and Danny Murphy. Six grown men in a canvas tent in Georgia was enough to convince me the Mexicans could keep California to themselves.

These boys had signed up for this – seeking glory and honor in Mexico – and in those first few days camped at Columbus they were having the time of their lives, yammering on in their thick brogues about the Mexicans they would kill and how they would bring Senior Antonio Lopez de Santa Anna to his knees. At the time, of course, it was President Farias we were off to fight as Santa Anna was still in exile (though Santa Anna would make his appearance soon enough), but Santa Anna's was about the only Mexican name any of those boys knew, and so he was the one going to his knees if the Jasper Greens got within rifle shot of him.

Not all of the Greens were from Ireland. Captain Jackson, for instance, was born in Athens, not far from my boyhood home of Scull Shoals. But they were all of Irish descent, and I suppose most of them were lately of the Emerald Isle.

It didn't mean anything to me whether they were Irish or not, but it wasn't the same with the men of some of the other companies.

In particular, the Kennesaw Rangers knew no bounds to their bigotry when it came to the Jasper Greens. Every other thing was whiskey this, potato that, and we couldn't go about without some fool or another calling us Irish Apes.

It was made worse, too, when Captain Jackson was elected to serve as Colonel of the Georgia Volunteer Regiment. From then on, any time there was a task that needed doing, it was the Jasper Greens who were called upon to do it. While this might seem a burden, camp life in Columbus was so exceedingly dull that any minor thing – going to fetch water for the regiment, going to the depot to get newly arrived supplies – was a treasured break from the monotony of life in camp.

Of course, the Jasper Greens didn't do anything to help their standing among their fellow Georgia volunteers. Anytime there was whiskey to be got at, they got at it with such exuberance and animation that it was never long before the entire encampment knew they were drunk.

Because of my association with them, I was on the receiving end of the bigotry as well, and I can tell you that it wore terribly tiresome. It would all come to a head before we reached Mexico, and the truth is I always have believed that the Jasper Greens gave to the Kennesaw Rangers exactly what was coming to them. [6]

At camp there were generally two forms of occupation: drilling and swatting at gnats. The gnats were intolerable, and all of the volunteer companies found the drilling to be just as bad as the pests, mostly because we were bad at it.

Having served in both regular army and militia and witnessed discipline in each, I can tell you that those volunteers headed for the War of '46 were a terrible lot. As we tried to learn to march and form up in squares to repulse imagined cavalry attacks, the layabouts and children of Columbus would come to watch us and, if you can believe the impudence, laugh out loud at us.

When finally our rifles arrived by train, I was among the Jasper Greens sent to the depot to collect the crates.

The Georgia General Assembly had seen fit to provide us

with Hall flintlock breech loading rifles. These Hall rifles were far more accurate than the smoothbore muzzle-loaders the Mexicans would be using against us, but not a damn one of us knew how to get the things open, having never seen breechloaders like this before. Eventually, some sergeant figured out what he was doing, and in addition to our marching drills we were soon firing away at mounds of dirt.

Until I actually reached Monterrey, I couldn't imagine that a battle could be any more dangerous than life at camp. Bullets were always zipping through the air as the fool volunteers played with their new toys. Just going out of your tent to relieve yourself could become a matter of life and death. Even at night, when there was no hope of being able to see what was downrange from the end of your rifle barrel, those damn fool volunteers would shoot off a bullet just for the sport of hearing the rifle's report. I always viewed it as a small miracle that we did not lose half our regiment to friendly fire in Columbus, Georgia.

I was in a funk that I could not shake. Fleeing the Jasper Greens was proving an impossible task as there was always somebody at hand. I was missing my life in Milledgeville and missing my wife and spending most of my time in a funk, regretting the decisions that had landed me here.

It did nothing to ease my mood, either, when I received my first letter from Eliza while we were encamped at Columbus.

It was the kindest of letters, full of endearments and cautions to "please be careful" and it truly made me miss her all that much more and wish to return to my life in Milledgeville.

"Granddaddy thinks you must have been suffering from a fever or some form of mental infirmity, but I am ever so proud of my daring and brave and gallant husband," she wrote. "There was even an entire story about you in the Southern Recorder, about how you alone stood above all other men in Milledgeville to brave the coming storm and fight for our Manifest Destiny!"

I hated to disappoint, but the truth was I'd made up my mind that if I was to find no avenue of desertion and found myself out west in Mexico, my plan was to skulk in the back, feign sickness or injury or do any other necessary thing to escape actual fighting, up to and including shooting off my little toe to be sent home as an invalid.

But not so the rest of the Jasper Greens. Those Irish boys were so ready to jump into the fray that I found it all rather alarming, and I saw the danger to myself in all their gleaming eyes. They didn't know, of course. They were not only Jasper Green, but they were truly green. None of them had ever seen anything of war and knew only about the fancy adjectives the newspaper editors were using to describe them – those same fancy adjectives my beloved wife heaped upon me in her letter.

Well, I hadn't seen war, either. But the leg up in understanding I had on those boys from Savannah was that I'd seen murder in a man's eyes before. I knew absolutely what a terrifying thing it was to have a man not only want me dead but committed to seeing the thing through. Sure, I didn't know then the whiz and snap of a musket ball, but unlike all those Irishmen, I knew what it was to have someone trying to put an end to me.

I wrote to Eliza almost daily. I offered her sincere endearments and earnest declarations of my undying love, and told her in desperate terms how much I missed her. It was all true, too. I know I'm a scoundrel when it comes to my dealings with the fairer sex, and I won't deny any charge leveled against me when it comes to my treatment of women, for if the specifics of the charge are false, the generalities will be true enough.

But in those days I was smitten still with my lovely, fair-skinned, red-headed wife, and all I longed for was to be back in her embrace and away from Moses Gleason and his incessant snoring.

We were not long in Columbus before we took a steamship

to Mobile and then to New Orleans. And, from there, we steamed through the Gulf of Mexico, and up the Rio Grande to Camp Belknap where at last the Georgia regiment met up with other volunteer regiments, and the regular army. At Camp Belknap, we encamped and began drilling and learning maneuvers in earnest. We improved a fair bit in our ability to form up and fire a volley. In fact, our improvement was so much that Eliza in one of her letters to me quoted from a newspaper report that claimed we were "much improved" from our time in Columbus. I have always believed it was a testament to just how poorly organized we were in Columbus that a newspaper should even comment on our improved drilling.

It was true enough, I suppose, that we were better, but it would have required a retraction had that newspaper report claimed we were anything close to being ready for combat.

During drills and maneuvers, the volunteers flatly refused to lug around their haversacks and spare ammunition. It was all the sergeants could do to get them to tote their rifles. It occurred to me then that when the real thing came we would find ourselves woefully unfit for duty, but I left my haversack, spare ammunition and bayonet in a pile with the others. Rifle included, it was 30 pounds or more of gear that they expected us to carry about, and in the heat of August on the banks of the Rio Grande, that was asking more than I cared to do.

Besides, you'll remember that when the real thing came it was my intention to have no need of rifle or spare ammunition because I intended to be in the back somewhere shirking my duty.

If anything, life at Camp Belknap was worse than it had been in our days at Columbus. At least in Columbus there were pretty girls from town who came occasionally to watch us drill or they would make fresh lemonade and bring it to camp, and we would flirt a bit and at least have the benefit of their appearances to break up the monotony of the days. But at Camp Belknap there was none of that. The only diversion from drilling, guarding and being bored was when the Jasper Greens got ahold of some whiskey from time to time.

During these days, I had done what I could to endear myself to the man among the Jasper Greens whom I thought was most likely among them to keep me alive. Sgt. Paddy Martin was a grizzled old veteran and knew his business. Before coming to America, he'd served in places I'd never heard of fighting to expand her Majesty's Empire, and he had countless stories of conflict. But there was something about his manner – maybe one coward can instinctively spot another – that told me he might have witnessed much warfare but always from a safe distance.

Sgt. Martin took to me, too. He was stout enough, but didn't stand more than five feet six inches, and I suspect he saw in me the right-sized lad for him to hide behind when Mexican bullets started coming toward us. When we drilled, he always seemed to be trying to keep me nearby him, anyway.

Camp Belknap was plenty bad – situated on high ground along the Rio Grande, there was little in the way of trees or grass to offer shade from the unmerciful sun or to break up the landscape. The camp – on a piece of ground about two miles long and one mile wide and mostly surrounded by water – was packed to overflowing with volunteers from across the country: Texians, Illinoisans, Mississippians, Alabamians and the entire regiment of Georgians were all there, and more, too, I suspect. It was at Camp Belknap that we began to experience the first indications that we would soon regret our slovenly ways, with a fair number of the boys falling ill with malaria and yellow fever and the like.

The heat, the sickness, the boredom, the cramped quarters and the overall lack of discipline among the volunteers finally began to take its toll when we were all crammed into that space on the banks of the Rio Grande with flies and mosquitoes all around. Getting so drunk on whiskey that you passed out in the sand was the only relief to be found.

Among the Jasper Greens was a young spark who fancied himself as fine a pugilist as ever raised his fists. And it's true enough that Private John Makin was a champion boxer. Camped right beside us were the Kennesaw Rangers, another Georgia Company, and they too had a champion boxer among their ranks.

Led by Capt. Nelson, the Kennesaw Rangers were the closest thing to regular army in the Georgia regiment. They were well disciplined and looked down upon the other companies with disgust. Most of all, they hated the Irish Jasper Greens and were as full of contempt for us "Irish Apes" as they were the Mexicans they come here to kill. It was said that Capt. Nelson was a preacher in his civilian life and conducted his drills as a Sunday school. The Jasper Greens, of course, were Catholic and they were also full of frolic that the Kennesaw Rangers despised. And somehow, the boys in my company were always able to secure for themselves a supply of whiskey, and the Kennesaw Rangers could not abide our drunkenness.

So we were always at a pretty high level of tension in camp, and it wasn't eased a bit when the boys of one company started debasing the champion boxer of the other company. Who started it I can't say, but it wasn't long before Private Makin was shirtless and face-to-face with the pugilist of the Kennesaw Rangers.

I joined with my fellow Jasper Greens in watching the event, and it was as fine a boxing match as I've ever seen. All the Savannah boys, and me with them, were well drunk and we were a loud and raucous audience. The Kennesaw boys were just as loud, and Sunday school class or not, I suspect a fair number of them were as drunk as we.

The Rangers' champion was a big, strong man and each time he landed a punch we all felt it, but Private Makin was livelier by far – dodging and weaving, ducking big roundhouse punches and jabbing away – and it wasn't long before the Irishman proved himself the better of the two champions, getting in a strong left hook that knocked out the big Ranger.

That should have been that, but the Kennesaw boys all took it as a defeat to the company's pride, and the Savannah Irishmen were too cocky to leave it alone. The tension that existed between our two companies only increased after Makin beat the Kennesaw boxer.

Early on the morning of August 31, it was Sgt. Martin who was rousting us out of our tent.

"Up with ye, Jackie Speed," Sgt. Martin said, poking his torso into our tent and shaking me by the shoulder. "C'mon the lot of ye. Cap'n McMahon wants ye all ta fall in and be ready to receive yer orders."

I rubbed the sleep from my eyes and tried to stretch out the stiffness of sleeping on the ground with nothing but a thin bedroll to provide comfort. Still stiff and sore, I crawled out of the tent to look for my boots.

We fell in like a typical lot of volunteers, no quickness to our step or enthusiasm in our purpose.

"It'll be more manooverin'," groused Danny Murphy in my ear. "I swear to all that's holy, this company knows how to walk by now."

But presently Capt. McMahon came to the forefront and there was something unquestionably altered in his expression.

"Lads," he began in a booming voice. "The time is at hand for you brave boys of Erin to show the stuff you're made of! We've been designated today to board the steamship Corvette which will take us down the Rio Grande to our staging ground, and from there to Glory!"

Those damned Irishmen in my company whooped and hollered, and I felt the cold grip of fear grasp my bowels. This was the moment I'd been dreading and believed would never come, but now it was at hand. I considered shooting off my toe right then and there, and it would not be long before I wished I had.

"Now lads," McMahon shouted out over the din the boys

were making, "we'll be encamping with the regular army, and we'll be well pleased with all the drilling we've been doing these last few weeks because it has perfected us into a fine sort of fighting unit. I am filled with certitude that the regulars will look upon us and envy."

The boys whooped and hollered a little more, and everyone but me was smiling and laughing satisfaction at finally being able to get at the Mexicans and Santa Anna and whatever else they thought they were going to do.

"Until this afternoon, then, you are dismissed!" McMahon shouted.

I groaned. Never tell an Irishman he's dismissed.

Those Irishmen immediately went out and procured some whiskey to celebrate the coming slaughter, and by noon they were all as drunk as, well, drunk as Irishmen who've been dismissed.

By the late afternoon the steamer Corvette arrived on the Rio Grande, and though they were in various states of inebriation most of the boys of the Jasper Greens began loading their gear onto the ship. A fair number of us were loafing on the shore, and I was among those, sprawled on a blanket and glad that the sun was finally setting and the coolness of evening was coming on.

It was our bad fortune that we were allotted to board the Corvette alongside the Kennesaw Rangers, who were still holding a grudge against us over Private Makin's victory over their own champion.

A prelude of what was to come came earlier in the afternoon. Private Makin and I were carrying luggage aboard the steamer when a couple of the Rangers, loafing near the gangplank, decided to hassle us.

"There goes a couple of Paddies," one of them called while the other sniggered. "Go it, Pat. You are now both loaded like a couple of jackasses."

Makin grunted. "Leave it alone, Johnny," I told him. The last thing I wanted was for Johnny to take the bait and me get caught up in a general brawl. Johnny took my advice and we both continued to lug our baggage up the gangplank.

It was that sort of incessant provocation that we endured, and so it was no surprise that later on in the day the Jasper Greens were going to answer the insults.

As evening approached, those among the Jasper Greens who were just now getting gear aboard the boat were singing and stumbling along the shore and up the gangplank. Michael Hoar – one of the younger boys in the company – and Charles Farrelly were carrying a footlocker up to the boat when Michael bumped into one of those Kennesaw Rangers. They were right at the gangplank, and when Michael bumped into him, the Kennesaw Ranger dropped his bedroll or some other thing into the water.

"You G-------d Irish son of a b---h!" the Ranger bawled.

And that was all it took. At the insult, Private Farrelly dropped his end of the footlocker and sobered up enough to land the hardest of punches on the bridge of that Ranger's nose. Farrelly was a big brawler sort and had a temper that ran hot at all times. The Ranger keeled into the Rio Grande with a bloodied and broken nose.

A couple of nearby Rangers started forward, and Private Makin, who was standing right there, raised his fists and assumed the posture of a man ready to take on an entire company. "C'mon with ye then!" he roared. "I'll take on any one of ye who thinks yer the man for it!"

In seconds, all those still on the shore – Ranger and Green alike – rushed forward looking for someone to fight, and chaos erupted all about. Drunken Irishmen were punching at the church ladies of Kennesaw, who were very quickly getting the better of their drunken adversaries.

I saw Danny Murphy swing his rifle and brain one of the Kennesaw boys, who toppled over into the sand. Someone on the deck fired a shot, I saw another of the lads trying to ram his bayonet through the neck of one of the Rangers. I got to my feet and started for the boat. I wasn't looking to get into the fray, you understand, but I didn't want to get caught down there on the shore with none of my fellows about and become a punching bag for those Kennesaw boys. As I dashed toward the gangplank, one of the Kennesaw troopers swung a right fist and punched me square in the gut, knocking the breath out of me.

I collapsed into the sand, and then scrambled over to a stack of barrels where I doubled up as the riot continued all around me. The Jasper Greens, sobering quick enough, started fighting as if they were storming Mexico City itself, and the Rangers were worse: Every man among them was screaming about "Irish Apes!" and brandishing bayonets or loading rifles, and it seemed that any moment the camp would erupt with an explosion of carnage and death.

I saw poor Danny Murphy disarmed and set about by a gang of three or four of those Kennesaw bastards. For a moment, I even considered dashing over to his aid, but common sense and good judgment prevented me from leaving the only safe spot within sight.

Up on the deck, the Greens heard the commotion and started for the gangplank to render aid to their companions, but Captain McMahon, his saber out, forced the boys back, and Captain Nelson, down on the shore, was also doing what he could to push back his Rangers.

And at that point it all pretty much died down. McMahon ordered all the Jasper Greens aboard the ship and Nelson ordered all the Rangers back down on the shore.

At some point during the fighting, an Illinois colonel who was, I think, the commanding officer at Camp Belknap at that point, grabbed together a band of men who'd been on a funeral detail and rushed to the steamer to seize control of the situation. When they arrived, the fight was still fully involved. They had no weapons among them and there was nothing they could do, so the colonel – Baker, I think was his name – went back to fetch up the entirety of his Illinois company.

The Illinoisans were not necessary, though, because

McMahon and Nelson had by now managed to gain control over their respective companies. McMahon ordered us to one side of the ship, and when we were there, Nelson brought his Rangers aboard. Someone tied a rope to the port railing and then crossed to the starboard railing where he tied the other end, and McMahon ordered us to stay on one side of that rope while the Rangers were ordered to stay on the other side.

Presently, though, Col. Baker and the Illinois company returned, fully armed.

At that moment, McMahon was raging at us and was in full fury: "Drunkenness and fighting with your fellow Georgians!" he shouted. "I'll have no further examples of that sort of disorder among my men! Yer lucky ye don't all face a court martial!"

Nelson, too, was giving plenty of the same to his own men, though I suspect he was leaving out some of the epithets McMahon sprayed so liberally at us.

And I'm sure in the growing darkness, with both men raging, it might have sounded like the riot was in full swing when the Illinois colonel came rushing up the gangplank with his now-armed company behind him. "Sir! I demand that you surrender over this ship to me!" the colonel was shouting.

Now, in fairness to McMahon and the other boys, I thought it was the Kennesaw Rangers demanding us to surrender the boat, too. None of us knew that it was a colonel just coming on deck who was shouting. And there was never a chance that the Jasper Greens would surrender anything to those Rangers. And so when the colonel came up the gangplank shouting about surrender, McMahon had heard enough.

His saber still clutched in his hand, our captain met the Midwesterner on the deck.

"Surrender your sword to me!" Baker demanded, his own sword drawn and held in front of him.

"Damn you, cross swords with me!" Captain McMahon shouted.

I believe he was still unaware that he was facing an officer of higher rank or anyone other than one of the Kennesaw Rangers.

The two engaged in a sparring contest, parrying and thrusting and slashing with their swords, and Captain McMahon was clearly getting the better of the Illinois colonel when one of the Illinois soldiers, seeing the plight of his colonel, shouted out, "Charge, damn you! Run your bayonets through him!"

One of those damn Midwesterners grabbed Capt. McMahon and dragged him to the deck. Three or four others went for him with their bayonets, and though McMahon was able to parry away most of the thrusts, one of those bayonets went into his mouth, pierced his cheek and pinned him to the deck. Even through the dimness of evening, we all saw clearly what was happening.

"Boys! They're killing our captain!" shouted Charles Farrelly, and with that every man aboard that ship (excepting me) flung themselves into the fray. Rangers, Greens and Midwesterners were all in a general brawl again.

I allowed the other boys from Savannah to storm forward and I stayed back in what I thought was a safe position, but in the ebb and flow of the fight the combatants started moving closer to me.

Presently, young Danny Murphy – who had taken such a beating just a short time ago from the Rangers who ganged up on him on shore – tackled one of the Illinois boys and the two of them fell at my feet. I took the opportunity to get my fun in, and stomped the Midwesterner in the face, crushing his nose into a bloody mass. I bent over and plucked Danny from the ground, and he turned to look for another victim. He didn't have far to look, though, for four of those stout Kennesaw men were rushing toward us. One of them caught Danny around the waist and dragged him to the ground. The Ranger pinned Danny's shoulders to the deck with his knees and set about punching him in the head and shoulders. Poor Danny was to take two severe beatings that evening.

That left three of those damn Rangers to set about me, and I had nowhere to run to. Backed into a corner and with three assailants preparing to do me harm, I looked about and saw a rifle leaning against the railing. I grabbed the thing up and, seeing it had no bayonet attached, began swinging it wildly like a club to keep those goons at bay. One of them, though, grabbed the butt of the rifle as I swung it past him and tried to wrench it from my hands. But I was stronger than he was, and I shoved him backwards so that he tipped and fell over the side of the rail and into the Rio Grande. If he broke his neck in the fall and drowned in the murky water, it was no more than he deserved.

That's when one of the other two grabbed me, and held me fast while his friend came at me.

A coward such as myself will do whatever is necessary to preserve himself, and as I've found too many times in my life, that necessary element to self-preservation is coming on strong and meeting violence with violence. And so it was here. With one of them holding my arms pinned to my side and the other about to land a punch in my face, I kicked out, catching that Kennesaw boy right in the breadbasket. He howled and doubled over. The fool holding me had a bigger fish than he could handle. I squirmed and shook until I was loose from his grip, and just then Johnny Makin stepped up, his face a bloody mess and a grin of pure delight showing through the black liquid. Private Makin was having more fun than he knew war could be. He jabbed with his right, then jabbed with his left, and the Ranger who'd been holding me was sprawled across the deck.

"Ye a'right?" Makin asked me.

With my guts churning and my heart racing, I issued some guttural noise in place of words, and just nodded my head.

"Right then," Makin said, clapping me on the shoulder. "Help poor ol' Danny boy there!" and he pointed and Danny Murphy, half conscious on the deck.

And then Makin turned back to the mass of fighting and

disappeared into the thick of it, leaving a trail of busted faces in his wake.

The Ranger who'd knocked Danny down was too winded by now to continue the storm of punches he'd been inflicting on Danny, and seeing that he'd abandoned beating the boy, I sought out a safe spot against the wall of the steamer's deck house. There I sank to the ground and watched as the riot raged in front of me.

Everywhere I looked was a mass of flailing arms. Occasional shots were fired. Men had armed themselves with rifles that they were using as clubs, with knives and with bayonets, and it was clear to me that it didn't matter to a man on that deck that he was killing his brothers in arms, just so long as he was killing. They were all maniacs. They'd come to Mexico to fight, and this was the first fight they'd found, and every man jack among them was intent on making it a good one.

Some of the Illinois company fired a volley into the mass of men fighting, killing our Cpl. Whalen, who was shot through the heart. One of their bullets, too, went through the back of the neck of their colonel, and he fell dead upon the deck as well.

I suppose it was the sudden violence of the volley, but presently the fighting began to subside.

The Rangers fell back to their side of the rope, the Greens stayed put on their side of the rope, and the Illinois company – their colonel dead on the deck of a ship where he never should have been anyway – retreated off the Corvette. [7]

At that point, Sgt. Martin – who was without bruise or scratch, I noted – came over and grabbed me under my arms and hauled me to my feet, saying, "Up with ye, Jackie Speed." Then together we helped the badly beaten Danny Murphy up, and Sgt. Martin left me with a damp rag to clean up Danny's brutalized face.

A company of Indiana soldiers were brought aboard the steamer to stand guard, but by then most everyone had lost whatever fight was in them. The next morning, they came to collect the wounded and dead from the deck of the boat and the shore.

For the next couple of days the boat was kept at anchor and the Greens and the Rangers were held aboard the ship while a court of inquiry was held. Charlie Farrelly was arrested as one of the ringleaders, as was Johnny Makin. Captain McMahon was also arrested and charged with drunkenness and mutinous conduct for attacking the Illinois colonel.

Our captain was convicted of the charges against him and he was ordered to be cashiered out of the army. Ultimately, though, our colonel interceded. The charges against Privates Farrelly and Makin were dropped, and the court remitted its sentence against our captain, and all were restored to our company for our trip to Camargo. Whatever else anyone might say of Henry Roote Jackson, his next action forever endeared him to those boys from Savannah – and me, too, for that matter.

The Jasper Greens were Col. Jackson's favorite company in the regiment, and of course we were because we were his company. After hearing testimony – from both us and the Kennesaw Rangers – of what transpired, Col. Jackson reached the conclusion that had the Illinois colonel and those men stayed out of it, then Captains McMahon and Nelson would have had the situation under control. Rushing the ship and shouting "surrender," Col. Jackson said, elicited the response from Capt. McMahon, and it was the Illinois colonel's intervention that led to the escalation of the fighting and the deaths. Col. Jackson declared to every man who would listen that the Jasper Greens could have done no more and certainly no less than they did aboard the Corvette. Seeing their captain set upon by a gang of Illinois soldiers attempting to kill him, the Jasper Greens were forced into activity. [8]

CHAPTER VI

After the court of inquiry, the steamer took us back up the Rio Grande from Camp Belknap to the staging camp at Camargo. Because it was September when we took the steamer upstream to Camargo, we were spared the full extent of misery the terrible trip many of the troops who went before us endured on their journey. All through June there had been heavy rains that flooded the Rio Grande and made the journey as rough as if they were at sea in a hurricane. By now, though the river was still overflowing its banks, the strong currents were eased some and our passage up the Rio Grande was not nearly as eventful as some of the other soldiers claimed theirs had been.

But when we arrived in Camargo, it was just in time to see the worst of that place.

Camargo. Say that name to any veteran of the volunteer regiments who was there, and you'll see them go pale with horror. Camargo. It was a hellish place, and I endured two weeks of that hell.

As something of a military man, I can look back at Camargo and tell you that we volunteers could have learned a lot and saved a fair number of lives from the example of the regulars, but the volunteers and the regulars never got along, in the Mexican War or any other. The regulars were, of course, as dimwitted as a man could be. If they were not drilled and disciplined to perform some activity, then that activity was beyond them to perform. Nevertheless, they were drilled and disciplined to keep their camps clean. The volunteers, being men of free will who did not cotton much to orders or respond well to discipline, could never be bothered with the menial tasks such as keeping a sanitary camp. We lived in absolute filth and we suffered for it.

Once, when walking downstream along the Rio Grande, I witnessed a group of Texas Rangers washing their horses in the river. A little ways farther along, I saw a company of Illinois volunteers washing their clothes in the very same water. And still farther down river I saw a company of Alabama's volunteers filling their canteens. And so it was that the Texas Rangers rode on clean horses, the Illinois troops wore horse dirty clothes and the Alabama boys all had a bellyache.

Yellow fever and malaria crippled the volunteer army. Nearly as many men died of sickness at Camargo as were killed by a Mexican bullet during the course of the war. Hundreds of men from every volunteer regiment were filling the hospitals. The flies during the day and mosquitoes at night tormented us without stop. The sun was brutal. And if it had been brackish water we drank at Camp Belknap, it was brackish mud we drank at Camargo.

Many of the volunteers had been at Camargo at least a month before our arrival, and when we stepped off the Corvette and onto shore in this place it was rife with sickness. If there was a man not suffering from malaria, yellow fever, diarrhea, measles, pneumonia or dysentery, I could not find him. Certainly some of our boys had fallen ill at Fort Belknap, but we were healthy enough when we stepped off that boat. That all changed soon enough.

Camargo had been a town of some size before our arrival, but the June rains that flooded the Rio Grande had sent the river into the town, and its citizens abandoned it. By the time we arrived, the river was out of the streets, but it had melted many of the mud buildings inside the town, leaving behind piles of clay and straw that had once served as roofs. The lagoons left behind when the river subsided were breeding grounds for mosquitoes and flies, and a body could not exist without serving as a buffet table for the damned mosquitoes.

To this day, upon hearing the name Camargo, I involuntarily swat at the back of my neck.

Camargo was all misery.

The volunteers camped along the banks of the Rio Grande. The regular army lived not much better than us, but at least had some semblance of cleanliness in their camps and suffered less from disease.

Those who were well enough drilled and carried out the never-ending chores of camp life, and rumor ran wildly through camp: One day we were being told that the Mexicans were preparing to make a stand in Monterrey and it was going to be one hellish fight, and the next day we were given to believe that the war would end without a further shot being fired.

Old Rough and Ready was being given a new nickname by everyone from President Polk all the way down to the newspaper editors. "General Delay" they were calling him. They were clamoring for some successful conclusion to the war, and their harassment of General Taylor only increased as they learned at home of the numbers of dead from sickness. [9]

We didn't know it, but the Georgia Regiment had seen all the fight it was going to see. After the Battle of the Boat, as they were calling it, General Taylor deemed us too unruly to kill Mexicans, and Camargo was as far as my Jasper Greens were going. [10]

Had I known this at the time, I'd have stayed put in camp and finished out the war drinking whatever whiskey Savannah's Irishmen could scare up and hoping to avoid sickness. But fate once again stepped forward to drag me from one hell to another.

Camp life was so bad that I found any excuse I could to leave camp, often wandering with the Gatehouse brothers or others from the company up and down the Rio Grande. I made my way into the camps of other companies looking for some diversion. The sickness was so bad that if you stood in one spot for too long, you were soon ordered to help on some burial duty, which meant digging a grave in heat that was as appalling as anything I'd ever encountered. Having suffered through one burial party, I determined to avoid any more if I anyway could.

And so I set about to make myself useful in other ways. I'd always had a knack with horses ever since I was young, and so I started volunteering to care for the Georgia officers' horses – watering and washing and feeding them. The horses generally lived better than a volunteer private, and though it was menial work it was better than being at camp where someone was always coughing in your face or sneezing on your food.

One afternoon as I was engaged in feeding the horses, a drunk Texian volunteer started shouting at a couple of regular army boys. What precipitated this incident I do not know, but it was clear that the regular army men were attempting to take the drunk Texian into custody for some offense or another.

"I'll be damned if any private will lay hands on me!" the Texian shouted, and stumbling forward he swung wildly at one of the privates and missed. Another one of the privates attempted to grab him, but the Texian shook the man off violently, throwing him to the ground. Now a group of privates – four or five of them – rushed forward to lend assistance, and the Texian was swearing oaths against them. He then drew from his holster the Paterson five-shooter the Texian volunteers all carried, and discharged two rounds at the privates stepping forward.

Chaos erupted, with men shouting and rushing forward either to subdue the Texian or assist him.

There were a group of mules in a crudely constructed enclosure nearby. Those Mexican mules were terribly skittish animals, forever starting and stampeding, and presently these animals broke the fence and stampeded off away from camp. Those of us charged with caretaking the animals began to scramble about in an effort to round up the stampeding mules.

Without thinking that it might lead to personal disaster, I saw an opportunity for a fine diversion. I saddled one of the horses and rode out after the mules that were by now breaking out over an open plain.

Taking great joy in my work because it was the first time I'd been astride a horse since my sudden enlistment, I rode out to the mules and hooted and hollered, riding round them in circles, until such time as I had them under control, and then I drove them back to the camp. Though they were the most stubborn beasts one could ever hope to encounter, I handled them well enough and made good work of rounding them up. It was a bit of a disappointment to ride them back into camp, for on the back of that horse I'd encountered the first decent breeze I'd felt since coming off the steamship to Camargo. And I can truly say that riding through that plain on the back of the horse and rounding up those mules was the first time I had found any enjoyment at all since coming west with the Jasper Greens. I had a fine time of it, and probably played it up more than I should have and, without question, I brought more attention to myself than I should have.

With the mules now in the hands of others, I dismounted the horse, unsaddled it and determined then to go and find some eatables.

"That was a fine feat of riding, sir," I heard a man say behind me. I turned and found myself facing the colonel of the volunteer Mississippi Rifles. He was a thin man and had the gaunt appearance of a convalescent. I assumed he was recovering from one of the diseases raging around camp. His eyes, though, were a bright, piercing blue. He was dressed in a blue officer's uniform and I only recognized him as a Mississippian because I'd seen him around camp.

"It was a good diversion, sir," I said.

"I assume you're one of the Texian volunteers?" he asked. The lack of any kind of true uniform for the Jasper Greens – just a green shirt and brown britches – more resembled the Texas Rangers, who adopted no uniform look but all just rode into battle in whatever clothes suited them.

"No, sir. I'm from Georgia," I said.

Now, anyone in my position would have been desperate to end this interview, because anytime a private was addressed by a superior officer it nearly always ended with him being ordered off to help dig a grave, and I was well hungry and had no desire to pick up a shovel.

"I had assumed, from your skill in the saddle, that you were one of the Texians," this colonel told me. It was high praise, you understand. The Texians – whose careers up to this point had been battling Comanches and banditos and, as such, had learned to live and fight atop their horses – controlled their mounts as if they were extensions of their own bodies. The Texians were the finest horsemen in the army, and that he was comparing me to them for my horsemanship was quite a thing. "It was all very quick thinking and good work. You rounded those mules up and delivered them back to the corral quite well. Have you always handled mules so well?"

I shrugged my shoulders and said it wasn't difficult work, and that I'd been working with the animals for a number of days.

"What's your name, son?" the colonel asked me.

"Private Jackson Speed, sir," I said.

"And what company are you with, Private Speed?"

"I'm with the Jasper Greens of Savannah, sir."

"Very well, then, Private Speed. I'll be speaking to your colonel. I am Colonel Davis of the Mississippi Rifles."

This seemed like an end to the interview, and I was well pleased to be getting away from Colonel Davis of the Mississippi Rifles without having been ordered to dig a grave.

Colonel Davis of the Mississippi Rifles meant nothing to me at the time, of course, but you'll know him well as the future President of the Confederate States of America. [11]

We'd been at Camargo several days when at last Taylor announced his marching orders.

Every healthy volunteer in camp (except me) was dreaming of glorious battle, and so it came as a punch in the gut to the rest of them when Old Rough and Ready announced that the regular army and only half of the volunteer army would be moving forward to Monterrey. Only selected companies were moving forward, and they were chosen based on their health and fitness for battle. The Jasper Greens and the entirety of the Georgia Regiment would be left behind at Camargo.

I took this news with mixed feelings. Having the advantage of knowing what would occur at Monterrey, you would be forgiven for thinking that I'd be glad to stay at camp with the Jasper Greens while the other volunteers went forward. But the rumor moving through Camargo was that the Mexicans were prepared to abandon Monterrey, and we would be moving into an undefended city to accept its surrender without firing a shot. At the time, they were even saying that Mexico would negotiate a treaty to give Polk the land he wanted and there would be no fight at all.

Camargo was hell, and so far I'd maintained my health by keeping with the horses as much as possible, but I felt certain that if I stayed there much longer I would soon be suffering from malaria and, likely as not, some poor gang of privates would be digging my grave. The thought of moving into an undefended city where decent water and eatables and other diversions were to be found was far superior in my mind than staying here in this damnedable encampment, where the ravages of disease were a certainty.

Faced with the prospect of dying of malaria, I was in as bad a funk as the rest of the Jasper Greens who had volunteered to come to Mexico to kill Mexicans and now found to their great disappointment that the extent of their service would be shitting their guts and providing escort for supply wagons.

And that's the state I was in when Sergeant Martin came to find me lounging in the shade of my tent in the mid-afternoon, swatting flies and mosquitoes. "Jackie Speed, I dunno what ye've got yerself up to, but it must be a world of trouble ye've caused, for it's Colonel Jackson who's wantin' ta see ya."

Sergeant Martin, hoping for some entertainment, escorted

me to our colonel's tent, where a captain was waiting with Colonel Jackson. I recognized the captain straightaway as being with the Mississippi Rifles because of his red shirt and white breeches.

H.R. Jackson, though he was seated on a stool, still managed to look down his beak nose at me and fix me with those hawk eyes. "Private Speed, this here is Captain Lewis of the Mississippi Rifles. He's delivered to me an unusual request from his colonel that I am inclined to approve, but, as it concerns you directly, I first wanted to ask your thoughts on the matter.

"It seems that Mississippi's Colonel Davis has been appointed to move forward with the rest of the army to Monterrey. As you know, it is our great misfortune to be left out of those who go bravely to battle. But Colonel Davis has requested that you be transferred to his regiment as he is in need of someone to procure for him and manage the mules and muleteers he intends to use for his personal baggage and the baggage of his officers.

"Obviously, as a Georgia volunteer it is your prerogative to remain here encamped with your company, but I do not believe anyone among the Jasper Greens would deny you the opportunity to go and seek your glory. Though there is likely to be little glory among the mules."

All this talk of glory just about had me ready to take my chances with malaria, but then H.R. Jackson added one more bit to his speech: "It's doubtful, of course, that you'll earn much glory in Monterrey. It seems likely that the army will face no resistance there."

"I'll go, sir," I said.

"That's my boy," Sergeant Martin said, and I cut my eyes at him and read from the expression on his face that he was satisfied staying here where there were no Mexicans. And so with that, I went with Captain Lewis to join the Mississippi Rifles and was immediately put to work procuring for Colonel Davis the mules he required for his and his officers' baggage.

When I think back on it, I am amazed at my naivety. I was young and foolish, and made rash decisions without any thought to the consequences. I knew nothing then of warfare or marching. I certainly did not know then that the first rule of staying alive is always, under every circumstance, avoid marching to battle with a band of lunatic officers who are convinced of the ease of victory. When they are certain sure of victory, they are always wrong. The same can be said, too, for camp rumors. If they're going around camp saying there will be no fight, you can bet the fight is coming.

On the first day of march, the damned mules in the baggage train again stampeded – startled, if you can imagine it, by the clanging of the cooking kettles and other gear strapped to their own backs. They scattered gear all over the road when we were not half a mile from Camargo, and those of us in the mule train spent the day reassembling all the gear and catching all the mules. After our first day of march, we camped within sight of Camargo. [12]

Each morning, the army set off in front of us, marching in the cooler temperatures of the morning, while the muleteers – the Mexicans we hired to handle the mules – packed gear and loaded the animals. It was always late morning before we got moving, and so we marched in the hottest part of the day. The countryside was full of cactus and mesquite and any other kind of shrub that grew thorns so that there was no breeze to offer any ease to our sufferings. The dust kicked up by the mules and wagons in the supply train was so thick that most of what a person breathed in was dirt, filling the lungs and congesting the chest. We tied bandanas over our noses and mouths, but this was nearly as unpleasant as it only contributed to the extreme heat. The heat and the dust and the bandanas were so choking it all combined to make it nearly impossible to breathe.

Like everyone else, when we first set out I gave no thought to how soon I might next get water, and so I drank liberally from my canteen at the start of the march and then found –

even when we stopped at night – that there was no fresh water to be had.

Often we passed soldiers who had fainted of sunstroke and were left by the side of the road, some to recover and others to die.

In the distance we could see the Sierra Madres mountains, and they promised cooler temperatures, breezes and fresh water, but they forever stayed in the distance and it seemed that no matter how much we marched we never could get any closer.

It was hellish, miserable marching, and the Mexican mules were impossible to move. No amount of whipping, beating or coaxing could get them to make reasonable time, and as often as not I took to whipping and beating the muleteers as well as the mules to give vent to my frustration.

After two weeks of marching, we at last reached our destination of Cerralvo in the Sierra Madres. This was where General Taylor and those other elements of the army that had gone on ahead of us had camped and waited for our arrival.

I can tell you that after that sun-baked, dusty road where there was no relief of any kind, being delivered into Cerralvo was like achieving the Pearly Gates of Heaven. In all my travels, I've seldom found a place so pleasant, and I was determined that I would not be moved from that place – not by Colonel Davis, not by Old Rough and Ready, and not by any encouragement or threat that man could make.

Cerralvo was resplendent with fresh springs and clean, clear well water. The townspeople grew all manner of fruits – oranges, watermelon, figs, lemons and even apples. There were pecan trees for shade and streams and a pleasant breeze in the higher altitude. The townspeople made a pleasant wine that I thoroughly enjoyed, and they were all so agreeable to the invading force that it felt like a holiday. One of the first things I did was bathe in one of the streams, and I nearly froze to death in the water. It was that cool and refreshing.

Clean water is a luxury, and those who have never suffered

without it cannot fully appreciate what they have.

Thinking back on it now, I am almost transported, and I cannot recall any other march with any other army into any other battle that can make me have such fond recollections as those of Cerralvo.

We were not long in Cerralvo, though, before we were back on the march to town of Marin. This march was nothing like the march into Cerralvo. We went through a valley where we enjoyed a constant, cool breeze from the mountains and there were numerous streams offering plenty of fresh water. Even at this late hour, most everyone was convinced that Monterrey would be had without bloodshed. Even those who had talked with General Taylor said that he anticipated General Ampudia and the Mexicans would retreat before we arrived.

From the plateau of Marin, we could see across the plain the mountains that stood behind Monterrey, and we knew we were close. There had been some rumor as we approached Marin that a company of cavalry was preparing to defend the city, but other than a brief skirmish on the road – well ahead and of no concern to me – there was nothing to the rumor. The townspeople, though, had gathered their livestock and left the town to hide in the countryside. Mexican soldiers had promised them that the American army would rape and pillage and murder.

The fact is, other than a few individual incidents, the Americans in Mexico behaved themselves rather well, and it wasn't long before the townspeople of Marin returned and discovered that they were safer with our men among them than they were with their own countrymen. Under orders from Taylor, we paid whatever price the Mexicans demanded for their goods. Compared to the Mexican cavalry – who had threatened to burn the town to the ground should any of the townspeople render us any assistance – the Mexicans much preferred having the Americans around making them wealthy. Often, the townspeople provided us with their own food and even rented rooms to soldiers.

Not me, of course. I was in a tent with the muleteers.

From Marin it was a short march to a small, almost deserted village. Nearly all of its inhabitants were gone when we arrived, having fled to the hills. It was here, just a few miles from Monterrey, that Taylor and the rest of the army began to realize that Ampudia intended to fight.

I wandered around the town and saw the Texians cleaning their pistols and the regular army boys setting up their pickets and camp guards and the volunteers were shining up their muskets. It was growing more certain that there would be a fight, despite the lingering rumors that Ampudia would abandon Monterrey at the last moment. I would be in the back with the mules and supplies and baggage, and among my duties, of course, would be guarding the mule train, but despite my proximity to the coming battle, I had little concern that I would see any activity.

Among those who believed that battle was imminent, everyone was confident that we would make short work of the Mexicans. The volunteers and even the regulars were chomping at the bit to get at Ampudia. It was hard to believe, looking about the camp at the well-drilled regulars and those ruffians from Texas with their slouched hats and thick beards, that the battle could be anything but a rout. General Taylor, it seemed to me, would be able to bust through the front door of the city and any Mexicans who didn't slip out the back would be bound to surrender.

The next day we marched a short distance and soon came to a plain overlooking Monterrey, and for the first time got a look at the place we'd been talking about for weeks. When the army first arrived, the city was shrouded in a fog, but it quickly burned away and was gone by the time I got forward enough to take a look.

I will say this: All the confidence went out of me when I first saw it. I was no military engineer, but it looked damned daunting to me.

Behind the city in the distance rose the Sierra del Madre

mountains, and those added immensely to a formidable impression I had of the city. To the east and south, the city was protected by the Rio Santa Catarina, and the river provided excellent protection so that we would be able to assault the city only from the north or west. That meant we would have slight protection through cornfields north of the city, but eventually we would step out of the corn and be in an open plain where we must endure fire from the city's several forts.

There were also several forts and any number of hurriedly constructed breastworks surrounding the city. Looking at it from where I was north of the city, there was El Teneria to the left (east of the city) that was couched between the city and the Rio Santa Catarina. The Black Fort was situated on a height in front of the city and offered a most fearsome sight. To the right (west of the city) there was Fort Liberty, and all along other breastworks had been erected. To the south of the city, atop a hill on the other side of the Rio Santa Catarina, there was the Bishop's Palace, plainly visible from our vantage point with the green, white and red Mexican flag flying above it. All of these forts offered the Mexicans plenty of opportunity to rain shells down upon any army advancing from the north.

Worse, though, the entire city of Monterrey had the appearance of one big fort. It was full of thick-walled, two story homes and buildings, every one like an individual castle, which lined narrow streets. Even if the Americans could get past the forts, once they entered the city they would be slaughtered.

General Taylor sent reconnaissance missions out, and even as I stood gaping at the impossibility of assaulting this city, cannon positioned at the various forts suddenly erupted, white smoke billowing away from the forts, and sending projectiles hurtling toward the engineers Taylor had sent to scout.

For now, I merely said a prayer of thanks that I would be in the back with the mules, and as another volley erupted from the forts I decided to go check on my charges. I'd determined that if it appeared on the morrow that the battle was turning against us, I would be well positioned to turn tail and run all the way back to Camargo if necessary.

"Private Speed," I heard my name called as I made my way to the baggage and the mules. I turned and saw that it was Col. Davis addressing me, so I saluted him. "Son, I know you didn't come all the way from Georgia to Monterrey, Mexico, to look after a bunch of mules." And then he examined me in my trousers and green shirt and suspenders, and he turned to a sergeant nearby us. "Sergeant, I want you to take Private Speed to the quartermaster. Get him uniformed like a proper looking Mississippi volunteer, get him a rifle and a Bowie knife, and put him in with your company." Then he turned back to me, his hollow cheeks bright at the thought of the coming slaughter. "We'll get you into the fight you volunteered for, Private Speed!"

And Jeff Davis clapped me on the shoulder and grinned at me, fully believing that this big, strong lad from Georgia wanted to rush in and take on the Mexicans in solo combat. Jeff Davis was no judge of character then, and he was no judge of character later, either, when he and I sat in his office in Richmond and he outlined for me how he would beat Abe Lincoln by wearing down the man's resolve. I knew 'em both well, and I can say this about them: I never cared for either one of them because from this day forward both of them tried their best to get me killed, but I had a begrudging respect for Abe Lincoln because I've never seen another man in all my life whose determination could not be turned.

So this Mississippi sergeant, who was no better a judge of character than his colonel was, grabbed me up by the elbow – all grins and enthusiasm – and set about dressing me like he was a girl with her toy doll. "We'll get you looking smart enough for them Mexicans," he assured me. "They'll take one look at you in our red shirt and surrender the city fer sure 'cause they'll think yer a great big Mississippi boy!"

We set off together to find the quartermaster who complained to no end about finding breeches long enough to fit my long legs (in the end, the trousers came to below my ankles, but shirtsleeves stopped well short of my wrists), and soon I looked like all the other privates in the Mississippi Rifles.

Davis was a West Point graduate who'd retired from the army to become a lawyer, and he'd worked hard to make his men look and act as much like professional soldiers as he possibly could. They were well drilled and well disciplined, and they looked smart in their uniforms. In the Mississippi Rifles, we wore red shirts with white tweed trousers and wide-brimmed white, straw hats. We wore a white belt with a thick shoulder strap from which we hung pouches for our spare ammunition, firing caps and rations.

The sergeant also secured for me one of the long-barreled Model 1841 Whitney Rifles all the Mississippians carried. They were useless at short range and did not fit a bayonet, so all the Mississippians also kept a long Bowie knife tucked in their belts for hand-to-hand combat. From a distance, though, the rifles were the best any regiment had, and Davis had used his position in Congress to secure the rifles for his regiment.

When we were done and I'd changed into the uniform of the Mississippi Rifles, the sergeant took me back to Davis so that he might admire me, and Davis laughed at the poor fit of the shirt but said I looked well enough and congratulated me for moving up in society from Georgia to Mississippi.

Daft as I was, and scared as hell that this man's intervention was steadily moving me closer and closer to the combat, I didn't know what to say but to thank him. Had I any sense, I'd have told him he could keep his red shirt and white trousers and societal advancements and I was walking back to Camargo where I intended to get exceedingly drunk with my Georgia Irishmen.

They called the campsite Walnut Springs, and I'll be honest

that despite its proximity to what would soon be a battlefield, it was a pleasant enough spot. I am told that the people of Monterrey liked to picnic there whenever an invading army wasn't occupying the place, and I could see why. Streams with fresh water, trees for shade, nice grass: It was an idyllic place had it not been for all the madmen showing their teeth in grins and snarls in anticipation of killing and being killed on the morrow.

The camp that night was full of confidence. Every American soldier in the place – all 6,650 of them – believed that we would take the city with ease.

As you might imagine, it was hours before I could fall asleep. Jeff Davis had thwarted my plans for remaining safely in the back, and I was in as deep a funk as ever I'd experienced. I tossed and turned and sweated through the night and only fell to sleep from absolute exhaustion. And I dreamed that night that I was advancing on Milledgeville with Jeff Davis standing in the rear shouting at me, "Onward, Private Jackson! Beat those Georgians and win the day for Mississippi!" and I could see the orange hair of my lovely wife who was on top of the parapets of the Georgia Capitol manning a cannon and she fired a shot that struck me in the stomach, leaving an enormous, gaping hole, and I woke up with a scream.

And there I found the other Mississippi privates getting up and starting their breakfast fires.

"Get a good breakfast in you, Speed," the sergeant who had dressed me was saying, "You'll want a good meal in you, for it may be some time before we get to eat again."

General Taylor's battle plan was to attack Monterrey from the west and south by sending half his army in a hooking maneuver around the city while distracting the Mexicans by sending a diversion in from the north. Old Rough and Ready sent General Worth with the Texians and a regiment from the regular army to envelope the city from the west, and he sent two regiments of the regular army under Garland and Butler to attack the city from the north. This diversion from the northeast was intended to give the Texians a chance to press in from the west. A company or two of volunteers were to fall in with the regulars under Garland, but I was relieved that the rest of the volunteers were all to stay back in reserve.

I prayed silently that the Texians would make swift work of capturing the city so that the reserves might be unnecessary or that at this late hour we might discover that Ampudia had retreated over night.

But presently the forts surrounding the city exploded in cannon fire, and it was clear that Ampudia intended to fight.

Though it was hell to stand around waiting all morning while the din of battle waged in front of us, I remained hopeful that the city would fall quickly. But it was not long before the walking wounded started arriving back in camp, and horrible rumors began to spread of how the battle was going, particularly in front of us at the northeast of the city. Americans were pinned down inside the city walls, being shot at from Mexican soldiers manning the roofs of houses. Cannon fire from the forts had devastated our ranks as they approached. Some were even saying it was hopeless or that General Taylor would need twice the force he'd brought with him if he hoped to take Monterrey. The rumors had entire companies being decimated.

And the Mississippi officers – Jeff Davis among 'em – moved among the men, promising us that we'd soon come to grips with the Mexican hoard.

CHAPTER VII

With my guts ready to explode, Jeff Davis came up to me and looked up at my face with those penetrating blue eyes. "Soon, Private Speed," he said, his voice barely above a whisper. "Your opportunity for glory will be here soon. I have every confidence that back in Georgia they'll be saying how Jackson Speed did his state proud."

Damn my state! I thought, but I muttered something about how maybe the Texians would win the day yet.

"Don't you worry about that," Davis said. "We'll be in the action presently."

By what I reckon as being late morning, General Taylor decided to commit more troops to the folly taking place on the northeastern side of the city. Taylor did then, and always would, refer to this action on the eastern side of Monterrey as a diversion. The Mexicans, not being privy to Taylor's battle plans, believed it was a full assault taking place. General Taylor committed almost two-thirds of his army to the east of Monterrey, so you tell me who was right.

Among those troops he decided to commit were the Tennessee volunteers, the Ohio volunteers, and – to my absolute horror – the Mississippi volunteers.

How I came to be here, about to charge the works of Monterrey, afflicted my mind. I wanted to cry out, "I'm from Georgia, b'God! Let me go home, or to Camargo!" But it would have done no good against the designs of these madmen. They were bound to charge the forts, and they would drag with them every able-bodied, however unwilling, man they could find, without consideration for whether or not he was from Mississippi or Tennessee or Ohio or Georgia – and certainly without any consideration at all as to whether or not he wanted to charge these forts.

And that's the hell of the army and war: Madmen with no thought for the lives and well-being of themselves are given the power to order other men to their deaths. Jeff Davis did not have a second's thought for whether or not he might have his chest pierced by a musket ball or his leg blown away by a cannonball, so why then would he care anything about my chest or my leg? "There they are, Speedy! Run at 'em!"

We were ordered to load our rifles, and shortly the Tennessee volunteers began to form up for battle. All around me the Mississippi volunteers were grousing because the Tennessee boys were getting a head start on us. Let 'em, I thought, maybe the Mexicans will run out of bullets by the time we get there.

As the officers gave the order to march, I found that my legs could barely work, my belly was churning, and I thought I would faint from fear. We were formed up in a column, and I can tell you those Mississippi Rifles under Jeff Davis had been better drilled than the Jasper Greens ever were. Those boys looked like regulars as they formed up in column and started forward.

I was near the back, which was as much as I could hope for, and as the Mississippi volunteers started forward with me among them, my feet wouldn't lift from the ground. For a moment – just a second – I thought they all might just march right past me and leave me standing there, but the damned private to my left caught me by the elbow and pulled me forward, and I found myself stepping in with the rest of them as we started off for the cornfield.

There, too, in the corn, I thought I might duck down, step out of line and lie down among the stalks where I might not be seen, but we were marching in such tight formation that from the left and right and from front and behind I had no choice but to continue forward. The cannon fire from the city was drowning out all noise, but even so the din coming from my churning belly seemed sure to give me away as a coward to those near me. Not that I cared a wit about that: All these boys from Mississippi would be dead before long and forever unable to tell anyone how Jackie Speed trembled and farted on the approach to Monterrey.

The only thought in my mind was getting behind something solid and staying put until the whole thing was over. If General Taylor won the day, I'd emerge from my hidey-hole and pat my fellows on the back for a job well done. If General Ampudia successfully defended Monterrey, I'd make my way back to Cerralvo, if I could, and retire in that pleasant little village until the war was over. Or, if I couldn't get back, I'd allow myself to be taken prisoner and spend the rest of the war in a Mexican jail and pray to God that I wouldn't be paroled. I found any of these options to be far superior to ever having to march into battle again.

And my thoughts naturally turned to Uriah Franks, and I caught myself wondering what would have happened if I'd allowed him to catch me there on McIntosh Street. I'd had that hatchet in my hand – maybe I could have put pay to him right there and then and avoided all these terrible weeks as a volunteer in Old Rough and Ready's army. And then I thought of Ashley Franks and how she had seduced me, tempting a too-young and too-innocent boy with her soft lips and round bosom. I thought of how she had corrupted me into this hell that my life had become, and I moaned out loud in despair at the thought that in moments all I was and all I'd ever been and all I'd ever be would concentrate down to the wound I would presently receive and the agony of death that would soon be upon me, and now I squealed with the knowledge of the pain I would feel as a bullet ripped through me – my chest, and I'd die in an instant? my gut, and I'd suffer for hours or days with my intestines turned to gravy? my face, and I'd bleed to death with a horrible visage of blood and bone and cheek torn open? or a cannonball that would shatter a limb and sever an artery and there on the field the blood would rush out of me?

Oh, there is no horror like that of marching to your death.

In the cornfield I could see nothing of what was coming, but by now the front of our column began to clear the corn. As we exited the cornfield into a plain dotted with small huts, we began receiving fire from the city. Some fool ordered us to form up into battle line, and the privates to my left and right manhandled me into formation.

We pressed forward over the open plain, now, and found ourselves under fire from the cannons from the Black Fort, Fort Teneria and a new fort – it was Fort Diablo positioned behind Fort Teneria – that we hadn't seen until now.

A cannonball fired from the fort on our left – El Teneria, the damned place – blasted through our ranks not far from where I was marching into battle formation, opening up a gap as men hit by the thing dropped to the ground with screams of agony. The lieutenants and sergeants kept us moving into position, and now all around me was the whiz and snap of bullets, men falling with grievous wounds and screams. Some simply dropped without a sound as a bullet crashed into their heads or breasts. All the while, the damn fool officers were pushing us forward.

All about were the bodies of men mutilated by cannon fire. Limbs and headless torsos littered the ground as cannonballs ripped into our ranks, bounced from the ground in front of us and flew just over our heads. In horror, I came upon a Mississippi volunteer who was on the ground screaming in agony, the crotch of his white trousers soaked red in blood where he'd taken a musket ball to the groin, and now I had a new horror haunting me: To have my bits and pieces shot away would be a fate worse than death.

By God, I was taller than nearly every soldier around me, and so many musket balls zipped near me that I was certain the men in the forts were using me as their target. I slumped down as low as I could so that I might find cover behind the men in front of me.

The Tennessee volunteers lined up on our left, facing El Teneria and we were marching with El Teneria in front and to our left so that we faced fire coming from El Teneria to our front as well as the shots from the Black Fort that were pounding into our right flank.

As we continued to advance, someone passed the order to act as sharpshooters and fire into Fort Teneria, and at this point some of the boys dropped to their knees or lay prone to take aim into the fort while others continued their slow march into the cannon fire.

This was my cue. I dropped to the ground, pointed my rifle at the fort and fired off a shot in its general direction. If it hit in the back one of the Mississippi boys still advancing, well that was nothing to me, and if it hit one of the Mexicans manning the cannons in the fort then all the better for it – but I'd done my duty and my intention was to stay there on the ground and wait the thing out.

But then a cannonball pounded the earth just a few feet away to my right – it was fired from the Black Fort – and skipped over me within inches so that I felt the breeze of the thing as it passed just over my back. If they could get that close once, b'God, they could get closer a second time, and I yelped and jumped up and rushed forward at a full run.

I tripped through one of those thorny bushes, and fell face first into the thing so that its jags ripped at my arms and face as I fell. In my effort to catch myself, I dropped my rifle and it landed just beyond my reach. Quite suddenly I realized that there was a rush of musket balls tearing up the ground all around me and snapping the branches of the bush, and I buried my face in my hands and wept as I tried to press myself into the ground.

A ball fired from El Teneria ripped through the sleeve of my shirt, cutting a line first across my forearm and then my bicep and it burned like blazes and I screamed and rolled through the thorns of the bush. I looked up, praying some soul would come and gather up the wounded and take me back to camp, but when I looked about I realized I had somehow run in front of the entire regiment.

No wonder the Mexicans were training their fire at me: Like a damned fool I'd rushed so far ahead that I was now their foremost target. I scrambled forward and grabbed my rifle and then ducked back down into the branches of the bush. It was no protection and no shelter, but it was something better than being completely exposed. My only options were to run back to the regiment and likely be shot as a coward by the Mississippians, or to run farther ahead and seek shelter among the walls of the city and then become an even more urgent target for the Mexican muskets, or to stay put and pray.

Unconsciously – I suppose to give me something to do to take my mind from the hell erupting all around me – I reloaded my rifle. I can't credit why I did it, maybe all that drilling they forced us to do at Camp Belknap took some effect upon me, but you'll see presently that it saved my life.

If it was a minute or an hour I cannot say, but eventually the Mississippians advanced to the place where I was, and the Lieutenant Colonel – who was leading from the front, you understand – grabbed me up out of the bush and examined me.

"You're a bloody mess," he said, but I couldn't hear the words for noise from the cannons and could only read his lips. "Come along, son, and we'll pay them back for that gash on your arm."

And he righted me on my feet and pushed me forward.

We weren't more than 60 yards from the fort now, and from our position we had a clear line of fire into a gap in the fort. I was doing my best to make myself small, but I realized that the fire coming from the fort was slackening. I didn't know what it meant: Had the Texians worked their way through the city and were now assaulting the fort? Had the Mexicans run out of ammunition? Maybe the Tennessee volunteers had found a way in from the east? But clearly, unmistakably, we were suddenly receiving only the slightest of firing.

I wasn't the only one to notice that the situation of the battle had altered.

The Lieutenant Colonel who had fished me from the thorns – McClung was his name – also realized that the Mexican fire from El Teneria had slackened.

"We can take it now!" he said to me, and there was insanity in his eyes. He was one of these full of piss and vinegar with no thought for his own safety but only for the glory of battle. And those who can have cannon shot and musket balls bouncing around them and still think of doing honor to their name – those are the ones who are the most dangerous to men who, like me, have common sense enough to wish to preserve their lives. "Why do they not give the order to charge?" he demanded. And then, looking directly at me, he yelled: "We can take it!"

"You and me?" I asked, outraged and in absolute panic that he was suggesting just the two of us could take the fort, but McClung didn't respond. He reached out and grabbed a sergeant by the arm and dragged the man to him.

"We can take the fort now," he said, and the sergeant nodded feverishly, clearly as insane as McClung.

And then the inevitable happened: No orders had been issued, but McClung swung his sword from its scabbard, pointing it at the fort, and he shouted out: "Charge! Charge!" Then, to prove he'd clearly lost his mind, he shouted out: "Tall big tree!" It was nonsense and meant nothing, but the madman dashed forward.

The sergeant shouted at me: "Follow him!"

"That maniac?" I asked, pointing at McClung.

I was all set to tell the sergeant that if he wanted to follow a madman like McClung to the "tall big tree" that was all the same to me, but I'd spotted a low wall off to the right, and my intention was to make to that wall and wait for the Mexicans to run out of bullets. But I didn't have the chance to make my argument. [13]

At that moment, the sergeant's head exploded in a cloud of

red mist as a musket ball burst through the back of it. One moment his face was contorted in battle rage, and the next moment it was just simply gone, and his headless torso was dropping to the ground.

And with the sergeant's head no longer obstructing my view, I saw, as clear as day, less than 50 yards away, four Mexicans with their muskets pointed directly at me. I could see their faces, the snarl of their lips, the whites of their eyes, their mustaches, the high blue collars of their coats. But most of all, I could see the black holes of their musket barrels, and I knew that in seconds those black holes would explode in flame and smoke and send their bullets to explode my head just as they'd exploded the head of the sergeant.

And I panicked and fled, screaming as I raced headlong, just behind McClung, who was charging toward the fort.

In my horror, not just at seeing the sergeant killed but also in seeing my own death down the barrels of those Mexican muskets, I outpaced McClung, passing him when we were within ten yards of the fort.

I leapt onto the parapets and looked down into a fort full of Mexicans. They were so startled by my appearance that at first not one of them reacted. A moment later, I was aware that McClung, sword drawn, was on the parapet beside me, still shouting about big trees.

McClung brought the Mexicans to life.

An officer drew his sword and dashed straight at me. I froze in my place, completely unsure of what to do. As he raced toward me, I saw another Mexican soldier draw his musket level to shoot McClung. Just at that moment, Lieutenant Patterson jumped onto the parapet where McClung and I stood and, seeing all these events immediately, shot and killed the Mexican who was about to shoot McClung. That act was enough to break me from my stupor, and I pulled the trigger of my rifle without aiming it. The officer charging me with his sword was immediately in front of my rifle barrel when I pulled the trigger, and the force of the bullet impacting his chest threw him back several feet, where he collapsed dead.

And now, McClung's charge had turned into a general charge and the entirety of the Mississippi Rifles – at least those who were not dead or dying on the plain behind me – were coming over the parapet, and the Mexicans were fleeing. It was a rout, b'God!

It's a bizarre thing. You won't find a bigger coward than I, and my every ambition in battle is to preserve my own skin. But even I was caught up in the moment. Americans were leaping by the dozen over the parapet and falling in with the Mexicans with murderous effect. The Mexicans, or most of them, were turning their backs and running for the back door. And in the midst of what was turning into not combat but slaughter, I gave vent to the turmoil that had been building inside of me, and I joined in the slaughter with abandon.

I jumped down from the parapet – though McClung stayed there, rallying the Mississippians: "Boys! Come on my brave boys!" – and using my rifle as a club I bashed in the brains of the nearest Mexican I could find. It mattered not at bit to me that he was in the act of surrendering when I swung the rifle butt into his head the first time.

Then I turned toward those who were making their escape out the back, and I rushed forward, thrusting my Bowie knife into the backs of first one and then another. All about me, Americans were sending Mexicans to their tombs.

Momentarily, Jeff Davis came rushing past me, chasing a handful of Mexicans who were fleeing out the back of the fort.

Enjoying this new bit of work so much, I charged in behind the Mississippi colonel, but as I came out the back of the fort and into the streets of Monterrey, a Mexican officer of some kind tackled me to the ground, knocking the breath out of me and the Bowie knife from my hand.

He was a small man, not more than five feet, four inches tall, and he could not have picked a worse combatant than me. With the knife out of my hand and a Mexican officer bent on killing me, all the bloodlust was gone from me now, and my mind had turned back to survival. I gasped for breath as the Mexican raised his fist, and I kicked out with my right foot and caught him in the groin. He gulped and fell away from me. I rolled over and scrambled to the Bowie knife, and I clutched it firm in my fist and turned back to my assailant. He was clutching at his crotch and gasping, and I rammed the knife directly into his throat.

All about me the Mississippians were accepting the surrender of the defeated Mexicans.

And now Jeff Davis was standing beside me. "They'll never believe you're not from Mississippi now!" he exclaimed, slapping me on the back. "First one over the wall! My God, though, you are a bloody mess."

I looked down at myself and saw the truth of it. My left arm was singed and crusted with dirt and blood where the musket ball had cut my flesh. Both arms, too, were scratched to bits from the thorny bush. My shirt and pants were stained with the blood of the Mexicans I'd stabbed.

Davis took a handkerchief, opened his canteen and wetted the cloth, and used it to wipe my face. When he withdrew the handkerchief I saw that it was covered in blood. "You look like you charged through every cactus in Mexico," he said, laughing.

He was delighted in the victory, and credited me and McClung for leading the charge. "The Hero of El Teneria," he called me. "I'll see you promoted for valor!"

McClung got the worst of it. Clutching his sword on that parapet and staying there to rally the men, two of his fingers were shot off by a Mexican bullet that then passed into his chest. That day, we expected he would die. [14]

But Jeff Davis' desire for glory was not satiated by the taking of El Teneria. Seeing that I had no rifle, Davis pointed out a discarded weapon not far from where we stood and said, "Get that rifle loaded. We're moving on to this next fort!"

He rounded up a handful of men – not more than 20 of us –

and ordered us forward into the city to assault Fort Diablo.

Now, if you're thinking the man was insane for attempting to assault a fortification with 20 men armed with rifles and Bowie knifes, I will agree with you and say that you're an excellent judge of character, but you can check in the official records – that's exactly what we did.

I protested that my wounds needed treating, and Davis laughed as if I was making a joke and ordered us all to follow him.

We crossed a small stream that ran through the city and advanced toward Fort Diablo. Both El Teneria and Fort Diablo sat on the eastern edge of town right up against the Rio Santa Catarina. Between the two forts was a distillery that was being utilized as a stronghold by the Mexicans. Already, others among the Mississippians had taken the distillery – Davis had led them, right through the back door at El Teneria and into the distillery.

To our left as our little band advanced toward Fort Diablo was the Rio Santa Catarina. To our right were the massive stone buildings of the town – each like its own fort. As we crossed a small stream that ran into the town, we began to take fire from Mexican troops at the fort and those on the roofs of the nearby buildings.

But here, at least, we had some level of protection, with walls to hide behind.

We came to a creek within a hundred yards of the fort, and there our advance was halted as we began to take fire from a group of Mexican soldiers shooting from behind a tall wall in front of Fort Diablo. A corporal with us was shot and killed as we returned fire at the soldiers behind the wall.

The cannon in the fort could not depress low enough to bring us under cannon fire, but now the dozens of Mexican soldiers on rooftops were concentrating their fire on us.

A few more Mississippians joined us – just enough that the madman Davis was confident of our success. Davis rushed forward, crossing the stream to an embankment that provided some shelter from the rooftop soldiers, and he called to us to follow him.

"I've had enough of running into carnage," I muttered. Nevertheless, I couldn't hold my ground for the fire coming from the rooftop soldiers.

I charged for a group of rundown buildings, hoping to find cover from there, and most of the other men in our band followed me, while Davis still howled at us to follow him and advance on the fort.

Lieutenant Russell, who had saved McClung and come into Fort Teneria just behind us, was now present and organizing us to assault Fort Diablo when I saw a messenger make his way to Davis' position. Davis suddenly became animated and anyone could see that he was furious. With that messenger in tow, he ran headlong to our position, somehow dodging musket balls the entire way.

"Dammit all!" he shouted at Russell. "We've been ordered to retire!"

Retreat! We're saved! I nearly shouted with glee. Someone, somewhere, with some shred of common sense, had ordered Davis back from this foolish endeavor.

"Ordered to retreat!" Davis raged. "The fort could have been ours in five minutes if only allowed to advance!"

The future president let fly a string of oaths, but I noticed not one among our group joined him in his fury. We discovered a house where the door was open, and we rushed in to find shelter from the enemy fire outside.

Davis continued to rage, but the rest of us collapsed. We were exhausted. Most of us had never seen anything of battle before, and we had just fought through some of the worst of it, and this madman in command didn't know when to stop.

While we holed up here in this house, all hell seemed to be transpiring outside. The booms of cannons shook the walls of the house and the musket fire never stopped. I huddled in a corner, too tired to cry or pray.

The maniac Davis was at a window, and began ordering

the men up. The Ohio men, who had gone before us in the morning's battle, had regrouped and were now attempting to assault Fort Diablo, but they were taking heavy fire from a battery down the street. Watching what was happening outside, Davis was talking about making an attempt on the battery.

"Captain Cooper," Davis said, looking about at an officer who was with us in the house, "take Private Speed and move into that house" – and he pointed out the window – "and fire upon those soldiers there on the bridge. The rest of you come with me and let us see if we can take that battery."

I was not inclined to move from the corner I was in. It was, by far, the safest place I'd encountered since we had first stepped into the cornfield, and I was too exhausted and too scared to consider moving. But I knew not to put up a fight – Davis wanted me to move from one house to another while he wanted the others among us to go with him to attempt to assault a battery. Of those two options, going with Captain Cooper was clearly the best option.

How many of the Mississippians were dead or mutilated I did not know, but it seemed evident that Jeff Davis wasn't going to be content until he'd killed off every man under his command. If his orders led me into a house where I was as safe as I could be with all the cannon and musket fire filling the air rather than down a street into the mouth of a battery, then those were the orders I would follow.

Captain Cooper and I made a mad dash across one of the narrow streets, where we were briefly exposed to fire both from down the street and from the rooftop soldiers who were firing down upon us. Amazingly, the door was not barred. All of these buildings in town had enormous wooden doors that were nearly impossible to break into without axes and crowbars – of which we had neither – and I was panicked that we would have to try to break into the house and our exposure to enemy fire might be prolonged in the effort.

But as I entered the house, I saw why the door was

unlocked. There, in the street, a Mexican woman was using her handkerchief to dress the wounds of a dying American soldier. I guessed this was her house we were going into. I ducked into the doorway – which opened into a tiny, walled courtyard – and stood sheltered behind the wall and watched her. If she intended to come home after dressing the American's wound, I was going to let her back in before barring the door.

But the woman, who was neither young nor elderly, moved from the American to a couple of wounded Mexicans not far away. She began treating their wounds, too, and offering them water. The musket balls in the street were so thick that I could not believe she was going about her business in such a calm, unconcerned manner. I nearly called to her so that she would hurry back and I could bar the door, but as I watched, she was hit by a musket ball and fell to the ground beside the two Mexicans she'd been tending. I watched for a moment more to see if she would get up, but from her posture I could tell that she was already dead.

I closed and barred the door and turned to find Captain Cooper at a window, carefully taking aim and firing off a shot.

"Got him!" Captain Cooper said. He turned to me. "Have a try."

He stepped away from the window to reload his rifle, and I stepped tentatively up to the window. We were receiving no return fire – it seemed that none of the Mexicans at the battery realized we were there.

I raised the barrel of my rifle out the window and took careful aim at one of the Mexican infantrymen stationed at the battery to provide supporting fire. He had just finished reloading and was propping himself on a wall of sandbags so that he could take his own aim.

I fired my rifle, which exploded in smoke in front of me, but I watched as the smoke cleared away to see if my shot had told. The Mexican I'd shot at was now clutching his shoulder and looked like he was about to swoon. I'd not mortally wounded him, but he was out of the fight. Now Captain Cooper was eager for another turn.

The carnage and death in the streets seemed endless, and from where we were we knew only that Davis had not been successful in storming the battery. When the command was passed to retreat, no one bothered to tell us, and if Captain Cooper hadn't seen some of the Americans fleeing toward the rear we might have been caught behind.

"I believe the others are retreating," he told me, turning from the window. "We should join them."

Leaving the safety of the house was against my better judgment, but getting caught inside the city while every other American in Mexico was outside that city was no better.

We unbarred the door and chanced a look outside. The street seemed clear enough, and Captain Cooper offered to go out first. I didn't offer any argument.

Cooper walked outside, his eyes on the rooftops. He hugged close to the buildings as he sidestepped down the street. Now I followed him, and I wasn't three steps outside the door when a gang of Mexican soldiers on the rooftop across the narrow street from us showed themselves and started blasting away with their muskets.

"Run!" Cooper said, but he didn't need to tell me, for I was already hightailing it past him and down to the end of the street. There I saw a group of Mississippians making their way back toward El Teneria, which was the only place that offered any amount of safety for us.

From the fort, in small groups and without any sense of order, we began retreating back across the plain and toward the cornfield through which we'd marched earlier in the day. We were taking fire from the Black Fort, and as I moved double-time across the field I heard someone shout, "Lancers!"

I looked back and saw that a Mexican cavalry force was bearing down upon us. They were spearing our wounded on their way to us.

Now the cowardice I'd experienced all morning swept through our ranks. Men threw down their rifles and muskets and dashed headlong toward the cornfield. As I ran with them, I kept my rifle, which you might think odd. I may be a coward, but ultimately I do what I must to survive. Even in flight, I try to keep my head together, especially when all around me are losing theirs. And it is solid advice, even for a coward: When there is death and murder about, always keep a weapon nearby. As you've seen, I have no fear in killing a man if it means saving myself.

The cornfield was a killing ground. Cannonballs from the Black Fort tore through the stalks, and the Mexican lancers were soon to be on us with the slaughter – cornfield or no.

Then I was aware of another of these madmen who was riding into the cornfield from the north. I didn't know it then, but it was Albert Sidney Johnston – the hero of the Confederacy and the general in whom Jeff Davis placed the highest esteem. In a booming voice that could be heard over the din of the cannon fire, A.S. Johnston began bringing order to the fleeing troops. He shouted at them to form a battle line at a nearby fence.

All day long these soldiers had followed the orders of their superiors – madmen like Davis and Johnston – and what had it got them? They were in piles in the city. Their body parts littered the plain and the cornfield. Not a man among them had survived through the day without seeing the man beside him torn asunder by a cannonball or a musket ball. These maniacs had led them over and over into the slaughter.

And now, with another one coming up and barking orders, they continued to do as they were told, forming a line of battle.

I couldn't credit it then and I cannot credit it now, though I've seen the same scene repeated over and over throughout the course of my life. When one of these maniacs came at me, frothing at the mouth and shouting for me to turn left or push forward, if there was any way to go right or pull back that is what I did. Well, nearly all of those men who followed the orders of madmen are now dead and in their graves, and I sit in comfort penning these memoirs and enjoying my grandchildren. You may judge for yourself if you would go hither or thither.

Nevertheless, Johnston's battle line was forming to the right, the Lancers were coming from the left, and if I did not find a better location I would get caught in the middle. So I fled toward the battle line with the intention of jumping the fence and running all the way to General Taylor's tent.

And now, as I reached the battle line, the lancers attacked, riding pell-mell for us. Johnston was riding up and down the line, encouraging the men – reminding them to remove the ramrods from their muskets before firing off a shot – and as I rounded the right flank of the line and prepared to find General Taylor, Johnston's horse stopped in front of me, blocking my path.

"We're nearly there, son," he said in the most damnably calm voice. "Turn and fire once more and let's drive those lancers back, and then all together we shall resume the retreat."

Well, I wasn't convinced, but Johnston was blocking me with his horse, and so I reasoned that the only option I had to survive was to turn, load my rifle and fire in the hopes of helping to drive the lancers back.

We fired a single volley and that was enough to convince the lancers that they had no easy prey here, and the men cursed them as damned cowards for cutting up the wounded but being unwilling to face our fire. I saw across the plain where another band of retreating Americans formed a line to drive the lancers away from them.

That was the last of it. I turned north and dragged myself back toward Walnut Springs. The shadows were already getting long and evening would soon sit in around us, and we looked like hundreds of walking corpses – bloodied and mutilated and exhausted – as we stumbled back into camp.

It was the evening of September 21, 1846.

I've seen worse days. I was at Gettysburg, wasn't I? But I'd seen enough to know that it was too much. But who else was there that day? You'll know all the names: Jeff Davis was there with A.S. Johnston; but so was Longstreet; Meade was there; and Sam Grant, riding his horse like a maniac through those streets of blood. Lee, McClellan, Bragg. Oh, hell, they were all there. These men – these architects of so much death and destruction – they were all there and, by God, that should have been enough for them. But they were madmen.

CHAPTER VIII

I sought out the hospital to have the wound to my arm treated, but the grim atmosphere of the place was more than I could take. The sawbones were hard at work, amputating arms and legs. Some of the men withstood it all with manly fortitude while others screamed and cried. Blood ran as freely in the hospital as it did in the streets of Monterrey, and I worried that if I got too close they might decide to take off my arm, too.

So I wandered back through the camp to the Mississippians. Everywhere there was sorrow. Some were writing to the wives and mothers of their fallen comrades. Some were sobbing silently to themselves. Some had collapsed where they were into fitful sleep. It was a scene that could not have been more unlike the one just the night before, when the men were all full of confidence and cleaning their rifles.

A thunderstorm came up, and I found a blanket with which to cover myself, and I slept in the grass. I remember my last thought before sleep overtook me: At least it is over and with his army devastated, Old Rough and Ready cannot hope to send us back in.

But I was wrong.

That night, a small force occupied El Teneria. Taylor refused to lose what had been gained at such a heavy cost.

I woke the next morning to the distant sounds of fighting. It was light outside, though the sun was not yet up, and a fog blanketed the city so that none of us in the Walnut Springs camp could have any idea what was happening.

The morning before, as we attacked eastern Monterrey in what was the costliest diversion you could ever hope to find, Texian volunteers and regular army infantry under General

Worth moved around the west of the city and crossed the Rio Santa Catarina. We didn't know it then, for there was no communication between Worth and Taylor, but the Texians had engaged in a pretty hot cavalry action before finishing their swing around to the south of the city and assaulting the works on Federation Hill and Fort Soldado.

They won the hills to the south of the city on the first day of battle.

On the morning of September 22, long before sunup, Worth's troops had recrossed the Rio Santa Catarina and assaulted Fort Liberty on a steep hill at the western side of the city, and those were the sounds we now woke to.

With El Teneria securely in our hands and Fort Soldado, also, Taylor's army had succeeded in the first day in securing a foothold in the eastern part of the city and securing the heights at the southern end of the city. Those heights, too, overlooked the Saltillo Road, and protected us from the thing we all most worried about – Santa Anna coming up from Mexico City with reinforcements.

Now the Texians and regular army under Worth were assaulting Fort Libertad – Liberty Fort – and there found themselves on the top of the same mountain as the Bishop's Palace. Anyone who knows of Monterrey knows these places. The Texians, who were already legendary for their exploits at San Jacinto and Mier and a dozen other similar places, were promoting their legend farther. Though there was no end to the difficulties – including scaling impossible cliffs – and resistance they encountered in securing Fort Libertad and the Bishop's Palace on top of Independence Hill, the Texians and regulars received few casualties in their assaults on these places. Though it took them the entirety of the day, they secured the western heights of Monterrey and now had a commanding view into the city. At the Bishop's Palace, they turned Mexican guns inward and, by late afternoon, were sending cannonballs into Monterrey.

Nothing Taylor could have done could have compelled his

army at Walnut Springs on the day of the 22 nd. We were whipped. Perhaps we could claim some level of victory for having taken El Teneria, but our losses were such that it was a hollow victory. The men were exhausted and had seen too much of the slaughter.

Taylor therefore offered no further diversion on the eastern side of Monterrey. Instead, he sent enough men to garrison El Teneria and the rest of us were left to lick our wounds at camp.

Fright and exhaustion had overpowered me, and though curiosity compelled me to see what I could of what was taking place across the city to the west, I soon found a mostly dry patch of grass under a walnut tree and slumped into a stupor. I do not think I slept. I had assumed the Texians and regulars under Worth had met as bad a fate as we had, and so I kept waiting for the order to withdraw that never came.

The groans of the wounded and dying haunted us all through the day in camp, and rumors spread first that the Texians were killed on top of Independence Hill and then that they had won the hill and were presently storming the western side of Monterrey.

But not until late afternoon when we saw the Stars and Stripes raised above the Bishop's Palace did we know anything for certain.

The rest of the camp hurrahed and cheered and celebrated, but the appearance of the American flag over the Bishop's Palace caused no celebration for me. A victory on the west side of Monterrey meant that Taylor would not abandon the place – though, if I'd known anything of the man's previous military experience at the time, I would have known that the "Ready" in his nickname indicated his readiness to continue throwing to the death the soldiers under his command in order to achieve his objectives. A victory on the west of Monterrey would mean, surely, further engagement on the east of Monterrey, and that would send me back into the fray.

The Texians, in their cool way, called it "warm work" when

the bullets flew all about them, but I thought it was scorching hot, and I'd been too burned on the previous day.

But any hope I had of shirking duty was abandoned later in the evening when Colonel Davis himself sought me out, inquiring about the arm.

"It's terrible sore," I moaned. My thought was he was determining who was fit for duty and if I played it up he might keep me with the wounded back at camp. "The Mexicans sure did a number on me, sir. It was a lucky shot, and I'm sick that it'll keep me out of tomorrow's action."

Davis took my arm by the wrist and examined the wounds himself in the dim light cast by a nearby campfire.

"This wound won't keep you out of the fighting," he proclaimed, and the maniac was grinning ear-to-ear, expecting me to celebrate his medical opinion. "We will have to see about getting you a new shirt. Tomorrow we are going to win the city," Davis said. "It is my intention that the Mississippi Rifles will be there to accept General Ampudia's unconditional surrender. And after your gallantry in the action of yesterday, I want you to be at my side throughout the fighting. Wherever I go, Speed, you will go with me."

I gulped in horror and tears welled in my eyes. Jeff Davis, fool that he was, mistook my weeping for some display of manly gratitude at being ordered forward at the side of my colonel. But I'd seen him on that first day of Monterrey – dashing pell-mell into the thickest of the fighting, rushing forward where not even his men would follow when ordered to go, not a thought for his own safety or for the safety of his men. His actions indicated clearly to me that Jeff Davis was determined to see himself slaughtered by the Mexicans and the more of his men that he could take with him the happier he'd be.

These men like Davis who seek glory in battle care not a wit for whether that glory is achieved in life or in death.

"And as I told you during the fighting yesterday, I have decided to promote you for your gallantry and valor in rushing to the parapets at El Teneria. I am brevetting you to Second Lieutenant and you shall serve as my aide."

Davis then passed the word among his men that the "Hero of El Teneria" had been brevetted to second lieutenant, and those among them who were still able to raise a voice hurrahed and cheered, no doubt because they knew as second lieutenant I'd be pushed up ahead of them – leading from the front, don't ye know – and would be well placed to block a bullet or two meant for them.

Years later, when George B. McClellan discovered I was a veteran of Monterrey and had been brevetted second lieutenant at the battle, he remarked rather coldly that when he arrived for duty in Mexico it seemed that every volunteer in the theater outranked him, and Little Mac left me at the time with the distinct impression that he was indifferent that I'd been an officer in the volunteers in Mexico. More right he was than he knew.

I was too horrified at the thought of having to serve side by side with this madman to think of what to say. I'm sure I mumbled some sort of gratitude because it seemed like the right thing to do, but my stomach did a somersault and I farted loudly and Davis laughed and clapped me on the shoulder and told me to be sure to get a good meal in my stomach so that I'd be ready for the fight in the morning.

He said, too, that he was absolutely certain my gallant exploits of the 21st would be overshadowed by what we would achieve together on the 23rd.

That night I found pen and paper and wrote my Eliza what I was sure would be my last words to her. Some men in their letters home would have gladly told loved ones that they had received a battlefield promotion for gallantry. I believe nearly all those men camped around me wished only for this. But I failed entirely to mention it. Instead, I gushed that it had been a terrible mistake that had led me to leave our wedding bed and come to this cursed place. I bemoaned my pathetic luck at being dragged to the front and told her that my only desire was to live through the day so that I could soon return to her.

My term of enlistment was only half expired at that time, and I saw no way that I would live through the next six months. All around me generals and colonels and captains were devising ways to push me farther into the death in a never-ending scheme to get me killed, and it seemed that in six month's time they would surely find a way to be successful. I did not eat nor could I sleep that night, and every thought that entered my mind was of a new and terrible death.

The promotion Davis gave me meant nothing. Had my brevet rank given me command of some group of men, I might be able to order them to form up around me and thereby shield me from the Mexican bullets and grape, but second lieutenant was just a name and offered no protection. The worst of it was this madman wanted me at his side. No doubt he believed that, tall as I was, the Mexicans would train their fire on me as the bigger target and spare him, the damned ass.

And when morning came, I was already up and wandering around the camp wondering if I could just start walking back down the road to Camargo to check on my Jasper Greens. Malaria and Yellow Fever now seemed far preferable to the scrape that Mexican bullet had left on my arm.

But soon Davis spotted me, full of glee about the coming battle, and told me to get together my rifle and Bowie knife and to be sure I had plenty of ammunition "because ere this day is out, I'll be introducing you to General Ampudia," he swore.

Some would say it was fire that I saw in his eyes, but I knew better: It was derangement.

It was then that General Quitman approached Colonel Davis, and I was near enough to hear the entirety of their conversation.

Our garrison at El Teneria had discovered with the dawn, Quitman said, that the Mexicans had abandoned Fort Diablo in the night. This was the fort where Davis had tried to get us all killed after we successfully stormed El Teneria.

Quitman ordered Davis to take some of his Mississippians and some Tennessee volunteers to occupy the abandoned fort. For the first time since my interview with Davis of the previous night, I had a glimmer of hope. Taking an abandoned fort sounded to me like absolutely the sort of warfare I was fit for.

In no time we were making our way back to El Teneria and then retracing our steps from the 21st from Fort Teneria to Fort Diablo.

A group of Mexicans in a redoubt fired on us as we advanced to the abandoned fort, but they were more than a hundred yards distant and their inaccurate muskets were rendered useless.

We took a handful of prisoners when we entered the fort, and the men set about fortifying the fort and finding what supplies they could, and I avoided any work by staying close to Davis. I should have known better, though, than to get too comfortable with the relative ease of the morning. Davis was determined to see Ampudia before the day was out.

"You and I are going to examine the works over there and see what might be done about advancing our position," Davis told me. "Taking an abandoned fort falls well short of my intentions for today, and we must determine what way best puts us on a road for the cathedral in the main plaza where Ampudia is supposed to have established his headquarters."

I wondered if he could hear himself, but then we were leaving the safety of the abandoned fort in favor of examining the redoubt. Quaking with fear, I stayed close to the buildings as the madman and I pushed into the city to reconnoiter the works that had been hurriedly constructed in the street.

We took with us a few other Mississippians and also the former president of the Texas Republic, Mirabeau Lamar. Anyone who knows about Monterrey knows that the Texians were the ones who best understood how to fight in those narrow streets. They'd had experience fighting in these similar towns in their war of independence. The grand movements of companies and regiments Davis and regular officers had been taught at West Point didn't work in these streets, and that had led to our slaughter on the 21st. But Lamar knew his business, and throughout the morning he'd been in Davis' ear, discussing how best to move into the city.

We pressed forward toward the redoubt, but it was well defended. Mexican muskets fired down upon us from the rooftops; well-hidden Mexican soldiers at the redoubt fired at us, and the cannon at the redoubt also threw a fair amount of grape at us.

We tried our luck with them, firing our rifles into the redoubt and at the Mexicans we could see over the parapets of the rooftops, but even the accuracy of the rifles wasn't enough to get at them.

Davis was too blinded in his quest for glory to see that any assault on the redoubt would spell disaster for all of us, but, thank God, General Quitman at El Diablo could see that, should we press forward any farther, we would all be cut to pieces. Quitman ordered Davis to withdraw to a safe position and await reinforcements.

Davis, Lamar and I, along with a few others from the Rifles, gathered behind the stone wall of a courtyard.

Throughout the morning, there was the constant noise of battle – either near as the Mexicans fired at us, or in the distance on the other side of the town where Worth's Texians were pushing into the center.

Though at the time I had little military experience, it was obvious enough to me what was happening, and even I could see that – mad or not – our officers were going to win the day. From the east, we were pushing in toward the cathedral and plaza in the center of town where Ampudia was making his stand. Meanwhile, the Texians and regulars under Worth were pushing in from the west. The Texians had the west and south secured. We had the north and east secured.

There could be no withdrawal for the Mexican army.

This whole time, Lamar and Davis were in constant discussion. Lamar saw the way: He swore that the Texians knew best how to fight through the city and told Davis that to advance through the streets was suicide (for my part, I could have told Davis that), but he said it was no matter to cut holes through the walls of the limestone houses and buildings.

"Rather than advance your men through the streets, advance them through the houses," Lamar explained. "You can easily cut into the roofs, too, and move men onto the rooftops. Take the rooftops from the Mexicans, and it will be us firing down on that breastwork!"

In our courtyard between the redoubt and Fort Diablo, we hunkered down and held the ground while Quitman sent up the remainder of the Mississippians. Davis encouraged Lamar to go back to Quitman and discuss with him the strategy for advancing through the city. Lamar returned to us and said that Quitman had seen the wisdom in it and was sending for the Texians who were not with Worth – East Texians serving under Henderson – who hadn't seen the first bit of battle yet.

It seemed like only minutes before the Texians were dashing through the streets – dodging musket balls – and coming up to our position. Henderson, their captain, arrived giddy to get into the fight. The Texians brought with them pickaxes and crowbars and even ladders. They were well prepared for this.

Lamar, when he returned, was riding a big white horse. The fool wore a bright red shirt, and he could not have been any more of a target. He rode through the streets, cheering on his men and encouraging them by calling out the names of the places where the Mexicans had slaughtered Texians: Goliad and the Alamo. All the while, musket balls and grape shot bounced through the streets, but Lamar continued to ride and cheer on his men.

You might think it strange, but I rather liked Lamar and his Texians. There could be no breed of man more opposite to myself – they thrived on the battle and were miserably unhappy if Mexican bullets weren't coming at them in sheets of lead – but they knew their business and they knew, too, how to survive among those bullets. And that's the part that endeared them to me.

Hadn't I been in the safety of the Mexican woman's house on the 21st, firing without concern at unsuspecting victims and enjoying my work tremendously? And if the Texians had devised some strategy of battle that kept us off those deadly streets and gave us the opportunity to win the day without having to stand up in the middle of the street to receive a canister of grape, then these were the men alongside whom I wanted to fight. Davis and the Mississippi Rifles could suffer death and mutilation in the streets; the Texians and I would hide out in the houses and fire our rifles through windows.

We set about the business right away.

Davis passed the word among his men to stick with the Texians and assist them in bashing in doors. Someone provided me with an ax, and Davis – madness gleaming in the eye – clapped me on the back and pointed to one of the big stout doors across the street.

"There, Lieutenant Speed! Let's get the door in on that house and you and I will have that redoubt quicker than we took El Teneria!"

The man's bloodlust knew no bounds. To dash across the street would mean exposing myself to musketry and cannon fire. A blast of canister would sweep everything in the street and leave my corpse in shreds.

"My God!" I yelped, unable to restrain myself. "You want me to run out there?"

Davis' blue eyes cut into me. For a moment, the man saw cowardice and could not believe what he was seeing. Looking into those eyes, I was certain if I stood there a moment longer, refusing to obey his order, he would run me through with his sword right there in that courtyard. But just then I heard the cannon belch and the grape shot clanged off of the limestone walls of the nearby buildings. I knew now was my chance. While they reloaded that cannon I could bash in the door before the next shot fired. And before Davis could come to believe that I was really on the verge of disobeying his order, I clutched my rifle in one hand and the pickax in the other and made my mad dash across the street.

I tossed my rifle ahead of me as I neared the door so that it slid to the foot of the door. I gripped the pickax with both hands and still at a full run I swung the tool as hard as I could into the heavy wooden door. Bits of it splintered away.

Foolishly, I'd thought the door would fall to pieces with the first blow, but these heavy doors were too thick. Screaming, I swung the pickax furiously, as if my life depended on it – which of course it did – raining blow after blow down on the door near its hinges.

A musket ball ricocheted from the limestone wall and caught me in the calf as I swung another blow against the door.

Now the door broke from its hinges, but with this final blow against the door, I reeled with the pain in my leg and dropped to the ground. Davis, damn him, drew his sword and stepped over me and into the house. All around musket balls were bouncing from the walls of buildings, hitting the ground and ricocheting up over my head. I rolled over to see the extent of the damage to my leg, expecting my calf muscle to be ripped from the bone.

But my trouser leg wasn't even ripped. The ball left quite a welt on my calf, but all its force was expended when it hit the wall. I pushed the pickax into the house, grabbed my rifle and limped inside the house just as the cannon spit out another shot of double canister.

"Empty!" Davis said. "Not a soul in this house." He sounded disappointed that we were not now coming to grips with an entire company of Mexicans.

I propped myself up on my rifle, tears streaming down my face.

"How bad is it?" Davis asked, looking at my leg and seeing nothing.

I took a tremulous step forward and the pain of putting weight on my leg was almost more than I could bear.

"Excellent!" he said, clapping me on the shoulder again. "Let's get to work on the wall." Then he stopped himself and looked back at me and said, "Good thinking to wait for them to fire that cannon before rushing into the street."

If he'd had a doubt about the valor of his recently brevetted second lieutenant, he had fixed it right in his mind, convincing himself that I was not questioning the sanity of his order – which is exactly what I was doing – but only questioning him on the timing.

Now Henderson and some Texians and a few more of the Mississippi Rifles were coming through the door.

Henderson took my ax and moved to the wall, chipping at the wall in spots with the tip of the ax. Then he swung the ax hard at a spot.

"Here," he said. "It's weak here. Knock a hole here and we'll cross to the next house."

Henderson handed me back the ax, and I set to work bashing in the wall. It was easier by far to cut through that stone than it had been coming through the door, and in minutes I had a hole wide enough for a man to crawl through.

The Mississippians in the room with us all stood behind me with their rifles trained on the hole so that if there should be Mexicans on the other side of the wall waiting for us they would shoot as soon as the hole was big enough to present a target. But as I cut away at the limestone an empty room was revealed to us.

I enlargened the hole enough that we were able to easily get through it. The Mississippians went through the house, checking upstairs, to make certain it was empty.

Henderson suggested that we should go through the roof here, and so he took my pickax and we all started to make our way upstairs. I could barely lift my leg to make it up the steps, and so I sat down and pulled up my trouser leg to examine the damage to my calf. Already there was an enormous welt, nearly the size of my fist, and the leg all around was bruised. I took a deep breath and tried to think of what I might do to extricate myself from my present situation. I'd been shot once, and I was desperate not to be shot again.

It wouldn't take much to play up my injury. I could tell Davis, in a manly and regretful way, that I couldn't go any farther and wish him the best of luck and to give Ampudia hell from me, but I suspected that would not do. So, using my rifle as a crutch, I hobbled up the remaining steps and, upon reaching the second level of the house, found Henderson standing on a table as he picked away at the ceiling.

"Here!" he exclaimed, jumping from the table and handing the pickax to one of his Texians, a big fellow dressed in the typical style of the Texians.

The Texian climbed up onto the table and began swinging up at the ceiling until rays of sun began to stream through. The Texians and Mississippians kept their rifles trained on the hole as the Texian opened it wider.

Then they stacked a couple of chairs up onto the table, and one of the Texians climbed up through the hole, getting a boost from the big man who'd just opened the hole.

One by one, the Texians and Mississippians went through the hole. Davis was the fourth man through, but it was more than he could stand to wait his turn. Other than the big Texian who was helping us all up, I was the last man through the hole.

When I arrived on the roof, the entirety of our small band was lying prone against the roof, and so I flattened myself down, too.

Each of these stone buildings had flat roofs and small parapets that ran along the sides. At the farthest building on our block there were a dozen Mexicans who were occupied with firing over the sides into the streets and unaware of our presence.

Henderson and Davis began ordering us to shimmy over to the parapet and prepare to raise ourselves over it to fire on the Mexicans. Other than Davis, Henderson and me, there were nine of us: a dozen against a dozen. We slid ourselves along the roof until we came to the parapet, and then all of us picked our heads up, leveled our rifles (still undetected by our intended victims) and let loose a volley. Immediately everyone except the Texians began reloading their rifles. The Texians all carried their Paterson revolvers and, when our initial volley was spent – with most of the Mexicans in the band falling dead or wounded – the Texians began firing their revolvers. Momentarily the Mexicans were all accounted for and they'd not fired a shot back at us.

And this is why I liked those Texians.

Now, with our guns reloaded, we ran crouching to where the Mexicans had been shooting. Five of them were killed – one having been knocked off the roof by the bullet that hit him – and the remainder were all in various states of injury. The Texians took away their muskets and dragged them clear from the side where Davis was picking out targets for us to fire down upon.

Our Whitney rifles were far superior to the Mexicans' muskets, and from our new vantage point we had clear shots at the Mexicans on other rooftops.

In most cases, the Mexicans firing from the rooftops offered only heads and shoulders as targets as they leaned over the parapets of nearby roofs. At first it was like shooting squirrels: Pick out a target, pull the trigger, shoot a man in the head, reload and find the next target. But as more Americans began appearing on other roofs, the Mexicans became aware of our presence. What had been a battle of Mexican soldiers firing down upon us had become a battle of all of us on a level plain shooting at each other. But only an unlucky musket ball ever found its target, and that was rare. Alternatively, the shots from our rifles almost always killed a man (as the only part of his body we could shoot at was his head).

Presently, the Mexican troops began falling back to farther rooftops, and as we ran out of targets Davis had one of his Mississippians use the pickax to break a hole open in the roof where we were standing so that we could make our way downstairs, across the street and into the next building.

Our ultimate goal was the redoubt, still a couple of blocks down the street from us. But being at the end of the block, we would have to exit the house we were in, dash down the street to the next block, bust down the door and start the process of moving down the block all over again.

Because of my limp, one of the Texians offered to rush down the street to the next house and knock the door off its hinges. That suited me.

The Texian set off with the ax and we watched as he swung it against the door. Twice while he worked the cannon belched out its grape shot, but the Texian was unhurt. He signaled us when the door was about to give way, and as the cannon had just fired we all ran down the street. Well, everyone else ran while I hobbled as fast as I could. Even without the grapeshot from the cannon, the musketry bouncing about in the street was enough to make me move faster than my leg comfortably allowed.

As I came up to the door, the Texian smashed it one more time with his ax and the door broke off its hinges and the Mississippians and Davis and the Texians pushed their way through the opening. Once they were all through, I limped in.

Unlike the previous houses, this one was not empty. A group of women and children – perhaps as many as a dozen women and at least two children for each woman – huddled together in a corner, clearly convinced that we were about to rape the women and brain the children. Or, based on what the Mexican priests had been telling the citizens of Monterrey about the heathen Americans, perhaps they thought we were going to rape the children and brain the women.

Either way, one of the Texians who had a bit of Spanish tried to settle their nerves as they were making a terrific din of weeping, praying and pleading. I could not help but notice, too, that a couple of the women and one of the older girls among this bunch were delightfully pretty.

There was no in between with Mexican women: They were either short, fat and ugly as sin or they were exceedingly gorgeous with big plump breasts and rounds butts and thin waists and soft full lips and almond eyes. Most of these women should have no fear of being raped, not even by one of those Tennessee boys who had only ever seen women who looked like men, but those three – even with grapeshot bounding down the street outside – might be enough to push some of us over the edge.

While most of our group went up the steps to make certain the rest of the house was empty, the Texian talking to the women, Davis, Henderson and I stayed downstairs. Henderson began working the pickax against the wall to open a hole into the neighboring building. With each crash of the ax on the wall, one of the women screamed, and they all continued to keep up their terrible sobbing noises.

"Sir, I've told them we would station a man here to keep them safe," the Texian said to Henderson.

"Lieutenant Speed will stay," Davis said instantly. Two thoughts crossed my mind at the same moment, and I suspect they are the same thoughts that have crossed your mind: I thought that was exactly the duty I'd been hoping for; and I thought, too, that leaving me in charge of these women was like leaving the fox guarding the chickens.

Davis turned to me, and I swear there were tears in his eyes. "It pains me, son, to order you to stay behind when we are on the verge of our objective, but your injured leg is an impediment to our ability to advance. I swear to you that when the moment arrives and we are on the verge of the plaza, I will send a man to relieve you here and another to assist you in getting to the plaza so that you might be there at that final moment."

I could have laughed with glee and hugged that bastard,

but I decided instead to play the part of the sorrowful champion.

"Sir, I am only sorry that my injury forces you to issue such an order." Then, to make it all sound a little bit better, I added, "I shall do my duty here and protect the virtue of these innocent women." I had no concern that men would be sent back to relieve me and fetch me up to introduce me to Ampudia, for I was convinced that, even with the assistance of the Texians, Davis would get himself killed before the day was done.

Davis was too choked up to say a word, and by that time Henderson had knocked enough of a hole in the wall that they could advance – without me, praise the Lord! – and so he simply clapped me on the shoulder, turned and charged through the hole with his sword out in front of him.

And to think – they elected that man president. The Confederate States of America never had a chance.

I was as good as my word, though. I eyed those Mexican damsels who, probably reading my thoughts a damn sight better than Jeff Davis did, eyed me back, but I never laid a hand on them. At length, one of them even got up and got some flatbread and offered it to me. It wasn't bad, either.

The battle continued to rage outside, and I admit I was nearly as nervous as those women. The longer I sat there by myself, the more I began to think of the possibility that some company of Mexicans would come through the door my Texian friend had bashed in. So I settled myself into a chair and kept my rifle on the door. Periodically, I would limp over to the hole that Davis and Henderson and the others had gone through. They had employed the same tactic we'd used on the previous block: Going through the first house into the second house, and then going through the roof of the second house.

At length, the cannon in the redoubt was silenced and fired no more grapeshot down the street. It seemed, too, that the rifle and musketry fire was moving farther away from me and closer to the center of town. Periodically, too, I would see groups of volunteers or regulars make headlong dashes down the street and past the doorway.

From the noises outside, I deduced that American artillery had entered the town. Braxton Bragg and his "flying artillery" were firing shells and canister back at the Mexicans.

The evidence I had, limited though it was, seemed conclusive: Taylor would have his victory in Monterrey before the day was out.

Perhaps it was an hour (but likely closer to two hours) after Davis had left me guarding the women, a Mississippian came running into the house through the doorway, and I almost shot his brains out before realizing he was an American.

"B'God man!" I exclaimed, "I nearly shot you dead."

It took him a moment to catch his breath. "I've had the devil of a time finding you, Lieutenant!" he said in response. "All these houses look just alike! Colonel Davis sent me to relieve you. Says he wants you up with him now."

My gut lurched. I'd been nervous enough guarding this house on my own, but it was a damn sight better than getting back to the front. "There's no way I can make it to Davis on this leg," I protested.

The Mississippian stepped back out into the street and started waving and calling, "The lieutenant's in here!"

A moment later, one of the Texians who'd been with us when I was still with Davis came into the building.

"Colonel asked me to come and lend you a hand," he said, and without formality or permission, the big Texian leaned his rifle against the wall and lifted me out of my chair. "Put your arm around my shoulder, and we'll get you up to the Colonel."

I carried my rifle and he carried his in one arm while supporting me with the other, and like this we started making our way to the center of town.

We passed the redoubt that had been Davis' initial objective – now empty and with the gun spiked – and soon came close enough to the action that musket balls were again passing around us, though with much less enthusiasm than they had earlier in the day. Here we stayed close to the walls of buildings, stepping into open doorways when we could and moving cautiously.

We stepped into a courtyard and stood for a moment. "We'll have to cross the street," the Texian said to me. But he stood still. Momentarily, we heard a cannon fire not far from our position, and as the smoke from the cannon drifted through the street the Texian and I dashed as best we could across the street, covered from view by the smoke.

"General Taylor's in town," the Texian said to me. "They say he's wandering around like he's on a picnic without a thought to all the musketry flying about."

More the fool he, I thought.

And now, with the action considerably hotter than it had been, we made our way down a street to where Davis and a now bigger group of Texians were gathered. I did not see Henderson among them, though he might have been there. They had piled every manner of furniture, horse saddle and other debris to construct for themselves a breastwork, and as the Texian and I came in to shelter ourselves behind it, Davis clapped me on the shoulder and said he was well pleased that I had arrived so that he could soon introduce the Hero of El Teneria to General Ampudia.

Indeed, we were just a block from the Grand Plaza. In front of us an active Mexican battery with cannon and dozens of firing muskets guarded the road leading to the Grand Plaza, Davis explained.

"We are at the corner of Santa Rita and Morelos," he told me, as if that meant anything. I know that few of Taylor's officers were provided with maps of the city, and I'd not seen Davis with one, so I did not know how he was able to tell me the name of the intersection. "If we take that battery, the plaza is ours," he said. "I have sent a messenger to General Taylor requesting artillery support be brought to us here. With it, we can either knock out that battery or, short of that, provide ourselves with enough covering fire that we might advance closer to it and have a better advantage on it."

I listened to what Davis was saying, but I kept wondering why he would drag an injured man forward and into the teeth of a battery. Why couldn't this man just simply leave me alone? What was it about me that Jeff Davis was so keen to see me dead?

Well, I'll tell you, this wasn't the last time he would drag me to death's doorstep, and that I managed to outlive him in spite of his best efforts against me is far more amazing a feat than storming El Teneria ever was.

But now Davis' messenger to Taylor was crouched down and running back up the street as the Mexican soldiers at the battery did their best to shoot him down with their muskets. He nearly dove into my lap as he jumped headfirst to clear the last few feet between him and the makeshift breastwork.

"Colonel Davis, sir," he said, breathing hard. "General Taylor's compliments, sir, and he says he's already ordered Bragg's artillery out of the city and therefore cannot provide the support you've requested."

Davis cussed a storm at this, but I knew better than to think he would be deterred. Instead, I suspected he would settle for a headlong charge into the battery that would likely as not leave every man among us in shreds at the intersection of Santa Rita and Morelos.

"Blast it!" he said. He cast about for some idea, looking first one way and then another. "Lieutenant, do you have any suggestions for taking that battery?"

My first thought was that we could retreat and let the Texians on the west side of Monterrey finish the job, but I could not find the right words to offer the suggestion in a way that he might accept, so I looked about.

"Onto the rooftop again?" I asked him.

Davis chewed on this for a bit, and I could see the spark in his eyes as he decided this would do. "Yes. I think that will do. We will split our force. You take some of the men onto the roof of that building across the street and fire down into that battery."

Damn my eyes! I thought. Why could I not have kept my mouth shut? "That building across the street," he had said. Without artillery or even smoke from the cannon fire to shield me, he wanted me to dash on my injured leg across the street to get to the rooftop.

"Give the rest of us enough of a diversion that we might advance ourselves along the street and get in a better position to move on the battery. It will likely come to a charge at the end, and so you must be prepared to provide us covering fire as we make our run into the battery."

I knew the maniac would want to charge that battery sooner or later.

But just as Davis prepared to issue the orders, a new messenger came running at the crouch to our position.

"Gen'l Taylor's compliments, sir, and he's sent me to inform you Colonel that he is ordering a general withdrawal of all American forces on the east of Monterrey. You're ordered to retreat, sir."

Davis went into apoplexy. He cursed Taylor and me and Texas and Ampudia and the battery and every other thing that he could think of. He was inconsolable that he could be so close – just a block away – and now ordered to retreat.

"Twice!" he raged. "Twice I have been on the very precipice of victory, and have been ordered to retreat! Unconscionable! Damn him! Why, oh why, oh why?"

He was near to sobbing. The poor man was devastated. Here he was, not 50 feet from a battery that would obligingly blast his intestines and mine all across the entirety of eastern Monterrey, and he was being ordered back from the brink. You know, if I hadn't been so worried that his next move would have gotten me killed, I believe I would have felt sorry for him. All he wanted was the glory, either the glory of succeeding in taking the Grand Plaza or the glory of dying nobly in the attempt, and here was Old Rough and Ready –

his former father-in-law, you'll remember – who once again was ordering him to retreat from the glory for which he so yearned.

But I didn't feel sorry for him, because it was my intestines, too, that he was willing to sacrifice for his glory. Instead, I quietly rejoiced that General Taylor had come to his senses.

Let the Texians in western Monterrey take the Grand Plaza! Wasn't that exactly what I was just about to suggest to Davis had I been able to find the right words? If the commanding general and I were thinking of identical battle plans, surely Davis stopped short in making me only a lieutenant.

In spite of that welt on my calf, I thought I could have danced my way back out of Monterrey.

Davis ordered all of us to fire off one more shot at the battery – a parting salute, he called it – and then hunched over and hugging the walls we made our way as quickly as possible back down the street, away from the battery, away from the Grand Plaza, away from General Ampudia and – because none of us had been killed in firing our "final salute" – away from Davis' glory.

Of course, Jeff Davis was right and Zach Taylor was wrong. All along the eastern side, little bands of volunteers from Texas, Tennessee and Mississippi and regulars from the 3rd Infantry were in the same situation that we'd been in. A block away. Had Taylor given Davis the artillery he requested or, short of that, just a little more time, we probably would have succeeded in clearing the battery and advancing on the Grand Plaza itself, and from the grousing we heard as we made our way back through the city and connected with other bands who had been as near as we had, a little time was all they needed, too.

But that was nothing to me. You'll remember, I was in Mexico on an ill-conceived plan to save my neck from Uriah Franks. Whether Taylor won or lost Monterrey was of no concern to me, just as long as he kept ordering me out of the fight.

Do you know, though, as we made our way back through the city, it was Jeff Davis who put an arm around my waist and supported me as I limped along on my sore leg? In his way, he genuinely liked me. The trouble with Jeff Davis was that he always tried to get those he liked killed.

CHAPTER IX

The Battle of Monterrey was over for me. If it lasted another week, not even future-President Jefferson Davis would order me back into it after supporting my weight on the retreat. And back at El Diablo, when I rolled up my trouser leg, no one could deny that I'd taken a nasty hit. The welt on my leg was discolored and swollen to the size of an orange and my entire calf all the way down to my ankle and heel was black and blue. Someone found a branch for me to use as a crutch and I hobbled about, reassuring the boys that they'd make good work of Ampudia tomorrow.

But Worth's men on the west side of town fired a few cannonballs into the Grand Plaza and it wasn't long before Ampudia was looking to parley.

The next morning, General Taylor all but doomed his career in Mexico (though you'll notice it didn't prevent him from becoming president) by allowing Ampudia to surrender and march his men with their arms out of town. The Americans (me included) lined the streets and shouted derision as each convoy of Mexicans left. It took them two or three days to get out of the town.

Monterrey was ours, but the Texians who were there to get revenge for a hundred insults handed to them over the years by the Mexicans were mutinous that Ampudia had walked. Taylor took the unusual step (for him) of increasing his personal guard because he feared the livid Texians might come after him. The Texians were not the only ones who were furious at Taylor. So, too, was President Polk.

In Taylor's defense, Polk had sent him into Mexico with instructions to treat the citizens well and kill as many of the Mexican army as he could, but to treat them decent while he did it. Polk, like any politician, wanted to find a political resolution. His aim at the start of the conflict was to negotiate a deal where the United States could buy up the property it wanted from the Mexican government.

But somewhere along the way he changed his mind and didn't bother to tell Taylor. Rather than treat them decent, Polk now just wanted Taylor to kill the Mexican army. [15]

The newspaper editors berated him. The public berated him. The Texians berated him. And Polk stripped him of his army.

None of which I cared a lick about.

With the armistice, there was a pause in hostilities, though there were still skirmishes in some places and banditos and rancheros took every opportunity to harass our convoys and attack small groups.

The next two months or so while the army occupied Monterrey, I continued to hobble around on my crutch, though my leg was plenty healed. Like the rest of the army, I enjoyed the fresh fruit, flatbreads and beef that the Mexicans gladly sold us for double a reasonable rate, and I used my leg as an excuse to shirk any duty.

The rumor spread quickly that the armistice would not last, and I intended to use any excuse I could to avoid further combat. My heroism and my busted leg, I believed, were enough to send me home, and I bided my time until the moment came when I could tell Colonel Davis that I thought I should be mustered out and sent on my way.

In the days immediately following the battle, Monterrey was covered in bodies and blood. Musket balls and grape shot were embedded in nearly every wall of every building. It was common, too, to find blood smeared across a wall. The work of burying the dead was gruesome business, and I was well pleased to be left out of it. The hospitals set up on the hill at Bishop's Palace and at Walnut Springs and in the Grand Plaza and everywhere else were full of miserable souls who had lost limbs and others who would soon be dead of their wounds. As bad as it had been for the Americans, the Mexicans took the worst of it. They had paid dearly for their efforts to try to hang on to the city.

I took a room in a house in the town. I paid my Mexican hostess well for a place on the floor of her parlor, with a couple of blankets for a pallet, but she kept me in beef and bread.

I spent my days wandering the streets. Monterrey was a beautiful town. The capital of Nuevo Leon, Monterrey housed many of the region's most important citizens in grand homes – many of which were now pocked with musket balls or had holes torn open in their interior walls and roofs. Fruit-bearing trees were planted in the courtyards of many of the houses, and though General Worth – whom Taylor had made governor of the occupied city – had ordered that all Americans must pay for whatever they took, most all of us picked these fruits and enjoyed them without payment.

I spent a lot of time observing the western part of the city where the Texians had fought. I will tell you that I was amazed when I saw the cliffs of Federation and Independence hills. In the dark of the night, those Texians had scaled 700-foot cliffs that rose straight up to get at Fort Libertad. How they had done it I could not fathom. And they took few casualties in the process, raising them even higher in my estimation.

Within a few days of the battle, the merchants in town quickly discovered that the Americans were paying excellent prices, and as they had at Cerralvo and Marin, the billiard rooms and taverns and restaurants and coffee houses opened up for us.

The entire region of Nuevo Leon is full of mines worked by English companies, and so many of the inhabitants of Monterrey had at least enough English while others were very fluent. The Monterrey valley is fertile and grows all manner of fruits and is rich in corn and livestock, and paying the prices we paid, the Mexicans fed us extravagantly.

I wrote Eliza daily and at last began receiving the first

letters I'd had from her since leaving Fort Belknap – many were weeks old.

"I cannot tell you with what pride I walk the streets of town," she wrote to me in one letter, "knowing that the other girls view me with such envy that my courageous husband alone among the men of Milledgeville stepped forward to offer himself to advance our nation's destiny."

Even the Old Man, she told me, seemed to hold his head with some pride when the other men of town came into the store. He was back working in the store every day, she told me, but he did not seem to mind. He continued to believe I had lost my mind, but was convinced my service in the war and my possible insanity would only advance my future political career.

As the Christmas season approached, I procured bottles of some of the locally made wines, as well as handmade jewelry and even dresses, and packaged them and sent these gifts home to Eliza so that she might think of me during the holidays.

When the order was finally given for the army to leave Monterrey and move south toward Saltillo, I decided this was the time for me to muster out and go home. I went to see Jeff Davis and told him in manly terms that I feared I would be an impediment to the army on the march to Saltillo and – as much as I regretted it – believed my days of service had reached an end. Davis took it rather well. By then, of course, we knew that General Winfield Scott was to get more than half of Taylor's army for a planned attack at Veracruz and then a march from Veracruz to Mexico City. Though Taylor was moving to Saltillo, no one truly believed there would be further opportunity for glory in Taylor's army.

Jeff Davis and the Mississippi Rifles were among those to be left with Taylor. Davis was crestfallen, believing his opportunities for glory had been cut short yet again. He'd been denied Fort Diablo on the first day of battle at Monterrey, and then denied the opportunity of taking the

Grand Plaza on the third day of battle, and now it seemed that the worst of the fighting would be moving south without him.

"There is little here left for men like you and me, Lieutenant," Davis told me in a sullen tone. "We who seek glory for our states and for our nation will find none of what we are after by occupying a captured city and marching to meet an army that will not be there. So I understand completely that you would want to return home. Your terms of enlistment will expire before you are fully recovered from your injury, anyway."

But then he picked up his head and looked at me again and smiled, consolingly. "But, of course, you have achieved some measure of glory, haven't you my friend? 'The Hero of El Teneria!' I shall never forget how you charged forward to lead the Mississippi Rifles into the breech. The image of your gallantry is forever etched on my imagination."

I continued on in my room at Monterrey as most of the army prepared to set out down the Saltillo road. They had received intelligence that Santa Anna himself was marching north and intended to take Monterrey back, and though I do not think anyone really credited the information, Taylor was getting restless and so prepared to go and meet the nonexistent threat. I had no pangs of regret as I watched my fellow Mississippians march south down the Saltillo Road. My intention was to wait for a convoy headed back to Camargo, catch a ride on the convoy and then find a steamer for New Orleans and from there make my way home.

So I came to Mexico a Georgian and mustered out a Mississippian.

And I would have been glad enough of that, except that the day before I was supposed to join a convoy headed back for Camargo I received a letter from my dearest Eliza, and in it was news that sent the old thrill of fear rushing through my blood again.

"My dearest, most gallant Lieutenant," she began – after her letter telling me of her pride in me, I wrote to her of my exploits at El Teneria and my brevet rank so that she might flaunt that among the other ladies of Milledgeville, and so now she always addressed her letters to her "dearest, most gallant Lieutenant" – "I so long to see my cherished love again. My heart aches in these moments when you are so far away, serving our nation in its time of trouble" – expansionism, more like – "and honorably and gallantly leading your men" – poor girl, she thought every officer commanded a regiment. "I was so pleased to hear in your latest letter that your injury is mending, and I pray daily that you continue to regain your strength so that you are fit and full when you return to me.

"Oh, and the most strange occurrence occurred on Monday last. A man who says that you and he are old friends came by our house to visit. I have never heard you speak of him before, and I must tell you that I found him to be wholly disagreeable and unpleasant. He was much older than you are and smelled poorly and looked very much like a barroom brawler. I am not sure that he was entirely sober when he came to the door. He was not the sort of man at all that I would expect you to associate with, and I asked him if he was from the war and he laughed and said that he was not and that he doubted very much if you were, either. What on earth kind of thing is that to say?

"He inquired a great deal about you and your affairs and seemed to find it unbelievable when I told him that you had been brevetted a second lieutenant. He asked if I knew if the Jasper Greens were still at the camp on the Rio Grande, Camargo he spoke of, for he had read that name in a newspaper article, and I told him that I did not know if the Jasper Greens were at that place, but that was no concern of mine because my husband was serving with the Mississippi Rifles in Monterrey.

"He found all of this very interesting and asked me for many details about your regiment and asked me to write down the name of Monterrey and the name of your commanding officer, which I did. It is Colonel Davis, isn't it? And he said that he was coming to Mexico and intended to try to find you because he desired to give you something. And he also asked that I not tell you anything about his visit because he wanted to be able to surprise you in Mexico. But there was something about his manner that made me dreadfully uncomfortable, and I decided it would be best to tell you, even though he asked me not to.

"Oh, and he told me that his name is Uriah Franks. Is he really a friend of yours?"

Whatever else she said in that letter I couldn't tell you, though I've kept the thing all through these years.

Uriah Franks. I felt the hot fear flash through my body. Was it true? Could it be? Would Franks really come all the way to Mexico to find me?

B'God he would.

Upon reading the name, I had dropped the letter. Now I scrambled to pick it back up. The date – what was the date on this letter?

A month ago! When I realized that her letter was a month in getting to me, I actually looked over both shoulders to make certain Uriah Franks was not standing behind me already.

In a month that man could easily have reached Mexico and be in Monterrey right now.

This sickening realization had me looking over my shoulder again, only this time I stood up to get a full panoramic view – neglecting my crutch and my limp entirely.

It was too much! I'd fled everything in life that I loved and entered the absolute hell of Mexico to get away from that man, and now he was chasing me all the way here!

I was in a terrible panic that any moment Uriah Franks would be upon me. The name itself sparked within me a visceral fear, and my experiences in Monterrey helped me to realize the reason behind my fear.

When I looked in Jefferson Davis' eyes, I saw madness. I

saw a man who was willing to have me killed for his glory. And my association with Jeff Davis made me expect that, likely as not, I'd be dead by the end of the day if I didn't duck into a house somewhere.

But when I looked in Uriah Franks' eyes, I saw murder. I saw a man who was desperate to kill me. It's a different sort of fear associated with a man who is *willing* to see you dead than it is a man who is *determined* to see you dead.

If my darling Eliza had written me that Jeff Davis was coming out for a visit, I'd simply adopt a limp and shake his hand and tell him I wish I could join him in the campaign, but the damned leg just wouldn't make it practicable.

But this was not Jeff Davis. This was Uriah Franks, bound for Mexico and looking for me.

Panic-stricken, I racked my brains for what to do.

Going home to Georgia seemed out of the question. I'd enlisted and fled Georgia for Mexico not only to escape Franks but also in the hope that a year in Mexico (or less, if I could manage it) would be long enough to shake him off me. Perhaps he would simply lose interest. Better yet, perhaps he would assume I had been killed in battle and never look for me again.

But now that I knew that Franks not only was still looking for me but had been to my Milledgeville home in search of me, knocked on my door and stood in my parlor talking to my wife, I knew I could not now go back to that place.

I did not know what I would do. Perhaps I'd find a place in Texas and send for Eliza. Or maybe Kentucky or Illinois or some other place a thousand miles away.

But for now, I had to come up with a plan to keep me safe with the expectation that any moment the man might show his face in Monterrey.

He'd be looking for me with the Mississippi Rifles – my loving wife had seen to that – so the first part of making my escape fast was already done. I'd mustered out of Davis' Mississippi volunteers. But ending my association with those boys wouldn't be enough. When Franks came to inquire about me, they'd tell him I'd been injured and gone home. So that would send him back to Georgia looking for me. So I could not go back to that place. Whatever I did next, I must make certain that the Mississippians did not know and could not answer when Franks showed up asking about me.

I had to buy some time. I couldn't just stay around in Monterrey waiting for a convoy to take me out. I had to get out of Monterrey and not go back to Georgia. I was sick with indecision and fear.

Though I had read Eliza's letter in the courtyard of the home where I was staying, I had now wandered out to the street.

Just then I heard the familiar sound of an oncoming rider charging through town, and I recognized him as the Texas Ranger Ben McCulloch. A big man with a thick, full beard that covered most of his face and neck, all that could be seen of his face between beard and slouched hat brim was those quick gray eyes that saw everything, McCulloch rode his horse like he'd been born on it. McCulloch and the other Texians had mustered out of the army with the armistice. It was said they were too furious over the terms Taylor had given Ampudia, someone for whom they held a specific grudge. But here was McCulloch, showing up again a day or two after the army had marched south.

McCulloch was a legend in the army. He'd known Davy Crockett and had fought Mexicans at San Jocinto and Commanche on the Texas plains. When Worth moved around to the west of Monterrey on the first day of the battle, he found a company or more of Mexican cavalry standing in the road in front of him. McCulloch led a charge of Texians right into the Mexican cavalry line, killing most of them and sending the rest running for cover.

McCulloch was exactly the sort of adventurous, reckless buffoon I had no desire to be around. McCulloch was a different species altogether; I've know dozens of them in my life: sheriffs, marshals, rangers and outlaws – gunslingers, all – and the thing they all had in common was that they were killing men. McCulloch lived and died bigger than life, meeting his end on a Civil War battlefield as a Confederate general. But you'll remember my experience with the Texians on the third day at Monterrey: Where Davis had tried to push his men (with me among them) right down the middle of the street to eat canister shot and subject ourselves to the Mexican rooftop snipers, the Texians devised a way to advance forward and keep our skin intact.

Other than abandoning Mexico altogether, the best thing I could think to do was try to get myself with these men who knew how to keep themselves alive.

Following the Battle of Monterrey, the volunteer Texians reached the end of their enlistments. Most decided to go home, and the volunteer Texas regiments that had proved so vital at Monterrey were no more. But McCulloch had told Taylor that if hostilities resumed, he would recruit a new company of Texas Rangers and return.

I followed McCulloch's ride part of the way down the street and saw that he was going toward the Grand Plaza where Taylor and Worth had established their headquarters. Luckily, a supply wagon was coming past me headed toward the plaza, too, and I asked the driver if I could hop on for a ride.

As we rode through the town I couldn't think clearly. Somehow I had devised a plan to avoid Uriah Franks by trying to join up with the men who were most known for their bravery. Was it insanity? Was I dodging one treacherous situation by jumping into another? But I couldn't see any way out. I could not go back to the Mississippians. I could not go home to Georgia. The remuneration I received when I mustered out wasn't enough to escape to another state, set myself up with something and send for Eliza.

It seemed the only option I had for survival was in some way staying with the army. Oh, I cursed the situation I found myself in – that the army could be the safest place for me was evidence that my situation was dire. Here I was, finally free of all the hell that Mexico had been, and I saw no way forward but to remain in Mexico and with the army.

By the time the wagon rolled up to the Grand Plaza, I had prepared a speech in my mind. I saw McCulloch's horse tied up and decided I would wait there near his horse for him to come out, assuming he was in trying to find Taylor's whereabouts.

My wait for McCulloch wasn't long, which was unfortunate because by the time he came out I had nearly reached the conclusion that this was absolute folly and was beginning to try to come up with new options. Had McCulloch delayed his return another five minutes, I would have given up on this ill-conceived plan and saved myself much grief.

"Major McCulloch," I called to him as he approached me and his horse.

He looked me up and down. "Mississippi?" he asked me.

I was still wearing the red shirt of the Mississippi Rifles as it was all I had. Fortunately, after the battle of Monterrey, they'd found me a new one that wasn't ripped to shreds from thorns and musket balls.

"Just mustered out of Davis' Rifles," I told him. "I'm from Georgia."

"What do ya want, son?" he asked.

Bravado and confidence, I told myself, was what would get me in with the Texians.

"My name is Jackson Speed. You might have heard of me from the storming of El Teneria on the first day at Monterrey. I received a slight wound and as a result mustered out of the Mississippi Rifles. I've convalesced and am now healed, and now I'd like to ride with you and your Texians," I told him, forward and up front and manly – just the sort of thing that would appeal to him.

McCulloch laughed derision at this. "You and half the rest of the army," he said. "Why would we want a Georgian riding with us?"

"I can ride as well as any Texian," I told him.

The smile dropped from McCulloch's face, and I swear for a moment I thought he was going to pull one of those Paterson five-shooters on his hip and shoot me dead. I was worried I'd overplayed my hand by too much.

Then his big beard cracked into a grin. "All right, son," he said with amusement in his voice. "If you think so, c'mon out to my camp later. We'll see what you can do. We're camping tonight up at Walnut Springs and intend to ride to Taylor in the morning. If you're as good as you claim, you can come along with us."

McCulloch mounted and rode back north out of town toward Walnut Springs.

I caught a ride on another wagon going north and arrived at camp and found McCulloch and a couple dozen other Texians – half of whom weren't even from Texas – lounging about.

"I expected you wouldn't come," McCulloch said, greeting me with a broad smile behind his mask of whiskers. "Gen'lmen, this boy here says he can ride as well as a Texian," McCulloch shouted to no one in particular, and a number from his band laughed at that.

McCulloch picked out one of his men. "Jim, take that Mexican lance there, ride about a hundred yards out across the plain, and stick it in the ground. Set yer hat atop of it, and ride back over here," McCulloch said.

"Ah, Ben, not my hat," the Texian griped.

"Just do it, Jim," McCulloch said.

The Texian threw a saddle across one of the horses tied nearby and picked up the lance McCulloch had indicated. Then he rode out across the plain a ways, speared the ground with the lance and set his hat on top of it.

"A'right," McCulloch said to me. "Pick out one of those horses from the corral over there. The best one you can find. And we'll give you a little challenge to see how well you ride."

Near the camp they had erected a makeshift corral where there were a number of horses. All of them looked good, but one in particular caught my eye. It was a mustang, of the type typically used by the Texians. It was a big enough horse, probably 15 hands to the withers, and it rippled with muscle so that I felt it could carry a man of my size on hard rides. He was white with big brown spots, including one on his side that reminded me of maps I'd seen of the state of Georgia, and with the decision resting on the spot that looked like Georgia on his side, I picked out that one.

"You know your horses, boy," McCulloch said. "Most of those horses belonged to Mexican cavalry, but that one belonged to one of our brothers who decided he wasn't coming back for the fight. The horse's name is Courage."

The irony was immediately apparent to me.

"Use this saddle," McCulloch said, tossing me a saddle and blanket and bridle. I put the gear on the mustang and mounted the horse.

"A'right," McCulloch said. "Take this rifle" – and he handed me one of the short-barreled rifles the Texians used because they could fire them while mounted – "and gallop out toward that hat as fast as you can. While still at a run, when you get to about twenty yards of that hat, I want you to shoot it off that there lance. If you can knock that hat off that lance at a full gallop from twenty yards, then yer fit to be a Texas Ranger and can join up with us."

I took the rifle from his hands and turned Courage toward the lance and hat. The feat seemed impossible, and I doubted that any one of those in the camp could have achieved it – McCulloch included – but I figured I'd give it my best shot and maybe if I made it look decent enough they'd let me in.

I spurred the horse forward and it took off into a gallop, closing the distance between me and the hat faster than I expected. I knew better than to squeeze too tight with my legs, so I kept my balance as well as I could, released the reins, and raised the rifle and sighted it onto the hat.

Just as I started to pull the trigger on the rifle, Courage bucked a bit so that my position in the saddle shifted just enough that whatever aim I had before I pulled the trigger was gone by the time the bullet was released. I grabbed up the reins and controlled the horse, slowing him down to a walk and turned him around as we'd already gone past the lance.

And to my amazement, the Texians were hooting and hollering and running out toward me. I looked at the lance and saw that the hat was on the ground, and even better, I hadn't hit the hat but my bullet had struck the shaft of the lance, splintering it in half. I rode over to the broken lance, hopped down off of Courage and snatched up the hat, then jumped back onto the horse and closed the distance between me and the huzzaing Texians.

I grinned as I rode up to them, and even McCulloch was smiling like a man impressed.

What happened next sealed my legend among those Texians, and I didn't even have to storm the battlements of a fort: I rode right up to Jim with his hat in my hand. I beat the hat against my knee to knock the dust off of it, and I handed him the hat. Then I looked at McCulloch and said, "That's the hat knocked off the lance, and no need to even patch a hole."

Those boys all started hollering and cackling laughter again, and just like that I was in among them: Lieutenant Jackson Speed, Texas Ranger.

They provided me with a rifle of my own and two of the Paterson five-shooters, along with a belt and holsters for the five-shooters. Having never before used such guns, they also gave me lessons in firing them – how to be sure my finger was out of the way when I cocked the hammer so that the collapsible trigger could be exposed – and advised me not to waste shots by trying to shoot at distant targets. [16]

"Get right up in with your enemy and shoot him directly," Jim told me. I think he appreciated my sparing his hat, and so he helped instruct me on the loading and firing of the pistols.

Other than those Paterson revolvers, the Texians wore no

uniform, though most of them wore buckskin shirts and slouched hats of the kind worn by the cowboys of a later era, so I continued to wear the white tweed pants, red shirt and white hat given to me by the Mississippians. I still had my Bowie knife, too, and that was as much a part of the Texian uniform as the revolvers.

We rode out down the Saltillo Road next morning to catch up to General Taylor.

CHAPTER X

I was mildly concerned that I might run into Jeff Davis and he might be perturbed that I'd healed so quickly after leaving the Mississippians and was now with the Texas Rangers, but when we caught up with General Taylor a few days later, I managed to avoid the Mississippians altogether.

Taylor mustered us into the army with a six-month enlistment period.

The army marched on to Agua Nueva, where Taylor made his headquarters, but McCulloch and the rest of us stayed in Saltilla a few days more to recruit more men and horses into the company and await orders.

There was little of army life evident among those Texians. In Saltilla we took rooms where we could find them and spent our time at leisure, eating and drinking and playing in the billiard rooms. A number of the boys found whores, but I was never inclined to pay to spend the night with a woman.

There were any number of Texians who'd mustered out after Monterrey who were still lingering near the army, and McCulloch found among these men more recruits.

I'll say this for the Texians, other than riding hard and fast into hell anytime the Devil seemed anxious for a fight, they were a good bunch to be around. Ranks and military protocol meant nothing to these boys. All they were interested in was having fun – drinking hard, chasing women, shooting off their guns, and telling anecdotes that were too much to believe. In these few days with them, I found them to be an agreeable bunch.

A few among them were vicious, though. Whenever the Texians rode into town, you could be sure that the reports of rapes and murder of the Mexican citizenry were going to increase. It was the murders, I believe, that forced Taylor to send them home after Monterrey. The truth is, a fair number of these boys were no better than outlaws. Had we not been at war, posses of Texas Rangers would have undoubtedly been riding after some of these boys looking to put them at the end of a rope.

I was just starting to get accustomed to the wild living that was part of being mustered in with the Texians when, on February 15, Taylor sent for us.

We rode from Saltilla to Agua Nueva, where McCulloch met with Taylor and then came to talk to us.

I can't credit it, but I wasn't the least bit nervous on that ride to Agua Nueva. For one, I'd chosen these Texians for a reason: They knew how to survive. For another, spending these last few days with these men had lulled me into a misplaced sense of ease. I'd forgotten the lessons of Monterrey – how one minute you're praying to God to avoid the Yellow Fever, the next you're dying of thirst on a dirt trail, then you're at your ease in the prettiest little village you'd ever want to see and then, just like that, men are dying all around you and Jeff Davis is charging forward with his sword out and expecting you to follow.

If I'd thought Jeff Davis a madman, Ben McCulloch was about to teach me that I knew nothing of madmen.

Something about his countenance – excitement, maybe, thrilled to be back in the fray, I suspect – made me squirm a bit as he approached where we were waiting with our horses. Quite suddenly, whatever ease I'd been feeling disappeared at the sight of the expression on McCulloch's face.

"The Gen'l wants us to scout down south near a hacienda called Encarnacion, where we've had reports of a Mexican cavalry amassing," McCulloch told us. "We'd be too big a target if we all went together, so I'm just taking sixteen with me."

I breathed a sigh of relief at this. Surely among this band McCulloch could find sixteen men he'd rather take to the death with him than me.

"Cap'n Howard, Lieutenant Clark and Crittenden," he called out their names. "You're with me."

He cast his eyes over the rest of us. One by one, he selected the men who'd been with him the longest, and I was prepared to find myself some diversion around camp while they were away, but my initial fear was confirmed when he called out the fifteenth of the sixteen he was taking with him.

"Speed," he said. "You're with us. And Jim. You come along, too."

It was late in the morning when we set out, keeping to the road as none of us were familiar with the area, and we rode throughout the day and well after sunset without incident. The night was black as could be, and with each mile my unease only increased. We rode slowly so as not to rush into trouble unawares, but in the darkness every distant shadow looked to me like the Mexican cavalry preparing to charge.

At length, we could see something up ahead of us.

"Look sharp, boys," McCulloch whispered back to us, and I heard a couple of boys cock their pistols. At that moment, the flash and report from a musket burst in front of us, and a group of a dozen or so Mexicans broke and ran toward a nearby ranch.

That was enough for me. We'd come face to face with Santa Anna's troops and could report back to General Taylor that indeed the Mexican army was here, but McCulloch determined to continue on.

I can tell you, old son, it's a hellish thing being in unfamiliar territory riding straight at an enemy army. Only the hoofs of the horses falling on the ground drowned out the rumblings coming from my belly. I was desperate for McCulloch to order us into the chaparral where we might find cover to disguise our presence, and when I ventured to suggest it he said we must stay on the road so as not to lose our way.

We continued on at not much more than a crawl, and McCulloch drew us up into a group so that we could repel an attack if it became necessary. I allowed the others to flank me so that, if the shooting started, I would at least have a body on each side and in front of me to keep me protected. I was already plotting what I would do if Mexican muskets erupted again and Texians started falling around me. My intention was to turn Courage about and charge as hard as that horse could run back to Agua Nueva.

"There's a fence up in front of us," someone said in a hushed tone, and I peered around those in front of me for a better view. Indeed, it appeared as though a brush fence of some sort had been laid across the road. We continued to ride forward cautiously.

But as we got closer, someone in the group hissed: "Cavalry!" and I felt my bowels dissolve.

From that shadow in front of us a voice called out in Spanish, but before anyone could respond, something approaching twenty muskets erupted in fire and noise. The entire volley passed overhead, and I was set to wheel Courage around and flee when McCulloch – doing his best impersonation of Jeff Davis – hollered, "Charge!" The whole of our group dashed forward, and Courage, the damned horse feeling the need to live up to its name, I suppose, outpaced all the rest except McCulloch, dragging me and him both to the forefront of the death.

In four seconds we were in among them and the Patersons were firing. How many of them we shot down I do not know, but I saw one fall dead for sure. The other Texians were shooting, but I was intent on trying to turn my horse back up the road. The Mexican cavalry, stunned that we would receive their volley and then dash into them like this, wheeled and fled in every direction. Courage, who I suppose thought it was some sort of game, dashed after the fleeing Mexicans. And, thank God!, the fool Texians continued their pursuit. Had the Texians fled at that moment when the Mexican cavalry broke and ran, I'd have ridden right into the Mexican camp all by myself, and you can imagine how that might have turned out.

Instead, it was me and the Texians all riding just as hot at the Mexican cavalry as we could go. The Mexicans were fleeing headlong back to where their entire army was encamped.

You won't credit it, but we charged after that cavalry right into the Mexican camp. It was a blur of insanity: Campfires and tents with Mexicans running this way and that, Texians jumping tents and knocking over other tents, ramming into Mexicans soldiers too slow to get out of our way, and the Texians shouting bloody murder the whole way so as to add to the confusion among the Mexicans. We rode fairly close together, but dashed first one way and then another so we gave the impression that our numbers were larger.

I released a ceaseless series of farts as my belly turned summersaults, and I screamed just as loud as the rest of the Texians hollered. By now I had one of my Patersons unholstered, and I fired it at random targets as they presented themselves before me. I do not think any of my shots told, but the reports of the pistol added to the din, and it was through this confusion that we rode pell-mell through the Mexican encampment.

Courage seemed perfectly content to gallop through the camp, trampling tents and shouldering aside soldiers who were attempting to load their rifles, and I had no ability to wheel the horse around at all.

And McCulloch, who knew his business, counted campfires as we dashed through the camp. Satisfied, he called to all of us and we wheeled and hightailed it back up the road toward Agua Nueva.

We rode at full gallop back up the road, and I have no idea how far we went before we finally slowed and discovered that there was no pursuit. And at that moment, the Texians all burst into laughter, riding up to slap McCulloch on the back, and all I could think was that I'd fallen in with another madman. But, unlike Davis, McCulloch wasn't in it for the glory. Davis was building a political career – if he could survive it – and intended to achieve some measure of famed gallantry with which he would propel himself into high office (it got him the presidency, didn't it?), but McCulloch was different. It wasn't glory he sought, but a good time. He absolutely enjoyed himself.

But even I realize now, and did then, too, on that road back north to Agua Nueva, that McCulloch's charge had probably saved all our lives. Imagine if we'd turned and fled after the volley went over our heads: The Mexican cavalry would have pursued, separated us and cut us down. But here we were, seventeen of us, riding headlong against what was probably a superior force, chasing them into their own camp where their comrades were caught unsuspecting, gathering up the information we needed and then getting out before anyone could raise a musket or saddle a horse.

And hadn't I done the same thing on a smaller scale? What about when I punched Eliza's suitor, Franklin? A strong, unsuspected manly show that caught a superior force off guard and saved my skin. It was no different in principle than what McCulloch had done. And, I learned later, this was simply Texian tactic. McCulloch had done exactly the same thing at Monterrey and every Texas Ranger who ever saddled a horse had done the same thing or something similar against the Comanche or the banditos.

Well, understanding the principle behind it wasn't the same thing as enjoying it, but these Texians riding with me had had the time of their lives.

"I estimated a thousand or more in the camp," Crittenden said to McCulloch.

"More'n that," Howard said. "Fifteen hundred's my guess."

"Fifteen hundred," McCulloch confirmed. "Cavalry."

"Was there any infantry?" Jim asked.

"I didn't see no infantry," someone else answered.

"Should we go back and check?" that fool Jim asked. I could have drawn my Paterson and shot him in the back at that moment. Those grinning devils would have enjoyed that too much.

McCulloch, thank God, said Taylor had information that a Mexican general was moving around behind him. "We can't take the chance that we don't make it back to General Taylor with our information while he has Mexicans moving in behind the army."

Had there been no Mexican cavalry in Taylor's rear, I believe that maniac McCulloch would have seriously considered riding through the enemy's camp one more time.

We made better time back, not having to worry that we might be approaching the enemy's picket lines or encampment. We camped very briefly on the side of the road in the early morning, and then woke before the sun was fully up and rode the rest of the way back to Taylor's camp where McCulloch reported to Taylor our encounter with the Mexican cavalry.

Our experience riding to Encarnacion was enough to convince me that spy work was as bad as infantry work, and I did not care for the cavalry any more than I liked being in the volunteer militia. The only advantage I could find was that in the infantry, when I turned heel and fled, I could only move so fast, but in the cavalry, when I wheeled my horse – if I could get the damned beast to cooperate – and fled, I could move like the wind and be beyond the reach of the enemy's muskets rather quickly.

With our evidence from the night ride in hand, the camp now took on the air of one readying for battle. All about, guns were being cleaned and bayonets sharpened. Most of the veterans of Monterrey had gone to Scott's army by now, though the Mississippians were still with Taylor, and the new regiments were green. They'd come to Mexico full of enthusiastic feelings of gallantry and patriotism and all those other things the newspaper editors promised they would find in Mexico, but upon arriving here they'd heard the stories of Monterrey. Most of those who had engaged in the victories of

Monterrey – the Texians and the Third Infantry regulars who had swung west of the town under General Worth – were with Scott now. And those who had received the worst of it on the first day and been ordered to retreat on the third day were the ones left in camp, and so the stories these green recruits heard were the stories of disaster.

On the eve of Monterrey every man jack in the army was thrilled to be throwing himself into the fray, and the camp was an atmosphere of excitement. The camp was boisterous.

Not so here at Agua Nueva. Here, the green recruits were nervous, quiet and thoughtful. It's always the same on the eve of battle, soldiers writing last letters home, some seeking out a parson, checking and rechecking ammunition pouches.

A day or two after we returned from our scouting mission, Taylor again ordered McCulloch to make another scout. He had not moved the army, but there was talk of falling back to Buena Vista if it appeared that Santa Anna was moving toward us in strength.

McCulloch determined it would be best to take only a few men. He was taking just half a dozen of us, all told, including a lieutenant from a Kentucky infantry regiment. This time, I was the first one he picked.

"Speed, you were so anxious to get into the front of our charge the other night, you join me on this scout," McCulloch said, and under my breath I cursed that damned Courage for being over-exuberant.

We started late in the afternoon to save water and arrive at Santa Anna's camp under the cover of darkness. We rode south for about six miles, not far from where our farthest most picket was stationed, when we came upon a Mexican deserter. He told McCulloch that Santa Anna was up with the cavalry now with twenty thousand infantry and was preparing to attack Taylor.

McCulloch ordered one of the boys to take the deserter back to the picket – not more than a mile behind where we were – and instruct them to take the deserter to Taylor so that he could receive the information, and told him to then ride hard to catch up with us.

"I can take him," I said immediately. I saw my chance. I could deliver the deserter to Taylor myself and then just stay at camp and avoid this hellish scouting mission. But McCulloch ignored me, and so we continued our way south.

When darkness fell, McCulloch decided to leave the road, which inspired some hope in me. Sneaking through the chaparral seemed a far better plan than riding down an open road, where surely there would be pickets and guards to challenge us. We touched the road only two more times on this scout, both times to cross the road and move back into the chaparral on the other side.

It was slow going, though. The moon was out enough to give us light as we weaved our way among the short trees, and not a man stirred for fear that the slightest noise might be overheard by Mexican guards. Late into the night, after hours of picking our way through the chaparral, the moon set and we were left with almost no light. But about that time, too, we came to a place where we could see Encarnacion out in front of us. The campfires were enough to tell us that the deserter's information was true. Encarnacion had become an enormous encampment.

As we moved along, McCulloch quietly whispered over his shoulder to the small band following him, "Picket to our left."

Indeed, a small group of Mexican soldiers were on guard not far from us where the road was. I held my breath and prayed that none of those boys around me would fart or sneeze or one of their horses snort and thereby give us away as we continued to pick our way forward past the picket. Soon we came inside the perimeter established by the camp guards.

Here, McCulloch dismounted and took Lieutenant Alston with him while the rest of us waited on our horses. The two crept quietly forward through the chaparral and other brush so that they could get a closer look at the camp.

The rest of us dismounted and took the opportunity to feed

our horses the corn we'd brought along and water ourselves. McCulloch and Alston moved so quietly through the darkness, that when they returned I did not hear them coming and nearly jumped back in my saddle when they came into view without making any noise.

McCulloch led us away from the camp a mile or so.

"Phillips and Speed, the two of you will stay with me," McCulloch said, and my heart sank. We'd come within the enemy lines, and I saw no sense in staying here. "The rest will go back with Lieutenant Alston to inform General Taylor of what we've found here. It looks to me like Santa Anna has added as much as twenty thousand infantry to the fifteen hundred cavalry we encountered the other night.

"Phillips, Speed and me will stay until daylight so that we can better ascertain the enemy's strength," McCulloch said. "We'll catch you up at camp tomorrow."

And like that, we went from being seven to being three. Even if it is only four men extra, there is always comfort to be found in greater numbers, and McCulloch's decision to send back four men and keep me with him, here in this godforsaken chaparral and among the enemy, had me near to whimpering in fear.

It was absolute madness, and he was keeping us here not because we needed additional intelligence on the enemy's numbers – b'God they had it, hadn't they? – but for the sheer sport of the thing. McCulloch was having the time of his life creeping around in the chaparral, and because we'd not been fired upon by a picket or chased by a cavalry unit, he couldn't bring himself yet to abandon the place.

I've said it before: These Texians were only truly happy if a sheet of Mexican bullets were flying at them like hail in a storm.

Our band split up as McCulloch ordered, with Alston and the others picking their way back north through the chaparral to get beyond the Mexican pickets and McCulloch, William Phillips and me riding back out to the road where McCulloch intended to cross to the other side so as to get around for a look at the encampment from the east.

Now we went back out of the chaparral to cross the road, and I swear I believe to this day that damned McCulloch did it on purpose. When we crossed the road, we were just a few yards inside the picket line, and the Mexicans saw us on the road.

One of them shouted a challenge in Spanish and for a moment McCulloch, Phillips and I came to a halt, looking at each other and back up the road at the picket.

And then the Mexicans started running for us, shouting and raising their muskets.

"This way!" McCulloch called to us, and we were dashing down the road to the south, heading straight into the enemy's camp, once again.

Less than twenty of us had caused commotion and panic in the enemy's camp when we rode through in the middle of the night on our previous scouting expedition, but now the enemy's camp was far bigger and we were far fewer and, having experienced our foolhardy charge once, I expected they would be far more prepared for it this time. I could not believe that McCulloch's strategy would be the same one he'd adopted just a couple of nights before.

We outpaced the picket and so they gave up the chase, probably assuming we were Mexican deserters trying to escape camp and feeling that they'd done their duty by chasing us back. We were less than half a mile to the camp when McCulloch turned from the road, back into the chaparral. I can tell you, I was panicked beyond belief at the thought of riding into an enemy camp of more than twenty thousand. I was nearly weeping when McCulloch led us off the road and back into the brush.

We picked our way along until we came to a hill and we rode to the top and there concealed ourselves until daylight.

When day broke, McCulloch used his spyglass to try to examine the Mexican camp, but the fires were burning green wood and so much smoke was settled in the valley that nothing could be seen.

It was a paralyzing fear that gripped me throughout the night. Every moment I expected to be overrun by Mexican infantry searching for the three men the picket had chased. Though McCulloch and Phillips were talkative – both of them absolutely enjoying the danger we were experiencing, damn them! – I said not a word. McCulloch and Phillips, both, too, slept for an hour or two, while I laid awake quaking and my belly gurgling loud enough to wake the Mexican army.

The night, in these hills, was cold, too, and I could never be sure if I was shivering from fright or cold, but I suspected it was a combination of the two.

Realizing that our night spent on the hill had been unnecessary – information I willingly could have provided when he sent the others off with Alston, if only he'd asked – McCulloch decided that we should return north.

But as we began to make our way back out toward the road, we hadn't gone far when we realized we were riding toward not one, but two pickets, stationed on two separate roads that forked away from each other.

"Hold your rifles down by the side of your horse," McCulloch told us, "so that the Mexicans cannot see the rifles. We are going to walk out slowly and deliberately, so that they might think we are Mexicans hunting up horses."

We did as he instructed, picking our way through the chaparral as if we were following the tracks of runaway horses. The soldiers at the pickets had started large fires and were engaged in warming themselves. Whether they did not trouble with us because there were only three of us – behind their lines, no less – or because they were too engrossed in warming themselves by their fires, I do not know. But they did not hail us or take any interest in us at all that we could see. In this way, we passed right through the enemy lines within sight of their pickets.

Presently, we came to another hill and there saw yet

another picket out in front of us. We stopped and tied up the horses in the chaparral and from the hill we watched the movements of both the picket and, using McCulloch's spyglass, the distant camp. By now the smoke from their campfires had cleared away as a breeze had picked up, and so McCulloch was able to confirm through watching the camp his estimate of their numbers and also determined that the army was breaking camp and preparing to march north.

McCulloch had hoped the picket might be called back into camp and thus provide us with a clear exit, but they remained in place. So, by midmorning, we decided to ride around the foot of a mountain and make our way back north.

I can tell you that even McCulloch was breathing relief when we were clear of the Mexican pickets and moving northward at a good pace.

It was frightful, hellish business spying behind enemy lines, made no better by the fact that I'd performed these duties with a band of madmen who took great delight in tempting fate.

At every turn when it seemed that we could avoid danger, McCulloch would turn straight into it.

But I will say this. In those few days that I rode with McCulloch, I learned some of the tricks that had kept him alive against the Comanche and against the Mexicans. Boldly surprising your enemies – doing that thing they least expected you to do because it was complete madness – would often buy you the time necessary to survive. Subterfuge, too, could be employed with effect, and the best subterfuge was that which was conducted right out in the open. Act like you're exactly where you are supposed to be and doing what you are supposed to be doing, and even those who are charged with the duty of challenging you will likely as not leave off if they have anything more enjoyable to do. I also learned about riding quietly and cautiously under cover of undergrowth.

These lessons were instructive to me and would serve to keep me alive when McCulloch was long dead.

Of course, it all took an extreme amount of bravado – more than I cared to muster, and while I learned from McCulloch and the other Texians, it was my intention at the time never to have to employ any of those lessons.

CHAPTER XI

I knew, as we rode back to General Taylor's camp, that self-preservation required me to get away from McCulloch faster than I'd gotten away from Jeff Davis. I did not know how I was going to make good my escape, but I was again leaning heavily toward the idea of deserting.

It happened all the time. Some deserters – particularly the Irish – went over to the Mexicans. Some just disappeared from camp. If anyone ever smelled anything of cowardice on them, they were assumed deserters; if they were brave men who'd stood with the army for any length of time, they were assumed dead at the hands of banditos or rancheros. The question was how I was going to procure for myself the opportunity to get away.

And, thanks to Old Rough and Ready, I didn't have to wait long for my answer.

When we returned to Agua Nueva, we found that General Taylor had not wasted time acting on Alston's information. Camp had been broken and the army was gone, having fallen back to Buena Vista. Only a few men left behind as a rearguard were there, along with General Taylor, who had not yet followed the army. The other Texians, too, were still at Agua Nueva awaiting McCulloch's arrival. The man was like a god to them – truly he was – and I believe if we'd fallen into Santa Anna's hands they'd have ridden south and attempted to free us.

We rode right up to Old Rough and Ready and, still mounted, McCulloch provided him the information from our scout. The most important bit of information we provided that Alston had not already given to Taylor was that Santa Anna was on the move.

"Very well, Major," Taylor responded. "That's all I want to

know. I am glad they did not catch you. I will need someone to ride to Monterrey and deliver a message there that Santa Anna is on the move. And then on to Camargo. Select a couple of your men to make that ride, and then prepare the rest for the battle. If not tomorrow, it will surely be the next day. We will make a stand at Buena Vista against overwhelming numbers."

And then Taylor mounted his own horse and rode toward Buena Vista.

We stopped in the deserted camp long enough to feed and water our horses and refill our canteens and get some food in us.

The whole time, McCulloch and Phillips thrilled the other Texians with accounts of our ride behind enemy lines. McCulloch told them certainly that we'd been within a few hundred yards of Santa Anna's tent – your guess is as good as mine of how he determined this, but that's how legends are made, isn't it? The chase put on by the Mexican soldiers at picket was played up to its fullest in Phillip's retelling.

The whole while I kept silent. The others took this as further evidence that big, silent Speedy was a fighting man through and through, a tough character who refused to tell stories of courage and daring and would rather allow his legend to be observed through his actions.

That I did not boast only further endeared me among these men. Hadn't they seen me on our first scout pass through the formation to get at the Mexican cavalry in front of all our band? Wasn't I the "Hero of El Teneria"? Wasn't I the one who was wounded in Monterrey and as soon as my crutch was cast aside stood to volunteer with the Texians?

Oh, I was their kind of man to the core, and these boys knew it.

But my silence had nothing to do with manliness. I'd heard General Taylor's words, and I'd discovered how the Hero of El Teneria could be as far away from Buena Vista as possible when the shooting started. Taylor needed to send word back up the road that Santa Anna was coming, and I knew which one of the Texians was just the man to carry that message in the opposite direction of Santa Anna.

And so I kept quiet and stayed close to McCulloch, to make certain that, when he started looking around for a messenger, I was readily available.

At length, we were the last of Taylor's army left at the Agua Nueva camp – our horses were fed and watered, our canteens and bellies full – and McCulloch decided it was time for us to be on the move.

"Either we go now, or we can stay here and face Santa Anna ourselves," McCulloch remarked, to which the Texians roared their approval at taking on the entire Mexican army. Damned fools.

We mounted and started on the road behind Taylor. It was then, as we were riding along, that McCulloch broached the subject of the message, and it could not have played out better for me if I'd wanted to preserve my reputation.

"Boys, it looks like we should expect a fight tomorrow or the next day at Buena Vista," McCulloch said. "Gen'l Taylor is determined to make his stand there. It'll be warm work, as Santa Anna far outnumbers us. I know all of you are going to want to be in it, but I'm going to need two volunteers to ride north to Monterrey, and then on to Camargo, to give them the message that Santa Anna is on the move."

Stone silence.

Here he was, on the eve of battle, offering any one of these men who was willing to accept it a lifeline, a chance to avoid what was sure to be slaughter. But not one among these Texians was willing to take him up on the offer.

"Someone's going to have to do it," McCulloch said. "If no one volunteers, I'll have to pick two out."

Still no one spoke.

"It'll be dangerous work, boys," he said, almost pleading. "It'll be just the two of you, and we all know the banditos and rancheros are operating in our rear. So it's not shirking dangerous duty if you step forward to deliver the message."

Still, nothing but silence. I timed it right, waiting for the moment just before I thought McCulloch would speak up again, and said as if it was the worst thing I'd ever had to say: "Oh, a'right. I'll do it, Major."

McCulloch looked startled that it was I who was volunteering. Like most of these courageous fools I've encountered in my life, McCulloch had completely misread me. Through bad luck and misinterpretation, I had already secured for myself a reputation for courage, and other men who were truly valiant were unable to see in me any signs of cowardice because they looked at me and thought I was just like them. And so McCulloch assumed that if anyone in his band wanted to be in at the death on the following morning, surely it would be me.

But he had his volunteer, and it didn't matter to him whether it was me or one of the others.

"Who'll go with Speed, then?" McCulloch asked.

My friend Jim, whose hat I had accidentally spared, quickly spoke up and said he'd ride along with me.

"Get moving, then," McCulloch told us. "When you arrive at Buena Vista, locate a couple of spare mounts to take with you so that you can ride hard the whole way."

And with that, Jim and I pushed our horses to a gallop and left Ben McCulloch and Santa Anna well behind us.

Jim Willcox was as dumb as a man could get, but he was equally kindhearted, and, for the kindness I'd shown his hat, he took to me right away. Jim was nearly 40 years old and older than most of the other Texians in our band. He had no wife and no children, and so I think he looked on me like a father might look upon a son. Or, at the least, like an uncle might look upon a nephew.

Jim felt a need to protect me and teach me, and so he'd instructed me on the use of the Patersons when I first joined up with the Texians, and that night of our first scout I noticed he was constantly at my side.

He was a big man, too. Not well-built, like me, but the kind of big man that leaves a horse's back sore. Too much camp bacon and Mexican flatbread and beer. He had a big, thick beard that hung in long strands down his chest. I suspect it was blond, like his long hair, but it was so matted with dust that it always appeared more brown than it really was.

His eyes were a pale blue and suggested an overall dullness of mind.

Nevertheless, I liked Jim, mostly because of the kindness he'd shown to me.

"I gotta say, Jack, I was sure taken aback when you said you'd do this," Jim said as we rode side by side at a trot. "You bein' so young, I figured you would be ready to get at the battle instead o' comin' off on your own like this. This is really the work for folks with more experience."

Now this caught me off guard. "What do you mean, 'more experience'?" I asked. "This should be light work, just riding up the road."

"Naw," Jim said, chuckling. "If we run into banditos or rancheros, we'll wish we were back bein' shot at by Santa Anna."

"How's that?" I asked, growing a bit worried. In my mind, running messages from one camp to the next was simple and safe work.

"This whole trail here is overrun with banditos and rancheros," he said. "Ya can't outrun 'em; ya can't outshoot 'em; ya can't outride 'em. The best you can do is hope to do is outfox 'em."

I'd heard over and over again talk of banditos and rancheros, and everyone in the army spoke of them with a kind of fearful awe. But I really didn't understand who they were.

"Are they part of Santa Anna's army?" I asked.

"Naw," Jim said, chuckling again at my ignorance. "Banditos are outlaws, and they've been harassin' our supply lines since we came south of Camargo. They're them same fellers we used to deal with before the war, always comin' up into Texas to rape and pillage and murder farmers and other innocent folks.

"They know what they're about, them banditos. Ornery lot. They travel in packs, like wolves, and their favorite thing is to catch a couple of messengers like you and me."

I gulped horror as he spoke. I'd not counted on me and Jim being easy prey. I'd assumed two men riding along the trail would be able to pass unmolested.

"Rancheros, now, they're different. Banditos just wanna kill ya and take yer horses and whatever else ya got on ya. Rancheros, though, they're kinda like volunteer cavalry. They're workin' with Santa Anna and attacking where he tells them to attack, and they'll be looking for a couple of riders like you and me on account of they'll know we're messengers. They'll be lookin' fer intelligence they can take back to Santa Anna. Letters, orders – anything like that.

"But the thing that makes me most nervous about them rancheros is how vicious they are. Brutal bastards. They own these great big ranches, most of 'em prob'ly are connected to the politicals in Mexico City, so they've got a bit of power in their towns, and they're out fer revenge against the invadin' army."

The words hung in my imagination as we trotted along the road. In the evening we reached the mountain pass of Buena Vista where the army was busily preparing for the coming battle. All told, Taylor was bringing just less than five thousand men against Santa Anna's force of almost twenty-two thousand. [17]

Observing the preparations, I decided that Jim Willcox could say what he liked about rancheros and banditos, but it was just fine with me to be heading north rather than standing the odds against Santa Anna.

Jim and I found a couple of spare horses in camp that we took from a company of Arkansas mounted infantry. They were none too pleased to be giving up a couple of good horses, but Jim told them we were acting "on orders from Gen'l Taylor hisself," and so they grudgingly gave us the mounts. It was true enough, I suppose, as far as it went.

We immediately switched horses to give our mounts a rest and allowed our mustangs to follow along beside as we kept up a fair trot north along the road.

By now it was full dark, but we pressed on as we could make out the road well enough. Jim's advice was to keep the pace at just below a gallop – that would keep the horses from getting too tired out, he reasoned, but at the same time allow us a good running head start should we encounter an ambush.

I cared not a whit for this kind of talk, but I accepted the advice as coming from a seasoned veteran, if not a smarter one.

We pushed hard on that ride. If Taylor's force was overrun, there was no one to save Monterrey and no force big enough in the north of Mexico to stop Santa Anna from going all the way to Camargo or farther if he wished. Taylor wasn't looking for reinforcements or support, but wanted what was left of the army at Monterrey to post pickets farther south and be prepared to abandon that city if Santa Anna should continue his march north.

On the third day of riding, we rode into Monterrey. We didn't know it, of course, but by then the Battle of Buena Vista was in the history books.

Jim and I opted to stay overnight in Monterrey, enjoying the hospitality of a Spaniard who lived there in the city. Señor San Something or Other. He was a wealthy man and pleased with every American victory because Ampudia, while he was still in Monterrey, had forced him to pay an exorbitant sum to support Mexico's war effort.

Our decision to stay overnight spared us the necessity to ride to Camargo, for the next morning a rider who had followed a day behind us came into Monterrey with news of General Taylor's victory.

My friend Jeff Davis had finally secured the glory he'd

sought – using his famous V formation to envelop and annihilate a Mexican charge and then aiding Braxton Bragg in saving an Illinois regiment that was cut off. Though Santa Anna had sent forth overwhelming assaults against the tiny American army, Taylor, Davis and Bragg with a mostly untested band of volunteers, drove off Santa Anna's army.

Davis got all that he wanted. He received a wound to his foot in the battle, and it wasn't long before he was back in Mississippi, moving about on crutches that were probably as unnecessary as my own, being toasted as a hero and running for the United States Senate.

Taylor managed to recover his own reputation, too, and in the course of the Battle of Buena Vista, the careers of two future presidents were cemented.

The best of it, from my point of view, was that the war in north Mexico was now essentially over. The only duties remaining to Taylor's army were those of occupation – dangerous enough as I was to learn, but no more charging into fortified cities or trying to sneak around to see what Santa Anna was having for breakfast.

However, while in Monterrey we also learned of the Ramos Massacre. A day or two prior to the Battle of Buena Vista, Mexican irregular cavalry – the rancheros – had attacked a supply wagon on the road from Cerralvo to Marin near the hamlet of Ramos. Fifty or more teamsters were slaughtered, while others fled for their lives, and the convoy's light guard was taken prisoner.

The Rancheros then assaulted Marin, but the Ohio volunteers guarding the city held them off until a relief detachment – which left Monterrey only hours before Jim and I arrived there – chased the rancheros off. The Ohio volunteers and the relief from Monterrey then abandoned Marin and started back for Monterrey.

CHAPTER XII

Each day, it seemed, someone new was coming into Monterrey from the north with more stories of ranchero attacks. The Mexican cavalry moving around in our north likely did not know of Santa Anna's defeat at Buena Vista, and they were still attempting to harass our supply convoys in an effort to help him.

After three days of this, Jim could stand no more.

"Let's you and me ride up to Marin and see what we can find up there," Jim suggested.

"I'd rather not," I told him bluntly. Seeing the disappointment on his face, I said, "Wouldn't it be more prudent for you and me to await Major McCulloch's arrival? If he wants us to go up and take on those rancheros, maybe we should all go."

"Aw, it wouldn't hurt nothin' to go have a look-see," Jim argued.

The trouble was we'd been hearing stories of the Battle of Buena Vista as riders came into the city, and Jim was yearning to get into a fight somewhere. He felt like he'd missed a great opportunity to do some killing.

"C'mon Jack," Jim coaxed. "You and me can just ride up to Marin. It'd be a good diversion. By now them rancheros will be gone and there won't be nothin' to do anyway, but there's nothin' to do here, so we might as well do nothin' on the road to Marin."

It was true that whatever Mexican cavalry had been haunting the road was likely gone, having been chased off by the Ohio volunteers. And it was equally true that there was nothing to do in Monterrey. There were enough regular army boys about, still policing the place, that we couldn't get up to any fun.

And so, reluctantly, I agreed to ride to Marin with Jim, but I made him swear that we wouldn't be on the road after sundown.

"No, no," he answered. "We'll get to Marin plenty before dark, and we'll stay the night there."

So I saddled up Courage, filled my canteen and bought some corn and oats, and Jim and I rode out late in the morning for Marin.

We had a pleasant ride north through the hills, and no sign of Mexican cavalry at all until we neared Marin in the afternoon. We were not two miles from the town when we observed on the road in front of us an odd sight: Buzzards were picking at the carcass of some animal.

"Is it a mule?" Jim asked as we approached. But presently we came closer to it and realized it was the body of a man. "Damnation!" Jim roared, and he rode hard up toward the birds, waving his hat and shooing them away.

Jim and I dismounted and examined the corpse. I'd seen plenty of corpses in the last few months – men with holes blown through their bodies, limbs and even heads ripped off by cannon fire. In a war, you get used to these sorts of sights. For weeks, as I limped around the streets of Monterrey on my crutch, I could still see walls splattered with blood where men had fallen, and of course in the days following the battle I had to literally limp over bodies if I wanted to move from one place to the next.

But there was something different about this one. The birds had only just begun to pick at the body, but the man's clothes were torn to shreds and his body was ripped like someone had abused him with barbed wire.

"Damn brutal bastards dragged 'im," Jim pronounced, looking at the corpse.

"What do you mean?" I asked him.

"It's them rancheros – it's the sport they love best," Jim said. "If they can get close up on an unsuspectin' man, they'll lasso him and drag him to death. It's how they best love to kill a man. They'll drag him for a mile or more until he's cut to bits – like this poor bastard – and he'll bleed out or crush his head against a rock or some such."

There was no wallet or anything else to identify the man, and so Jim said we should bury him. Together, we set about digging a shallow grave off to the side of the road.

It was now growing late, and even Jim seemed anxious to hurry into Marin. There we asked around until we found a family that was willing to take us in. At first they offered to let us sleep in the courtyard of their house, but Jim said that wouldn't do as we were paying for our accommodations, and he expected a bed to sleep in. So they increased the price, and Jim bunked down in a bed and I slept on blankets on the floor.

We ate flatbread and seasoned beef and spent the evening talking with the family. The owner of the house was an older man who said the Mexican army's depredations in the north had won them no friends among the people. Where the Americans asked for anything they wanted and paid for everything they received, the Mexican army simply came and took. The Mexicans, too, threatened the citizens with violence if they were caught aiding the Americans.

Everyone in Marin, he told us, wished that the Americans would stay and keep the Mexican army away.

"Put yer guns and yer wallet under yer pillow," Jim encouraged me as we bedded down for the night. "Don't want them sneakin' in here and stealing from us."

"They seemed nice, though," I said, even though as I said it I slid both my Patersons under my pillow.

"They'll forever tell ya what they think ya wanna hear," Jim said. "But half the time they'll say one thing and steal your wallet while ya sleep. In the morning, I think we should ride up to Cerralvo."

I didn't care to tempt fate, but Cerralvo was not far and, my memories of the place being so pleasant, I agreed to make the journey.

We rose the next morning, pleased to find our wallets and

Patersons under the pillows where we'd left them, and we breakfasted with the family that had taken us in. The man had two young sons who chased each other around the table while we ate a meal of steak and eggs. We paid him well for the meals and the night's sleep and saddled our horses, which had spent the night in the courtyard of the house.

On the way out of Marin we found an orange tree with fresh fruit, and we picked a couple of oranges a piece that we ate while we rode north to Cerralvo.

Our journey there was brief and uneventful, but when we arrived at Cerralvo we encountered an American convoy that was resting while coming down from Camargo. The convoy's guard were my old friends the Kennesaw Rangers. None of them recognized me in my Mississippi red shirt, or with my dust grimed and now-battle-hardened face.

"Y'all run into any trouble on the way down?" I hailed them as we rode up to them. Those same cold mountain streams that had provided me so much relief when I first came through Cerralvo were now providing fresh water for the Kennesaw boys, who were washing themselves and filling their canteens by the side of the road.

"About six miles north of here we had a band of Mexicans ride down on us, but we fired a few shots and they scattered," one of the Kennesaw boys answered. It was odd to me to hear that Georgia accent again after so many months of Mississippian and Texian accents.

"Have ya heard yet of Buena Vista?" Jim asked, and without waiting for an answer he began to tell them of how Ben McCulloch had scouted out Santa Anna's camp, giving Taylor the information he needed to prepare at Buena Vista.

"Me and him was with McCulloch," Jim said, indicating me. "We rode within a half mile of Santa Anna's tent."

By now Jim had half the company gathered around him, and they were asking for more details. When Jim started recounting the battle of Monterrey, I decided to ride on into town to see what I could get up to.

I found a tavern where I got a beer and then I wandered around town for a bit.

While in the town, I happened to see a young woman walking out of a store with two young girls – one of them looked to be maybe four years old and the other younger – who I took to be her daughters. The woman carried in both arms a basket of edibles.

Though I'd seen plenty of fine women in Columbus and New Orleans, and even a few good looking women in Monterrey after the battle, this one caught my eye in a way that no woman had since leaving my dear Eliza. I'll tell you, old son, I felt a stirring. Even thinking about her now, after all these years and seeing that fit and full body in my imagination, this old man still stirs.

Her long hair was parted right down the middle and pulled into a tight bun in the back. She wore a bright red blouse and a black dress that twirled as she pushed her young children forward with her knees. She had necklaces of colorful beads streaming down the front of her blouse. Her bosom filled her blouse so that it was near to bursting, and her thin waist spread out into a nice plump rear. I could see the shape of her legs as she strode forward and imagined those thighs squeezing around me.

But it was her face, I think, that really struck me. She had high cheeks and full lips, the beautiful almond colored eyes common among Mexican women, and dark eyebrows that arched up over her eyes. Her skin was an even shade of tan, and, gazing upon her, I determined that before this day was over I'd be sharing her bed.

At that moment, one of the little girls tripped and fell and began crying. Seeing my opportunity, I dashed forward, picking up the little girl in one arm and brushing off her dirty knees with the other. I shushed her and smiled at her and made faces at her, and in a moment she was smiling.

"Señora," I said, setting the girl down on her feet, "can I take that basket for you?"

She was reluctant at first, but finally relented and handed over the basket to me. "Gracias," she said, and, while she was polite enough, there was no bright smile or light in her eyes as I was accustomed to seeing when putting on the charms. She took her two daughters by their hands and led our little parade down the street.

"Do you live far?" I asked, trying to see if she had any English.

"Not far," she said, pointing vaguely ahead of us. She had an accent, for sure, but her English was better than half the Texians I'd encountered.

"My name's Lieutenant Jackson Speed," I said. "I'm an officer in the United States army."

She nodded her head but said nothing.

"Is your husband at home?" I asked.

"My husband," she said with a bit of coldness to her tone, "the father of these two little girls, was killed by an officer in the United States army."

There wasn't malice in her voice, but all the same I saw my chances diminishing.

"I am sorry about that," I told her. "A lot of good people have been killed in the last year." It was weak enough, but I had nothing else to say.

We walked on in silence for a bit and came to the edge of town. "I can take that the rest of the way," she told me, her voice still cold.

"Oh," I said, offhandedly, "I don't mind. Allow me to carry it for you."

I'd lost any hope that I'd be bedding her. How could she be convinced to sleep with a man who – whether I pulled the trigger or not – she clearly viewed as being representative of the man who had put her husband in the ground? Nevertheless, I felt a little bit of guilt over the woman's dead husband, and so I figured the least I could do was carry her groceries for her.

Her hacienda was about half a mile from town. It was a

nice spread with gardens and fruit trees and a spacious place. When we arrived there I expected she would take the basket from me and shut the courtyard gate on me, but she allowed me to follow her through the courtyard and into the house. It was a delightful place with big windows that gave plenty of light and white walls and spacious rooms and lots of decorative tile work. Whatever her husband was before he was killed by an officer in the American army, he'd clearly been a thoroughly wealthy man.

"For your kindness, please stay and have dinner with us," she offered. She said it with a hint of a smile, and I felt like the offer was sincere. And I also saw my chances improving a bit. Though clearly older than I was, she was still a young woman – maybe in her mid-twenties – and I've only ever encountered a few women of that age who could resist me for long.

"Well," I said, acting as if this wasn't exactly what I wanted to do. "My horse is still tied up in town."

"Go and fetch your horse," she said, "and come back and eat with us."

And so I did. While I was in town I ran into Jim, who'd finished telling his stories to the Georgians who were now again headed south.

"Find your own place to stay tonight, Jim," I told him. "My intention is to be occupied."

He gave me a knowing wink and a slap on the back and told me to be sure to keep my Patersons under my pillow.

I rode back out to the hacienda, and found the little girls playing in the courtyard. I tied Courage to a post in the courtyard and unsaddled him and fed him from a bag of oats I'd bought in town. Then I knocked on the door as I stepped inside. She was already putting out plates with bread and seasoned beef and fruits – sliced apples and oranges.

When I stepped into the house she smiled brilliantly at me – the first smile she'd given me, and it revealed beautiful, white teeth. Her entire demeanor had now changed.

"I am Marcilina de la Garza, Lieutenant Speed," she told me. "I am sorry if I was not courteous in greeting you."

"Oh, that's a'right," I told her in an offhanded sort of way. "Times are tough all around, no doubt about that. And sometimes manners and pleasantries ain't that important."

"I am sometimes bitter," she said, and the smile had already vanished. "I am twenty-three years old. I have two small daughters. And I am a widow. But it is unfair of me to blame you. You are a nice young officer, and you have done nothing to merit my rudeness toward you."

"Oh, think nothin' of it," I said, flashing her my best smile. "All is forgiven, and I'm famished."

She called her daughters into the house, and the four of us ate together at the table. The girls were curious about me and giggled at me a lot, and I was playful with them, endearing myself to their mother the whole time, don't ye know.

Marcilina told me that she was the daughter of a Spanish gentleman who had moved to Cerralvo and married her Mexican mother and that she had grown up in this place. Her family had traveled to America often, though, and she had learned English as a result. Her husband was a Mexican gentleman who had answered the call to arms when the Americans invaded Mexico. She told me that he was a much older man when they married. When she talked about him, I got the distinct impression that she did not miss him but only worried about what kind of life she could make for her daughters without a man to take care of her.

She talked through the afternoon like a person who has been a long time without a confidant, and would you believe as we sat there talking and the shadows grew long I caught myself actually feeling sorry for her situation?

It grew late into the evening. She lit candles and eventually took her daughters to bed while I sat waiting for her.

Most of the conversation so far was depressing stuff, and I was determined to try to change the tone. Ashley Franks and Eliza both had taught me that if you wanted to bed a woman, the best thing for it was to get her laughing. But my lighthearted approach was not well received. At the most, I got a polite smile back from her dark countenance, and I began to believe that she was the kind of woman who never laughed.

Now it was late into the night and darkness had settled completely outside. A fire in the fireplace and the candles gave us light in the sitting room of the house, but I was growing tired and could not stifle a yawn.

"May I rent a room from you for the night?" I asked.

She did not speak, but stood up and walked outside into the courtyard. A moment later, she came back with an iron pot filled with water.

"You may rent a room," she said, hanging the pot over the fire. Then she went into another room and came back momentarily with another plate of sliced oranges. "Please," she said, offering me the oranges. I accepted them gratefully, as the fruit was as good as any I'd ever tasted.

She then walked back to the fire and put a finger into the pot of water. She hefted it up and carried it into the back of the house. A moment later she came back to get me.

"Come with me," she said, taking me by the hand. She did not smile, but the touch of her hand filled me with a warmth I'd not felt for a long time.

She led me to a room at the back of the house where there was a large washtub. She picked up the bucket of water, and dumped about half of it into the tub. Then she turned to me and began to unbutton my red shirt. She unstrapped my belt and set the belt and holsters with their Patersons on a table. She led me to a chair and ushered me to sit down, and she knelt down and slid my boots off my feet. Then she took me by both hands and led me back to my feet. She unbuttoned my trousers and slid those off of me, too.

I was now stripped of all articles of clothing. She took me over to the tub and sat me down in the shallow water. It was still very chilly, not having warmed much at all over the fire, but I wasn't in much of a mood to complain about the temperature of the water.

She took a sponge and a brush and a bar of soap, and she began to wash me.

I don't know if you've ever had a beautiful Mexican señorita bathe you, but I highly recommend it if you ever have the opportunity. It is one of the most erotic experiences you can enjoy.

I'd washed myself in some streams from time to time, but the fact is I was covered in the dust and muck of almost a year's worth of marching and riding and warfare.

She ran the water from the bucket over me to rinse me and then laughed for the first time. "I need more water," she said, her eyes lighting up. "You are filthy."

I sat there in the tub and waited while she went out to fetch another bucket. I was near to freezing by the time she returned.

"It's cold," she said, and poured some of it over me. She wasn't lying, either. That water was freezing cold, but I didn't say a word. I didn't chatter my teeth or shiver.

I didn't speak. I couldn't. I was overcome with emotion. Lust. Love. Longing. Whatever it was. As she washed me, scrubbing my hands and fingernails and feet and toenails, running the sponge over my chest and stomach, I felt as if all the horrors of the past few months were being cleansed from me.

She was so soft and sweet, so careful and thorough. She had almost bathed me into an absolute trance.

And then she bid me to stand up and step from the tub, and she fetched a towel with which she dried me as carefully and tenderly as she had washed me.

And then she led me into her bedroom.

She was nothing like Eliza, who giggled and played her way through lovemaking, or Ashley Franks, who demanded everything and took it all.

Marcilina was a passionate lover. Everything was intense:

staring into each other's eyes by the candlelight, kissing deeply as if it might be the last kiss ever – not the last kiss that we would share, but the last kiss on Earth. Her body shuddered under mine, but she did not make a sound. She clutched my ribs with her hands as if she were going to pull my sides away, but only the slightest gasp escaped her.

And there was no talk when it was done. Instead, she propped herself over me as I lay on my back and she caressed me with her fingertips, running her fingers over my muscles, tracing their lines on my body.

I was well built in those days, and the privations of army life had only amplified the cut of my muscles. Marcilina, I believe, came as close to any woman I've ever been with to worshiping my body, and I can tell you that's a hell of a flattering thing.

I was so relaxed that I drifted off to sleep with her still propped on her elbow and running her fingers over my chest, arms and stomach.

When I woke the next morning, light was flooding the bedroom. Marcilina was not there. I searched around and found a robe to wrap around myself, and then I wandered back into the room where she'd bathed me. My clothes were not there, but the belt and Patersons were on the table where she'd left them. I checked the pistols and found they were both still loaded. Even after that night, when I'd experienced more passion than I'd ever known, I was still in the middle of a war and found that trust came hard.

Now I walked through the house and found it deserted. I peered through a window and saw Courage still in the courtyard, but there was no sign of Marcilina or her children.

But at length I found my clothes. She had washed them and hung them on a line outside to dry.

I went out and fetched them and dressed myself, even though my trousers were still a bit damp. I waited for some time longer, but began to get nervous about tracking Jim down.

I certainly didn't want to find myself alone in Cerralvo and have to brave the road back to Monterrey alone.

And so I decided to leave. From my saddlebag I got paper and pen and ink and wrote a letter to Marcilina. I told her that I was sorry not to have a chance to say goodbye to her, but that I would visit again. I told her, too, that I wanted to pay her for the room. And I left the note and five dollars on the table for her. It was a lot of money in those days, but I felt compelled to help her.

Then I saddled up Courage and rode back into Cerralvo, where I found Jim waiting for me at a tavern. He was all grins and winks when I walked in clean as a whistle and looking like I'd just arrived in Mexico.

"What have you been up to, Jackie Speed?" he asked with a knowing tone to his voice.

"I found adequate lodging and a bath at a reasonable price," I answered, grinning back at him.

"Well, I found meself a whore in town, too, but she didn't offer me no bath," he said.

I had a beer or two with Jim and then we decided to set off for the ride back to Monterrey. If we pushed pretty hard, we could make the journey in one day and arrive back not long after sundown. I was dubious about being on the road past dark, but Jim was insistent that by sundown we'd be close enough to Monterrey that we wouldn't have anything to fear.

Just as I mounted up on Courage, I heard my name. "Lieutenant Speed!" I turned and saw Marcilina coming down the road, almost at the edge of town, on foot and almost at a run.

"I'll be with you presently," I said to Jim.

I rode back to the edge of town where Marcilina had stopped to catch her breath. I expected she was looking for a goodbye kiss, but when I hopped down from Courage's back with a smile on my face, she spat fury at me – throwing at me the coins I'd left for her on the table.

"I am no whore," she said, her eyes blazing. "What I did

last night with you I did because I wanted to, not because I expected your money!"

I was taken aback. Honestly, when I'd left the money, the thought had never entered my mind, and I said as much. "I left the money because I told you I wanted to rent a room. I left the money because I thought it would help you. I wanted to help you, and I told you I'd pay you for the room."

She glared at me, fury in her eyes.

"I swear," I told her, pleading that she would believe me. "I promise you! I left the money because I wanted to pay you for the room – as I told you I would – not because I thought you were a whore."

She glared at me, still, but a moment later her eyes softened, and she began to weep. I put my arms around her and held her close to me. "I didn't mean it as an insult," I told her. "I was just looking to help you."

And then she grabbed my face in her hands and dragged my lips to hers and she kissed me passionately. I held her pressed tight to my body, and I could feel that she was trembling. "I have been so sad," she said, tears streaming down her face. "Last night was the first taste of happiness I have had in so many months."

I released my grip on her and I bent down and picked up the coins. Then I held them out in my open hand. "Please," I told her. "Please take this money. If you will not take it for yourself, then take it for the sake of your daughters."

She hesitated, but then she took it.

"Will I see you again?" she asked, and her tone was desperate.

"I will come to Cerralvo every opportunity I have, and I will make opportunities when I have none." And I picked up her chin with my forefinger and thumb and held her face so that she was looking into my eyes. "I promise you."

I can tell you that quite suddenly my feelings toward Mexico had altered, and I was in a fine mood as we rode back to Marin and then onto Monterrey.

CHAPTER XIII

The ride was uneventful – we passed neither convoy nor messenger on the road, and the only thing close to a scare we had was when we saw a couple of Mexicans on horseback in the distance. Jim and I both had our hands on our Patersons as we came closer to them, but then realized that they were both riding on mules and our concerns passed away. When we got even with them, we also realized that one was an old man and the other a boy.

When we arrived back at Monterrey, Taylor and the bulk of his army had returned, along with McCulloch and the rest of the Texians. Jim delighted in telling them that I'd had a bath, and McCulloch warned me to keep an eye on the women that they didn't cut my throat in my sleep.

Over the next few days, we all stayed in town, finding houses among the locals who were willing to rent a room for a night or for a few days. We paid severe prices for these rooms, but the comfort of a real bed and a good meal was so superior to life camped beyond the city we paid the prices they asked.

McCulloch was hot after hearing the news of the Ramos Massacre, and he pestered at Taylor daily to turn us loose on the countryside. McCulloch wanted the Texians to ride the Camargo Road and hunt out the Mexican cavalry.

Instead, around the first part of March, Taylor finally sent a column under Major Luther Giddings to run to Camargo. McCulloch sent me and Jim and a couple other of the Texians to act as messengers.

"Stay outta the fight," McCulloch warned us. "If Giddings needs reinforcements, he'll need the two of you to ride back for help. Ya can't do that if you're shootin' at Mexicans."

It sounded like sage advice to me, and Jim swore he'd stay out of the fight if Giddings needed us to ride back.

I wasn't at all nervous as we set out from Monterrey. Giddings had more than two hundred infantrymen and a detachment of field artillery. We also had more than a hundred wagons along, and those were slowing our progress quite a bit.

On the second morning out from Monterrey, we were nearing Cerralvo and I was yearning to visit Marcilina. I figured if I rode ahead of the army I'd have enough time to pay her a visit and be ready to go by the time Giddings got up to Cerralvo.

"I'm going to ride on ahead to town," I told Jim.

"I'll come along," he said.

"Naw," I said. "I'll go alone."

Jim laughed out loud and bid me farewell.

I pushed Courage pretty hard and presently came into the outskirts of the town. People were milling about by the streams, and I immediately sensed something was amiss. The men all seemed to be watching me from under their hats. The Americans had always enjoyed a good rapport with the citizens of Cerralvo, and it was odd to me that there would be a suspicious atmosphere as I rode up to town.

Feeling uneasy, I decided to skirt the edge of town, by the stream, and ride to Marcilina's hacienda. As I approached it, I saw her outside picking oranges in the small stand of trees at her house.

I rode up straightaway and hailed her.

She looked at me as if she'd seen a ghost. First she looked one way, then another, and then motioned me toward her house.

"Hurry," she said. "Inside. You cannot be seen."

The urgency in her voice had me convinced. In a flash I was in the courtyard, tying Courage to a rail and then in her house with one of the Patersons in each fist. Marcilina followed me through the door. "How are you here?" she asked me. There was fear in her eyes and panic in her voice – not at all the welcoming I'd been hoping for. "Have you come alone?"

"There's a column south of Cerralvo," I told her. "I rode ahead that I might come and visit."

"You cannot be here," Marcilina said, and her voice was barely more than a whisper. "The cavalry is near town and they plan to attack the American column. If you are seen here, they will come here and kill you and kill me, too. You are in terrible danger here."

I can tell you, the thought of walking outside her door terrified me, but I believed her that they'd come to her house looking for me. And every layabout in town had just seen me ride along the stream toward her house.

"You must get back to your column," Marcilina told me. "You must hurry, and warn General Taylor to turn back."

"Taylor ain't with us," I said, then realized it was no use to argue the point. Then another thought occurred to me: "What about you? Will they know I've been here?"

Marcilina stepped over to a wardrobe against the wall and opened the door. She took out a rifle. "I can protect myself if I need to," she said. "Now, you must go. You must hurry."

There was real fear in her eyes and her voice trembled, and I wasn't sure that it was fear for me or for herself. But I didn't argue. I dashed out the door and mounted Courage at a run. I galloped through town, the reins in one hand and one of the Patersons in the other. Every man I saw looked like a ranchero – horse or not – but I didn't slow down enough to see if they would pursue.

I rode headlong back down the road and it wasn't long before the convoy came in sight. Jim was the first to see me coming, and he met me out in front of the convoy.

"Cavalry," I said. "They're planning to attack the convoy. My girl in town told me. She was scared to death when I saw her."

That was all Jim needed to hear. He wheeled around and charged straight to Giddings.

Once in among the convoy, I dropped down off Courage to give the mustang a break and to catch my breath. I checked my rifle to be sure it was loaded and with a cap in place.

All about me now was activity, as Giddings organized the men into a defensive perimeter and men prepared for battle.

I'd not been back with the convoy more than a few minutes before we saw the Mexican cavalry riding down on us from the rear. They rode hard into the perimeter, firing their muskets at the teamsters who were mostly gathered in the rear. They threw torches into wagons and then wheeled to retreat as we returned fire.

Giddings moved some of his infantry back down the road to serve as a rearguard. We lost a few wagons and some of the teamsters were killed, but my first concern was for Marcilina. Could you possibly credit it? She bathes me up once, and a coward like me actually thinks first of her. But I wasn't going to check on her by myself. I needed Jim to ride with me.

"Jim," I told him, "if it hadn't been for her, we'd have been ambushed. I've got to go back and make certain she's safe."

He chewed on this for a moment. "Well, if you're goin'," he said, "then I suppose I'd better go with you."

This was exactly what I was aiming for. I had no desire to ride into the town alone, though I believe I would have if Jim had refused to join me.

We rode hard, and decided it would be best if we took a trail that wound around the town to avoid it altogether, and so we actually came in from the north as we rode up to Marcilina's hacienda.

Four horses tied up in the courtyard suggested to me right away that something was wrong. But as we rode closer to the house, Jim was the one who spotted them beyond a grove of pecan trees over near at the stream. There was a huddled mass of human beings there.

"Doesn't look right," I said to Jim.

"Ride hard, right into 'em," he said. "Guns out."

And with that, Jim charged ahead. Courage made to bolt, but this time I was ready and held the mustang back a split second. There was no reason both Jim and I had to be at them first, and I didn't mind letting him get to them first with me coming in with time to see how they would react.

As the horses charged forward, I could see what was taking place at the stream. There were four Mexican rancheros there, all looking down into the water. Two of them were standing, but two were kneeling at the stream. Between the two who were kneeling, I could see Marcilina – they were holding her face down in the stream and trying to drown her.

The two men who were standing were both laughing and didn't hear Jim until the last moment.

When they looked up at the big Texian, he was riding hard toward them with his reins loose and a Paterson in each hand. I heard the report of first one gun and then the other, and I watched in amazement as both of the standing Mexicans dropped to the ground, dead right there. He might not have been the smartest man I'd ever encountered, but Jim Willcox was a damn good hand at killing Mexicans.

One of the kneeling Mexicans made to stand, but Jim's horse crashed into him and knocked him backwards into the stream. Jim's momentum pushed him on across the stream and once he was clear on the other side he made to wheel his horse and come back for another charge.

The other of the two kneeling Mexicans had stood, now, and was leveling a musket at Jim. Marcilina, coughing and gagging and sobbing, pulled herself up onto the bank.

And then I was on top of him. Courage stopped short and I tumbled head over heels from the saddle. Honestly, it was as if the horse had purposefully catapulted me from the saddle to use me as a projectile. I hit that Mexican square in the back. He broke my fall and I sent him reeling. The musket discharged, but the aim was gone and the ball flew wildly away from harm.

Now the Mexican that Jim had knocked into the water was pulling himself from the stream, and I was the first person he saw. I scrambled quickly to my feet as he drew a long knife from his belt. In a panic, I tugged at one of the Patersons and it came loose from its holster. I raised my right arm just as the Mexican started at me and I fired the Paterson once, hitting him in the chest and knocking him back into the stream.

I turned my attention now to the only one left alive, the one that damned horse had flung me into. He was sprawled on his stomach – stunned by the weight of me crashing into him. I did not wait for him to get his wits about him. Instead, I leveled my Paterson at the back of his head and fired one shot. His body shook and went rigid, and then he was dead.

I ran over to Marcilina and helped her to her feet. "Are you a'right?" I asked her, but in response she threw her arms around my neck, weeping into my shoulder and soaking my clothes with the water from the stream that drenched her.

Jim now rode across the stream.

"Let's get these bastards buried," Jim said. "We can't just leave 'em here, or they'll be comin' after the girl again."

Marcilina provided us with a couple of shovels, and we dragged the bodies away from the stream. We dug a deep hole that we tossed them all into. By now it was growing late, and Jim and I both agreed that it would be foolhardy to try to locate Giddings' column before sunset.

We stayed the night at Marcilina's hacienda, Jim in another room and me reaping the benefits of having saved her from the rancheros.

She guessed, though did not know, that people in town had seen me ride out to her place earlier in the day. When the rancheros came upon Giddings, the column was stopped and formed out for battle, so the rancheros knew we'd been warned about the attack. They'd obviously concluded that Marcilina had provided the warning.

As we prepared to leave the next morning, intending to ride back toward Monterrey to catch up to Giddings, I left Marcilina with one of my Patersons, fully loaded.

"If they come back," I told her, "let 'em get close to you and then shoot them in the gut with this."

She kissed me and bade me to be cautious and return to her soon, and I swear she was in love with me.

"She ain't no whore," Jim remarked as we rode down the road – again skirting the town so as not to draw further attention to Marcilina.

"No," I said. "She ain't."

What we did not know was that another column from Camargo was coming south and by now had reinforced Giddings' column. Jim and I both assumed after the attack that Giddings would turn back toward Monterrey, but in fact they were already moving north of us.

When we arrived back to Monterrey late in the evening, McCulloch asked us to pass on the information of the attack on Giddings directly to Taylor.

McCulloch was hoping that, if confronted with the firsthand account of an attack on a strong column, Taylor's hand would be forced and he would finally send the Texians north along to the Camargo Road to root out the rancheros and put pay to them.

And probably McCulloch was right. Even though the Texas Rangers at this point were few, no other company or regiment was better suited to find the rancheros and dispatch them. With McCulloch at the lead, the Rangers would gladly slip off the Camargo Road and take the back trails and find the rancheros where they slept. Sending columns up the road – even well-armed columns full of infantry, as Giddings' column had been – only provided the rancheros with a target.

Well, McCulloch's ploy worked, to a point, but it was Humphrey Marshall's Kentucky cavalry regiment that Taylor decided to send. Taylor decided an entire regiment of Kentuckians was better to send than a single company of Texians.

He was probably wrong.

Jim and I remained employed in riding messages back and forth between Taylor and Marshall. When moving between the cavalry and Monterrey, we rode hard up and down the

Camargo Road so as not to give the rancheros the opportunity to attack us. Even with Jim there, I can tell you that I rode with a constant tossing and turning in my gut.

The biggest fear I had was that I would feel the bind of the lasso come around me when I was watering my horse or in some other way occupied and that I would be yanked from my feet and dragged to death like that poor bastard Jim and I had found shredded to bits.

"If it happens, the best you can hope for is that you smash your head against a rock and it kills you right away," Jim mused once when we were talking about it. "Can you imagine, bein' drug to death? How long do you live before they've drug the life out of you? A mile? Two miles? Three miles, mebbe, if you're strong like you and me? Can you imagine it?"

The fact was, not only could I imagine it – I was imagining it all the time. Whenever we got caught on the road after dark, I was forever seeing in the distance shadows of rancheros with their lassos swinging above their heads.

One night we were on the road coming into Camargo and it was well after dark. I remember the desert stretched out before us for miles, and off in the distance I spotted shadows moving in the road.

"You see that?" I asked Jim.

"Mebbe," he said. "Can't be sure."

We continued to ride forward, and in the chaparral I imagined I could hear whispering. I thought my bowels would explode, and only the bouncing in the saddle muffled my constant farting.

"C'mon," Jim said, and he urged his horse forward at a gallop. I thought we were going to try to flee past the spot where I'd seen the shadows, and I pushed Courage forward at a run behind Jim.

But as we got up to the spot where I'd seen the shadows, Jim reined in his horse abruptly and, waving his hat in the air over his head, began shouting like a madman.

"Here! Here they are, boys! C'mon and get 'em!"

Courage – the damned horse had a mind of its own no matter how much I tugged on the reins or spurred him forward – reared up alongside of Jim.

At that moment, a pack of turkey buzzards came scattering out of the chaparral and I thought sure I would lose control of my bowels at the sight of them.

Jim, though, thought it was the greatest joke he'd ever witnessed and guffawed like a moron as I slid down off my horse and tried to calm my nerves.

"Whoa-wee!" Jim hooted. "Here you and me was scared of a bunch of buzzards!"

It was good enough ruse, I suppose – ride forward to the point of danger and make believe that you're leading an entire regiment – but the buzzards didn't seem as frightened as I was.

In addition to the Kentuckians, Taylor sent the Mississippians along the road and even left Monterrey himself to lead the convoy. Eventually, Taylor also sent another company of Texas Rangers under Captain Mabry "Mustang" Gray to seek out the Mexican cavalry under General Urrea – those who had been most responsible for the attacks on our convoys. Gray never found Urrea, who by now had moved his operations away from Monterrey.

Even so, Taylor continued to send escorts of mixed arms with every supply convoy, and Jim and I stayed employed in riding up and down the Camargo Road, delivering messages and warning convoys if there was any word of a potential attack. But truly, we did little that was worthwhile.

On these trips, I stopped in Cerralvo every opportunity I had to visit Marcilina. Sometimes I spent the night or two nights, sometimes I was there for only a couple of hours. Jim would always find a room in town or wait for me at the tavern. Marcilina's daughters had taken to calling me "Uncle Lieutenant" and were forever waving at me from down the road anytime I approached the hacienda.

It was a regular marriage I had now. Marcilina welcomed me into her home and into her bedroom regardless of whether I was there for a week or there for an hour. She fed me. I slept there and generally made myself at home as if it was my hacienda.

I spent an entire week with her once when Jim was down with a fever. He stayed with a whore he'd taken up with in town and she nursed him while he was sick, and I spent the week with Marcilina, enjoying the leisure of eating well, sleeping well and making love every time her daughters were outside or asleep.

One of the most delightful experiences of my life occurred at this time. In the plaza in town they'd planned a big fiesta – a fandango, they called it – with all sorts of food and wines and dancing. It was a cool evening and they had hung lanterns and lit candles so that the entire plaza was illuminated with soft light. Some of the old men played music on their guitars. Other Americans from the army who were loafing about town attended, as well as every man, woman, boy and girl from town, and there wasn't the slightest bit of tension among them.

Marcilina danced in such a way that I was at a loss to keep up with her – fast-paced Latin dances I'd never encountered before. She wore a soft cotton dress that clung to her frame, and I didn't care to take my eyes from her for a moment. I danced with her daughters, too, and they laughed and frolicked through the evening.

Marcilina, too, was caught up in the gaiety of the evening, and she laughed at me as I tried to dance with her, and she threw her arms around me and kissed me openly. She was by far the most beautiful of the women in Cerralvo, and all the Americans eyed me with envy, and those boys couldn't take their eyes from my Spanish lady.

You've heard 'em say, no doubt, that a person moved as if their feet never touched the ground. Well, b'God I've seen it. Marcilina danced and skipped and laughed and kissed me and gathered up her daughters in her arms and danced with them and the woman's feet never touched the ground.

It was delightful, and there's no other word for it. And if I had spent the rest of my life dancing with that Mexican beauty in the plaza of Cerralvo, it would have been a life well spent, in my estimation.

And when the music was over and we carried her exhausted daughters home – one in her arms and the other in mine – and we put them in bed and then retired together to her room and made love, she smiled at me throughout and as I convulsed and shook in absolute ecstasy, she looked up into my face and whispered, "I love you, my American lieutenant."

And, do ye know, I loved her back.

Marcilina de le Garza's passion never wavered and never ceased. She threw herself into lovemaking with me with an intensity that I've never experienced with any other woman. Other than that fandango, she still seldom smiled and never laughed, but I can feel the strength of her kiss against my lips now, and see the longing in her deep, dark eyes. I've forever remembered those dark nipples and the smoothness of her skin. Not many women managed to haunt my memory in the way that Marcilina de la Garza did, and I suppose some reason for that goes beyond the way she clung to me as her body shuddered beneath mine.

I suppose one of the reasons that Marcilina remained forever in my mind was that she saved my skin.

CHAPTER XIV

On my last ride as a messenger for General Taylor – I suppose it was late April – Jim and I had stopped in Cerralvo on our way from Camargo to Monterrey. Jim left me at Marcilina's hacienda and went into town to visit the whore he'd taken up with and visited whenever we stopped there.

Marcilina and I spent the afternoon harvesting corn and apples from her garden. We ate. She put her daughters to bed, and then we retired to her bedroom where we engaged in a passionate tête-à-tête that lasted late into the night and left me completely spent and exhausted.

So it was that I overslept that next morning, and that probably is what saved my life. Had I left Marcilina's hacienda and met Jim in town, as I usually did, I'd have been alone when I left the house and Marcilina would not have heard the shot that brought her to my rescue.

But I'm getting ahead of myself.

It was Jim pounding on the outside door and hollering that woke me. I'd been in one of those deep sleeps that, upon waking, left me disoriented. Marcilina was there beside me, sound asleep herself, with one leg thrown over my legs and an arm draped across my chest. She was an outstanding beauty, lying there like that without a stitch of clothing in the soft morning light. I considered, for a moment, rolling her onto her back and waking her with a taste of what had exhausted me the night before, but then Jim went to pounding on the door again.

"Jackie Speed!" he called. "We gotta git on the road, son!"

"Gimme a minute, Jim!" I hollered back at him.

Now Marcilina stirred, and I kissed her on the forehead.

"Must you leave?" she whispered, her voice thick with tiredness.

"I must," I said back. And I slid out of the bed and began dressing myself.

Marcilina dressed and cut an apple for me that I ate while I saddled up Courage. I kissed her goodbye and mounted up, and together Jim and I started away from the house, back down the road toward Monterrey. At that time we were returning from carrying a message from Taylor with a list of necessary supplies he needed shipped down with the next convoy.

It was a clear day and the air was crisp, almost chilly there in the mountains. We could hear the stream near Marcilina's hacienda and there were birds chirping, and never for a moment did I think about an ambush. Oh, they still happened from time to time, but on a morning as pleasant as this one in such a pastoral location, a man could be lulled into a sense of peace.

"Now what's this?" Jim asked, pulling his horse to a halt.

Courage pulled up, too, and snorted. I saw coming toward us from the pecan grove near the stream a single rider. There was nothing hostile about his posture – he was just at a walk, and whether he was riding to us or merely toward us I could not distinguish.

"He ain't a Mexican," Jim said, as the man grew nearer and we could distinguish more about him.

For a moment, the thought occurred to me that I'd seen the man before or knew him, but it was a fleeting thought, and I turned Courage to head back down the road. Jim, though, stayed where he was.

"Hallo!" Jim called to the man. I looked over my shoulder, and realized that Jim was now riding up to him, so I turned Courage back around and rode up towards the man, too. Now I could not see him at all because Jim had positioned himself between the stranger and me.

So I was all the way up to them, just a few feet away, when Courage stepped to where my line of sight was clear of Jim and I could see the man's face for the first time.

Fear shot through my body in such a forceful way that I thought certain they would smell it.

There, with a pistol leveled right at Jim, was Uriah Franks.

What he might have said to Jim as I was riding up to them, I do not know. But now Franks didn't utter a threat, he didn't caution us against any sudden movements. He simply pulled the trigger, shooting Jim right in the chest and killing him instantly, or near enough to it.

The big Texian, my companion on all these journeys and my friend who had a great love for fun and who looked upon me as a son, crashed from his saddle and hit the ground with a thud. He let out two labored, gargling breaths and then stirred no more. His horse started and ran.

But not my damn horse.

I was paralyzed with fear. I could not move or react, even if I could think fast enough of what to do.

Just as quick as Franks pulled that trigger and killed my friend, he raised up his other hand where there was another pistol.

"I've got you now, you bastard," he said, and there was venom in his tone.

Uriah Franks looked poorly. He looked malnourished and sickly, what was left of his hair had turned all gray, and I believed he was not long for this world. But that same burning hatred was in his eyes, that lust for murder. My murder.

"You try to ride away, and I'll shoot you dead before you ever wheel that horse around," Franks told me. "You go for one of those pistols on your belt, and I'll gut shoot you."

There was suddenly color coming to his cheek, and only two thoughts were in my mind: How bad will it hurt to die? And why doesn't he just go on and pull that trigger?

But vengeance, true revenge that eats away at a man's soul, is a hell of a thing, as Uriah Franks had clearly discovered. For so long the only thought in his mind was to see me dead, and I could see clear that his desire to kill me had ruined his health. And now here I was, at his mercy and without a hope of escape, and the moment was too much for Uriah Franks. He needed to draw it out. He needed to see me suffer. He couldn't just shoot me dead and put a close on his only reason for living, for I believe if he'd shot me dead there and then it would have ended his will to survive, too.

"I'm going to kill you, you despicable miscreant, you vile, contemptuous reptile," he said, and he spat as he spoke barely above a whisper. "But before I do, I want you to know the misery you've caused.

"You burned down the mill at Scull Shoals," he said. "Dr. Poullain – from his own pocket – is paying wages for the people of the town as the mill is rebuilt. You done that!" His voice raised into a shout and he pointed the pistol at me in an accusatory way. "My wife, that slut – I banished her from our home and she has gone back to whorin' in Athens." [18]

The phrase caught me off guard, and before I considered what I was doing I repeated it back to him, as a question: "Back to whorin'?"

"Once a whore, always a whore!" he spat, and the venom was rising. "That's right! I found her a whore and thought I could provide her salvation, but once a whore, always a whore!"

I assumed for the past two years he'd told himself that over and over again: "Once a whore, always a whore."

The shouting had caused him to start to cough, and though he kept the pistol leveled at me, he shuddered and shook and spat as he coughed up blood. Tuberculosis. He was near to death. If I'd just avoided him a little while longer, he'd never have bothered me again.

After the coughing fit, he returned his glare to my face. "And me, you damnedable, contemptible reprobate! I have chased you all the way to this godforsaken country. I have lived off of rats and snakes and sought you out in every army camp from the Rio Grande to Veracruz.

"I have contracted the disease that will be the end of me, but before I pass, I shall see you in your grave so that you may pay for the sins you have committed against so many better folk!"

The hand gripping the pistol shook, and I thought for sure this was going to be it.

Throughout this interview – which lasted only a few moments – my bowels were erupting and fear had grabbed hold of my chest so that I could barely breathe and I racked my brains for some way out, but nothing – no bit of inspiration – came to me. If I tried to get to one of my pistols I'd be dead before I could pull it from its holster. If I tried to flee, he'd shoot me – if not in the gut then surely in the back. I was just far enough away, too, that if I had the courage – which I did not – to try the Texian trick of surprising him and riding into him, he'd have plenty of time to pull the trigger.

But presently I saw something that gave me the slightest bit of hope.

There, coming through the pecan grove, I could see two riders coming nearer to us. They must have been messengers from Camargo, or maybe my fellow Rangers, and if I could stay alive long enough I was certain they would be my deliverers. I dared not look at them directly for fear that Franks would be alerted to them and shoot me dead before they could stop him. But if they could come up on him and arrest him or, better, kill him, then I could be rescued from this miserable fate.

And so now I just had to keep him talking long enough for these damned fools to step to it.

"Surely you can't blame me for all of this. You said it yourself, she was a whore. I'd say you share some of the blame for bringing a whore to Scull Shoals." I said, and it was so offhand the way I said it, so cool-as-you-please, that I surprised Uriah Franks and me both by my tone.

"Insolence!" he shouted, and now went to coughing and sputtering again.

And now, from the corner of my eye, I could see them coming with a purpose!

The two riders were at a gallop and closing the distance between us. Franks' coughing muffled the sounds of their approach so that he did not even know they were upon him. And just as they were up to us, I chanced a look at them.

I can tell you, Ol' Speedy's been in some tight spots in his life, but when I saw those two Mexicans with their lassos coming up over their heads – one to ensnare Uriah Franks and the other to ensnare me – my guts exploded in a frightful way.

There was nothing for it. That damned rope was pinching my arms to my body before I could think, and as the rancheros passed us with a yelp and a holler and continued on at a gallop, I felt the sudden lurch as I was dragged from my saddle and through the air.

The wind was knocked out of me when I hit the ground, and I couldn't breathe or cry out. I couldn't struggle to free myself as I was dragged over the rough earth. I couldn't move my arms to try to get to my pistols.

The rocks, the dirt, the broken branches, even the blades of the grass were ripping me to pieces as I tumbled over the ground.

The pain was like nothing I'd ever imagined. Each scrape and scratch sending flashes of agony through my body.

I could not see him, but I could sense that somewhere nearby Uriah Franks was also being dragged to his death.

I thought of poor Jim, dead now, and missing this great chance to answer his question: How long could I last being dragged to death like this?

My face, my back, my arms and legs were all being ripped to pieces. Death had chased me all over Mexico and now had finally caught me. I could feel my life ebbing away as unconsciousness overcame me. My head bounced off the ground again and again and everything throughout my body was pain. My last clear thought was that I was all but certain that bastard Franks would be satisfied as long as his last breath came after mine.

And then I heard the shot from somewhere in the distance and my body slid to a stop.

I couldn't credit it. I couldn't imagine what had happened. I could not think of why the tumbling over the earth had stopped or why I might still be alive, lying here on my broken and battered back, looking up through the limbs of the pecan trees at the blue sky above.

"Jackson!" I heard my name. It was Marcilina screaming. "Jackson! Jackson!"

She was coming nearer.

I could not move. I could not turn my head. Everything ached. I felt as if everything in me was broken.

And now Marcilina was over me, falling to her knees and grabbing my head in her hands. "Jackson! Jackson!"

"Get this blasted rope off of me!" I yelled at her, but all that came out was a groan.

She understood, though, and began to try to loosen the rope. But the rope had dug its way into my flesh, and as she pulled on it every fiber of the rope seemed to tear open a new wound, and I screamed. Marcilina drew the Bowie knife from my belt and cut the rope free. Now she tried to pick me up and raised me up from my back.

I rolled over, and Marcilina let out a gasp of shock when she saw my back. It looked like raw, shredded beef.

I was on my knees and elbows now, and I lifted my head enough to look around. Not far away I saw what I was looking for. With whatever strength I could find, I pushed myself to my feet and stumbled, first to the base of one tree and then to the next, until I reached the object of my current obsession. Marcilina, filled with worry and fright, followed me along as I went, with her hands outstretched toward me as if to catch me should I fall.

I leaned against the trunk of a big pecan tree. I looked down on the face of my aggressor. Uriah Franks was as bad off as I was, torn and bloodied and only half alive. He was still bound fast by the lasso.

Marcilina stood there, with her hands out to catch me. She looked at me, looking down at Franks.

"Do you know him?" she asked.

"Aye," I mumbled.

And without ceremony or speech, I drew one of the Patersons from its holster, cocked it, and fired a shot into Uriah Franks' face.

His expression of hate never changed, but I do believe there was a moment when he heard the cocking of the pistol, when I saw a trace of realization pass over him: Realization that he had failed in his overwhelming desire to kill me, realization that it was I who would be ending his existence.

Whatever it was, in my pain, I took some delight in knowing that Uriah Franks spent his last moment knowing his failure was about to put him to the death.

To escape him, I had fled to hell and that damned Franks had followed me here. It wasn't my fault the fool had married a whore who had seduced a teenager and left him a cuckold. He got what he deserved, if you ask me, but I paid for it in Mexico.

I fired the shot and stumbled a few feet away, and then I collapsed.

I could not tell you how she did it, but Marcilina managed to get my shredded body from the pecan grove to her house. She stripped me and applied ointments to my numerous wounds and bandaged me, and for the next several days she nursed me as I suffered unconscious.

She was a good woman, that Marcilina.

When I was well enough to open my eyes and communicate, she told me what had happened after I shot Franks, and I'll say I was well impressed by her.

"I found Jim," she said. "He was shot. I do not know if you knew that."

"I did," I told her. "The man I shot, the one who was dragged, he killed Jim."

"Is that why you shot him?" she asked me.

"It is," I said, not seeing the necessity of going over any other details.

"I rounded up the horses – your horse, Jim's horse, the horse that belonged to the ranchero who was dragging you, and the horse that belonged to the man you shot," she told me. "I have all of the horses here, still, and have been caring for them. I buried Jim in a grave where he fell because I could not move him. I used one of the horses to drag the other two bodies into the woods and left them there."

"Was it you who shot the ranchero?" I asked her.

"After you left with Jim I heard a shot. I ran to a window and I saw you and the other man – the one you shot – among the pecan trees. He was holding a pistol pointed at you, and Jim was on the ground dead. I ran to get my rifle, and as I came outside, I saw the two rancheros ride up and throw their lassos over you and the other man. They dragged you first one way, and then back through the pecan trees and toward me.

"As they came nearer to me, I shot the one who was dragging you and he fell from his horse. When I shot him, the other ranchero dropped the rope that was dragging the other man and he fled, so that the other man was left there near you, where you shot him."

"Thank you," I said. "Thank you for saving me."

In all, I spent almost two months with her while I came back to health. The first few weeks were because I was too weak to stir and the next few weeks because I was enjoying the daily baths, ointment treatments and other diversions Marcilina and I could get up to.

But by then there was a gnawing in the back of my mind.

Back in Georgia I had a wife who was yearning to see me again after being a year away at war and, though I enjoyed my days with Marcilina, this was not home. Also, back in Georgia there was no man waiting to kill me as there had been before.

As I began to feel better, I would take Courage out for rides of increasing distances to get my strength back up and be active again.

And finally, I decided I was well enough to leave.

I did not tell Marcilina what I intended to do, though I suspect she knew.

Jackie Speed had had enough of Mexico, enough of killing and enough of people trying to kill me. It was time for me to go home.

I waited late in the day so that I could ride by night when it was cooler so that the horses would not be overburdened in the heat. I took Courage and Jim's horse so that I'd have a spare mount. Marcilina and her daughters had gone into town to buy edibles.

Before I left, I searched through the ranchero's saddlebags, and the saddlebags that had been Uriah Franks' and Jim's. The ranchero and Jim both had enormous amounts of cash on them – surprising amounts, really. Between them, I found almost sixty dollars in gold, coins and paper money. Franks, too, had some money in his bag, though not much.

I took twenty dollars so that I would have enough cash to get me home and then left the remainder on Marcilina's table. I also left her the three saddles and the other two horses, all of which could be sold.

Wearing civilian clothes that had belonged to her husband – all too short and too wide for me – I saddled up Courage and led Jim's horse and started north on the Camargo Road.

My plan was to skip well wide of Camargo, where too many people might recognize me, and ride all the way home to Georgia. Having come so close to death, I had no interest in steamers or trains. Besides, though the damned horse had a mind of his own and seemed constantly as willing to get me in at the death as ever Jeff Davis had been, he rode well and I'd grown attached to him.

I didn't know or care how long it would take, just as long as I could get north of Mexico and start going east. I just wanted to put all of this damned hell behind me.

You won't credit it, and I don't blame you, but over the years, I continued to send money to Marcilina. She'd saved my life and nursed me back to health and provided me no end of love during a time when I needed it. I never put a return address on the money I sent her – the last thing I cared to have happen was for her to come find me and have to introduce my Spanish Lady to my Southern Belle – but I always enclosed it in a letter that said simply, "This is payment for the room."

It's a bit softhearted, I'll admit, but the kindness I continued to show to Marcilina de la Garza would pay me back one day, saving my life when I found myself in another tight spot.

I didn't know it then, but the money and the horses were not all I left Marcilina to remember me by. In February of 1848, my first son was born in Cerralvo, Mexico. He would grow up there hearing stories of his father, the brave Texas Ranger who had stolen his mother's heart and, though he'd disappeared one afternoon, had continued every year – two or three times a year – to send money for the care of her and her three children.

So that was me, done with war. As I rode off through those picturesque mountains, down into the rough countryside toward Camargo, I grew increasingly eager to get home to Milledgeville, to my wife and to a life that seemed a hundred years away. Each mile that Courage took me from Monterrey and Encarnacion and those madmen bent on seeing me at the death seemed to cleanse me of the hell that Mexico had been. I did not know then that my time in Milledgeville would be a short stay, that in the coming months I would take my bride off to find our fortune, and I did not know that fate would step in my way time and time again to drag me back in to the death and hell of war and violence. I suppose riding away from there I was as content and happy as I'd ever been in my life, for I believed then that I was done with corpses and bullets, done with the thunder crash of cannons and the gut wrenching fear of violent death.

I believed that I was riding east to my beautiful wife and peace and a decent life as a shopkeeper, maybe a lawyer. I dreamed on Courage's back of attending lectures at

Oglethorpe University and maybe becoming the sort of politician that Old Man Brooks would really hate – a greedy, selfish man who used his office to get rich and live in luxury. But that was another man's life. Not mine.

California and Baltimore and Gettysburg, Pinkerton and Lincoln and Grant and Lee and, damn 'im, Jefferson Davis, and William Bonney and by God the Devil himself and a host of other maniacs would make certain that my life would be one spent fleeing for safety. If Ashley Franks hadn't tempted me with her peach cobbler, I'd have probably lived my life as a content blacksmith in Scull Shoals, Georgia. But I ain't complaining.

Because I had my wits about me whenever the bullets started to fly, I survived every bit of it, and if I've lived to be an old man I suppose I owe part of it to Mexico where I learned most everything I know about surviving.

the end

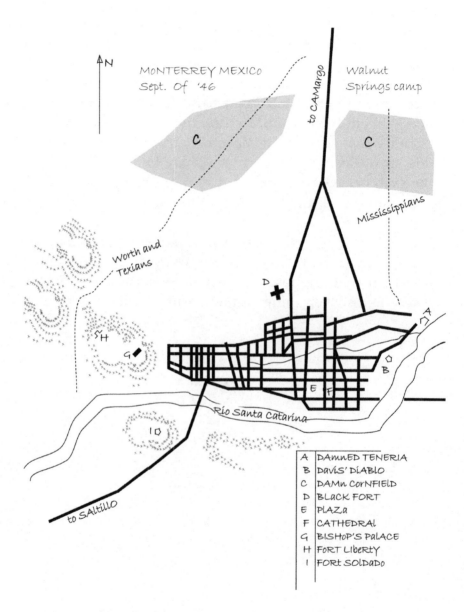

A map showing points of interest from the Battle of Monterrey. This map was found with Jackson Speed's memoirs along with a note t hat he drew the map while avoiding burial duties, presumably after the battle and before joining with McCulloch.

The Mexican-American War

The Mexican-American War is often overlooked in American history, overshadowed by the war that came 15 years later, but its importance in the shaping of the United States is important.

The Treaty of Guadalupe Hidalgo, signed February 2, 1848, gave the United States the disputed portion of Texas west of the Rio Grande, and ceded to the United States present-day California, Nevada, Utah, New Mexico as well as most of Arizona and Colorado and parts of Oklahoma, Wyoming and Kansas. The United States paid $18.25 million for the land which was considerably less than it had offered Mexico prior to the outbreak of war.

It was also the first time that the United States military found itself in the difficult position of serving as an occupying army. While there were unquestionably atrocities committed by Americans serving in the occupation force, on the whole many in northern Mexico welcomed the Americans. One reason, which Speed noted, was that the Americans mostly paid for supplies where the Mexican army often demanded money and supplies and threatened the populace. Another reason, not noted by Speed, is that in the sparsely populated areas of northern Mexico that eventually became United States territory, many of the settlers there were already Americans who had moved into these western territories with little or no concern about what government they lived under.

American soldiers, too, got their first taste of urban warfare on the streets of Monterrey and other Mexican cities, and learned tactics on those streets that are still employed by American troops who in the 20th and 21st centuries have found urban warfare more common.

Many historians make the case that the American Civil War

was so gruesome and raged on for so long because its generals learned their trade at West Point and on the battlefields of Mexico. Speed notes their names: U.S. Grant, Robert E. Lee, Albert Sidney Johnston, James Longstreet, Braxton Bragg and the list goes on. Speed's commanders in Mexico were both prominent in the Civil War – Jefferson Davis was the president of the Confederate States and Ben McCulloch was a general with the CSA who was killed in the battle of Pea Ridge.

Though the war unquestionably opened up vast new areas of expanse for the United States, it was also controversial. By war's end, many people – including U.S. Grant who called the war "unjust" – began to question its legitimacy. Grant concluded, too, that the American Civil War was "punishment" for the Mexican-American war.

President James K. Polk, a Democrat, faced opposition over the war from his Whig opponents, but by the end of the war and with victory, the Whigs muted their opposition and made Zachary Taylor their candidate for president in 1848.

NOTES

[1] In October of 1905, the New York Giants beat the Philadelphia Athletics four games to one in the second World Series. This reference seems to place the writing of this memoir in 1905, when Jackson Speed would have been 75 years old.

[2] Though a minor detail, Jackson's memory must be playing him false here. "Safety Matches," as they were known – those with the red phosphorous tips that were struck on sandpaper on the outside of the box – were not patented until ten years later than this episode in his life. Johan Edvard Lundstrom of Sweden patented the Safety Matches in 1855. More likely, the matches Jackson used were white phosphorous "Strike Anywhere" matches.

[3] In 1845 the Georgia Legislature, determining that Marthasville sounded too feminine, voted to rename the two-year-old city that had been established as a major railroad junction for Georgia. Georgia General Assembly Act 109, approved by the legislature and signed by the governor in late December of 1845, changed the name of Marthasville to Atlanta.

[4] Henry Roote Jackson was Captain of the volunteer company from Savannah known as the Jasper Greens when the company was called to serve in the Mexican-American War. Formed just three years prior to the war in February of 1843, the Irish Jasper Greens consisted almost entirely of Irish immigrants or those of immediate Irish descent. Two other infantry companies volunteered from Savannah, but the Jasper Greens were called upon to help fill the ranks of the

single Georgia regiment called to war in 1846. Jackson, who was 26-years-old at the time of the war, would be appointed colonel of the Georgia Regiment. H. R. Jackson, born in Athens, Ga., studied at Yale and set up his law practice in Savannah. After serving in the Mexican-American War, Jackson returned to Georgia where he was a noted orator – delivering a speech on "Courage" at the University of Georgia in 1848. During the mid-1850s he served as Minister Resident to the Austrian Empire and in the late 1850s was a prominent lawyer and prosecutor in Savannah. Notably, he unsuccessfully prosecuted the owners and crew of a slave ship in 1859. During the Civil War, H. R. Jackson served as a judge in the Confederate Army before being promoted to Major General of the state militia. He was captured at the Battle of Nashville and held prisoner in Fort Warren, Massachusetts until the summer of 1865. After the war, he was named Minister to Mexico for the United States, worked as a lawyer, railroad executive, banker and was the President of the Georgia Historical Society until 1898, the year of his death.

[5] That Speed was unable to hear the address being made at the Courthouse in Macon may explain why he mistakenly thought the city's mayor was making the address to the Jasper Greens. In fact, it was Samuel Blake, Esq., an honorary member of the Floyd Rifles, who spoke. A newspaper account of the event also notes the difficult observers had in hearing what Blake said: "We regret that we are unable to lay it before our readers. His speech was replete with the noblest sentiments of patriotism; but our distance from him and the frequent interruptions of his remarks by the deafening cheers of the multitude, prevents us from venturing to give even an outline of the speech. Speed is also correct that none of the volunteer units escorting the Jasper Greens through Macon went to war in Mexico; however, the Macon Guards – not to be confused with the Macon Volunteers – were part of the Georgia Regiment forming in Columbus.

[6] The Irish Potato Crop Failure of 1845 sent nearly a million Irish to America, though most arrived in 1847. This sudden, mass immigration was met with the sort of bigotry typically found in any mass immigration through the history of the United States. At the time, the Irish were widely depicted as slothful, immoral drunkards and destructive. Some scientists of the time believed that the Irish, as well as Africans, were more closely related to apes than to human beings. The surprise here is that Speed, who could rightly be considered a bigot himself, was able to empathize with those who suffered intolerance because he had been on the receiving end of it.

[7] Speed's portrayal of the incident aboard the Corvette corresponds generally with the sometimes conflicting news accounts of the time, though as an eyewitness he provides details not to be found in any other surviving account of the "Battle of the Boat." He gets one detail incorrect, though he can be forgiven for it: Col. E. D. Baker of Illinois, shot in the back of the neck, was not mortally wounded. The ball passed through the back of his neck and into his mouth, knocking out a single tooth. Col. Baker underwent surgery and survived his wound. In 1861, leading Union troops at the Battle of Ball's Bluff, Col. Baker was killed. Captain McMahon recovered from the wound he received. One of the Illinois men was killed and as many as ten men disappeared, assumed killed and knocked overboard. As many as 30 men, all told, received wounds that prevented them from continuing on in the war. Reports that appeared in newspapers were wildly exaggerated – one report even had Col. H. R. Jackson shooting down some of his own men. Col. Jackson, though, had already gone down river with other Georgia companies and was not at Camp Belknap at the time of the riot aboard the Corvette.

[8] Clearly Speed was never aware of the full extent to which the 26-year-old Colonel of the Georgia Regiment stood up for

his men, in part because he thought Col. Baker of Illinois had been killed. Col. Baker refused to accept the blame for the escalation of the incident, and Col. Jackson went so far in his defense of his men's honor as to informally offer a duel to Col. Baker. The duel never took place, but Col. Jackson at least seemed prepared to risk his life to champion the honor of the First Georgia.

[9] General Zachary Taylor, who after the war would be elected 12th President of the United States, was appointed by then-President James K. Polk to lead America's forces in Mexico. Polk sought to force Mexico into negotiations that would allow the United States to buy what is, essentially, the present-day Southwest United States: New Mexico, Utah, Nevada and California and parts of Arizona, Colorado, Texas, Oklahoma, Kansas and Wyoming. To keep open the possibilities of negotiations, Polk asked Taylor to go to war but to take care in his dealings with the Mexican citizenry. As such, the invading force was often viewed more favorably by Mexicans than the Mexican army. The Americans paid high prices for food and supplies, whereas the Mexican army simply took what it wanted and, in some cases, forced wealthy Mexicans to pay additional taxes to support the military. By the time of the Mexican-American War, Taylor already had an impressive military career, established during the Black Hawk War and the Second Seminole War. He was known by his soldiers in the Mexican-American War as "Old Rough and Ready."

[10] When General Taylor began moving troops south from Camargo on the Monterrey Campaign, Taylor had misgivings about the quality of many of the volunteer regiments. He hand-selected and took only about half of those volunteers available to him (Taylor's Army moving on Monterrey consisted of just more than 6,600 volunteers and regular army). The entire Georgia Regiment was left at Camargo.

[11] Jefferson Davis, remembered more for the role he played as a U.S. Senator prior to the Civil War and then as President of the Confederate States of America than for his military exploits, was a West Point graduate. He served in the United States army under Zachary Taylor during the Black Hawk War, but resigned his commission when he eloped with Knox Taylor, Zachary Taylor's daughter, against her father's wishes. After the marriage, both Davis and his new bride fell sick with a fever. She died before she had been married three months. Davis recovered, though he never lost the gaunt look of a convalescent. Following the death of his wife, Davis spent 10 years studying and practicing law, remarried and was elected to Congress. When the war drums began to beat, Davis resigned his office and returned home to Mississippi to raise a volunteer regiment, the Mississippi Rifles.

[12] Speed's details, both of camp life, General Taylor's decision to leave half or more of his volunteers encamped at Camargo, and the march from Camargo to Taylor's forward base of operations, Cerralvo, are accurate enough as far as they go. However, it is impossible that Speed witnessed the events he describes on the first day of the march, and some of his other recollections are almost certainly confused. General Taylor made his decision which regiments would move on to Monterrey in mid-August, before Speed and the Georgia Regiment arrived at Camargo. Further, Taylor sent the first of his men forward from Camargo under General Worth on August 19, well before Speed arrived at Camargo, and it was General Worth's mule train that lost its entire first day of march to the incident with the stampeding mules. It is likely that in the 60 years from when he experienced these events to when he penned his memoirs, Speed, whose accounts of historical events are typically accurate and add much to the historical record, were confused with what he personally witnessed and what he later heard. It is possible, too, that the

incident involving General Worth's mule train repeated itself when the last of the regiments left Camargo, though that seems unlikely. Speed's recollections of time and distance are often vague, and here he has incorrectly recalled the length of time he spent at Camargo. The Georgia Regiment would have arrived at Camargo probably on the second or third of September, and Speed would have left with the last of the men going to Monterrey on September 6, putting him at Camargo not more than four days. That those four days, over the years, were remembered by him to seem more like two weeks might be forgiven as conditions at Camargo were so poor. It is also likely that Speed's initial encounter with Jefferson Davis took place at Camp Belknap, though it could have happened at Camargo.

[13] Speed's recollections of the battle correspond precisely with official records as well as other written reports from soldiers who participated in the battle. The first day at Monterrey saw heavy American casualties as General Taylor pushed more troops forward as a "diversion" on the east side of the city at Forts Teneria and Diablo. Others who heard Lieutenant Colonel McClung recorded (probably more accurately) that he gave the command: "Charge! Charge! Tombigbee Volunteers follow me!" Prior to his promotion to lieutenant colonel, Alexander McClung had been the company commander of the Mississippi Volunteer Company K, known as the "Tombigbee Company."

[14] When Lieutenant Colonel McClung fell, several of his men moved him to a safe spot at the foot of the fort and treated his wounds. He stayed in that spot as the battle raged for the rest of the day, and back in camp that evening Colonel Davis remembered his second in command and asked for volunteers to go back and fetch him. The entirety of the Tombigbee Company volunteered, and four men were selected. It was dangerous work, with the battery at the Black

Fort firing at them as they went to El Teneria and as they returned across the plain. Carrying McClung on a stretcher on their shoulders, the men dashed back toward camp. One of the cannonballs fired from the Black Fort actually passed under the stretcher and between the men carrying it.

[15] Indeed, as Speed says, President Polk's position toward the Mexicans changed. Initially, he believed the Mexicans would negotiate the purchase of land. While Santa Anna was in exile in Cuba, Polk and Santa Anna had been in communication, and Santa Anna had made assurances that once restored to Mexico he would push for the negotiations Polk sought. The American President allowed Santa Anna to leave Cuba and return to Mexico, believing him to be an ally. But when Santa Anna returned to Mexico and took up arms against the Americans, Polk was outraged. He adopted a policy of taking what he wanted through force. Unfortunately for Polk's general in the field, no one conveyed this change of policy to General Taylor.

[16] The Colt Walker Revolver, designed by Samuel Colt in 1847 at the request of Texas Ranger Samuel Walker, is more often associated with the Mexican American War, but in 1846 the Texas Rangers were still using the Paterson Revolver. Patented in 1836, the Paterson was the first repeating firearm with a revolving cylinder and multiple chambers that was sold commercially. It was not particularly successful and Colt's business failed in 1842. However, the Paterson, with its odd folding trigger that engaged when the hammer was cocked, became a favorite weapon among the Texas Rangers fighting the Comanche prior to the Mexican-American War. There were various lengths and calibers of the Paterson. Probably Speed carried the "Number 5 Holster" or "Texas Paterson."

[17] McCulloch, and Speed, overestimated the size of Santa

Anna's force. Historians believe Santa Anna assembled an army of about 22,000 in San Luis Potosi, but on the march north that army dwindled by some 7,000 troops who deserted or fell out from exhaustion. Nevertheless, Taylor at Buena Vista – as he had at Monterrey – faced a foe of overwhelming size. Where it had been closer to three-to-one odds at Monterrey, Buena Vista was odds of more than two-to-one.

[18] In 1845 a mysterious fire destroyed the mills at Scull Shoals. We learn in his memoirs, for the first time, that it was Jackson Speed who was responsible for the fire that destroyed the Fontenoy Mills. The owner of the mills, Dr. Thomas Poullain, did in fact pay from his own pocket to support his employees while the mills were rebuilt. The mills were rebuilt and back in operation by 1847, but it is likely that Uriah Franks would not have known that if he had spent several months in pursuit of Speed. The mills, rebuilt in 1846, were now made of brick and were three and four stories.

Printed in Dunstable, United Kingdom